DESOLATION RIDGE

LAVONNE GRIFFIN-VALADE

SEVERN RIVER PUBLISHING

DESOLATION RIDGE

Copyright © 2022 by LaVonne Griffin-Valade.

Severn River Publishing
www.SevernRiverBooks.com

This is a work of fiction. Names, characters, businesses, places, events and incidents are either the products of the author's imagination or used in a fictitious manner. Any resemblance to actual persons, living or dead, or actual events is purely coincidental.

ISBN: 978-1-64875-555-2 (Paperback)

ALSO BY LAVONNE GRIFFIN-VALADE

Maggie Blackthorne Novels

Dead Point

Murderers Creek

Desolation Ridge

Poison Spring

To find out more about LaVonne Griffin-Valade and her books, visit

severnriverbooks.com

For Tom

In memory of my mother

1

MORNING, NOVEMBER 12

A brutal wind battered the small modular that held our Oregon State Police station. It occurred to me nature's lashing of the structure was some kind of omen. Being a cynic, I was betting it had something to do with my upcoming trip down the aisle—my third such venture.

Sherry Linn Perkins and I were commiserating about the weather when the main office line rang shortly after eight thirty. She took the call, and I walked to the pod of officer desks tucked behind the service counter out front.

My phone buzzed before I'd barely had the opportunity to sit down and log on to my computer.

"Hey, the call that just came in?" Sherry Linn said. "I think you'll want to check out the report right away."

"Thanks." I pulled it up, skimmed through her notes, and shivered. A timber thinning crew had been spooked by a large male cougar prowling in the vicinity of their worksite near Desolation Ridge, deep in the Umatilla Forest.

I tapped Mark Taylor to drive out and assess the danger. He specialized in the enforcement of wildlife law and was somewhat of an expert about game mammals in particular. And I knew he'd be anxious for everybody, including the big cat, to remain calm.

About an hour later, Sherry Linn patched through a call from a woman reporting a domestic disturbance at her neighbor's place. She lived in Dale, an unincorporated village a few miles south of Forest Road 10, where Taylor was already headed. Since the caller made it clear the altercation was violent and appeared to be escalating, I radioed him.

"Mark, have you passed Dale yet?" I asked when he picked up.

"Nah, it's another twenty minutes up the highway. What's going on?"

"I'm waving you off the stalking cougar and sending you to Dale. A guy named Charlie Archer's beating the crap out of his wife or girlfriend. His next-door neighbor in the local trailer park just contacted us. Said it sounded like Archer was slamming the woman against the walls, punching and kicking her."

"I know right where that trailer park is, too. Can't be more than six or seven mobile homes on the entire property."

"The mobile homes don't have individual house numbers, but apparently you can't miss Mr. Archer's abode. The neighbor, uh…Patti Hutchens is the name, said it's a small, older Fleetwood, lime green and white."

"I know Patti. She's a member of my church."

Well, of course Patti Hutchens was a member of Taylor's church, along with half the damn county.

He continued. "I'm bumping up my speed and switching on the siren. Should make it to Dale in no more than fifteen minutes."

"Hollis and I are heading there pronto in case you need reinforcements, and I'll send Doug out to check on the animal."

"See you when you get here."

"Stay safe," I said.

Taylor let out his usual nervous giggle. "No worries, Maggie. Got it covered."

I dashed to Doug Vaughn's desk. He looked up from his computer. A pretty smart guy and good at his job, he was occasionally aloof. Or maybe *sober* was the better word.

"Doug, I need you to take over for Mark."

"The cougar call, right? Out near Desolation Ridge?"

"Yeah." I handed him a copy of the police report. "Gives the directions to the timber thinning crew's location just off of Road 10."

He read it over. "I better get out there before somebody decides to rile up the cat and ends up killing it."

As Vaughn closed down his computer, collected his gear, and retrieved a container of bear spray, I returned to my desk just across from my patrol partner's. Hollis Jones and I went way back, and we were close buds. I trusted him with my life, and I liked to think he felt the same about me.

"So we're headed to Dale?" Hollis asked.

"Yep. You know how DV interventions can go south."

"I do indeed."

From John Day, I sped west on Highway 26, my cop Tahoe's siren pouring it on while Hollis dictated what he'd gleaned about Archer from various online data troves.

"Charles Sean Archer, age twenty-seven, six five, a hundred and ninety pounds," he began. "Owns a 1980 International Scout—orange in color—with Oregon vanity plates, M-U-D R-U-N. Lived in the Portland area most of his life. Managed to serve a couple of drunk-and-disorderly stints in the county jail there. And apparently, he likes to fight other drunks in city parks. Wears a pair of nasty steel-toed boots to tromp on his opponents."

I shrugged. "Charming. Too bad a good portion of the males in Grant County could brag about having a similar profile."

"And he's a gun collector, I guess you'd say."

Hollis turned the mobile comp screen toward me, and I caught a glimpse of Archer displaying his cache of weapons.

"Jesus, just like a kid showing off his new toys from Santa."

"Like a kid with money, maybe. Which he's definitely not. He's lived mostly on the margin. Skipped out on jobs or paying rent a bunch of times."

We had turned north and were speeding up Highway 395 toward Dale when Sherry Linn contacted us by radio.

"Patti Hutchens just called again," she said.

"Let me guess, she figured out Archer and the woman had the volume turned up on some movie they were watching, and there was no domestic disturbance."

"Afraid not. Something terrible happened." Her voice, typically clear and strong, was now breathy and strained. "Mark's been shot. And Archer fled with the woman."

Fuck. "Has an ambulance been called?"

"She contacted Life Flight in both Pendleton and La Grande, but it's too windy to chance it, I guess. So she called the closest ambulance service. In Long Creek."

"Dammit."

I knew that was likely the best option available, but Dale was twenty-five miles north of Long Creek. Which meant that once the EMTs loaded Mark in the ambulance, they had to turn around and drive back south another sixty-two miles to the Blue Mountain Hospital in John Day.

"Patti wasn't happy about that either, but fortunately she's a retired RN. She's staunched the bleeding and bandaged Mark's wound. She thought it best not to move him indoors but is making sure he stays warm, and she's outside with him monitoring his vital signs until the ambulance arrives."

"Sounds good. Her phone number, please," I said.

Sherry Linn read it out slowly and repeated it.

"How are you holding up?" I asked her.

"I'll be all right. Would you like me to call Ellie?"

God. Ellie, Mark's wife, would freak out. "I think that should be my job. I'll reach out to her after we report the shooting to regional dispatch."

"All right, Maggie. Update me when you can."

"I'm going to alert regional," Hollis said after I signed off.

I nodded, and he put in the call requesting an APB for Archer's apprehension and arrest. After the requisite back-and-forth with dispatch, he volunteered to contact Ellie.

"I'm supposed to do that, remember?" I said.

"You're behind the wheel and barreling up the highway. Plus, you probably don't want that call to be broadcast over the speaker." He hesitated. "And I might know Ellie a little better than you do."

Code for his tendency to be more responsive to the listener in sensitive situations.

"Let her know the person tending to him is Patti Hutchens. Mark told me she attends their church."

Listening to Holly's side of the call, it was clear Ellie was distraught, but I was still compelled to ask about the obvious when he clicked off the line.

"How'd that go?"

"Like you'd expect. She's pretty upset, but was pleased Patti Hutchens was there with Mark."

"Goddamn, I hate this, Holly. I should've been the one traveling out to the DV, not Taylor."

"Even though he's technically part of OSP's Fish and Wildlife Division, he's a trained law enforcement officer like we are. You made the obvious call, Mags."

"Doesn't mean I made the right call." But I'd have time to kick myself about that later.

For half a second after hearing the news Mark had been shot, I'd considered redirecting Doug Vaughn to the shooting scene but then thought better of it. Those two were tight friends, which could be problematic when it came to keeping a cool head. And all things considered, Mark was in good hands and an ambulance was on the way.

I handed my phone to Holly and asked him to dial Patti Hutchens's number.

"I'll call her. You need to keep your mind on the road."

"I talked to her earlier, so she might be more comfortable if the call came from me. Besides, I'll be using Bluetooth."

Holly dialed the number and placed my phone on the center console.

"Hello?" she answered.

"Ms. Hutchens? This is Oregon State Police Sergeant Blackthorne."

"Oh, of course. I recognize your voice. You've heard the news about Mark?"

"Yes. Can you update me on his condition?"

"He's unconscious, but his breathing and heart rate are stable. He was wounded outside the trailer house, but with a friend's help, I managed to get him into a down sleeping bag and jury-rig a tarp for shelter. Afraid we weren't equipped to safely move him inside."

"He's lucky you were there."

"I'm doing lots of praying, Sergeant."

"We all are," I fibbed. "Do you know the name of the woman Mr. Archer attacked?"

"I'm sorry, I don't. Neither is very friendly. And the only reason I know *his* name is because somebody came around looking for him a week ago or so. I'm not a busybody, but I wrote the Archer fellow's name down just so I'd know who my neighbor was."

"Was he driving his Scout when he took off?"

"Have no idea what a scout is, but he was in the orange truck he usually drives."

"And to be clear, the woman was with him?"

"Yes. I saw him push her down onto the front floorboard as he drove away."

"Appreciate your help. We're on our way. We'll want to talk with you briefly when we get there."

"All right, Sergeant Blackthorne. I should go. I hear the ambulance coming."

We had begun to climb higher through a steep-walled gorge formed by the cleaving power of weather, time, and the rushing waters of Beech Creek, a snow-fed tributary flowing south toward the John Day River. As I drove, a tempest swept through the Miocene ravine and rocked the Tahoe.

I worked to steady the vehicle. "Jesus, I see why Life Flight was reluctant to send a copter."

"Yeah, my MomMom would've called this a derecho."

I remembered his MomMom was his grandmother but had no idea what a derecho was.

"A wild Oklahoma windstorm," he added.

"Huh." I glanced at my watch. Eleven ten. "Is anyone going to the hospital with Ellie or taking care of the kids?"

"Her mother lives with them, so she has a built-in babysitter. And as for emotional support, she plans to reach out to your old landlord," Hollis said.

"Dorie Phillips, the guardian angel of Grant County."

"Especially for you, Mags."

"No doubt about that. Been there for me a million times over."

Dorie had appointed herself my surrogate parent after my mother's suicide, and she'd gone beyond goodness. She'd saved my life.

I accelerated, nudging the Tahoe into the narrow canyon's series of S-curves, the bucking creek below us now, hidden behind a mangy knot of mixed conifers, snowbrush, vine maple, and melting snow.

"Holly? When did you start calling me Mags?"

"I've called you Mags before."

"Don't think so."

"Maybe you're right. I guess I sometimes refer to you as Mags when Lil and I are talking about work."

I decided to let go of the *Mags* matter. After all, he'd put up with me calling him *Holly* all these years.

Highway 395 gradually rolled up from the gorge, and the road now cut through a series of tawny mesas striated with bands of igneous scarp. Mid-autumn sunlight broke through the purple-black clouds rolling swiftly across the sky and lit up the juniper, sagebrush, and dark veins of basaltic rock. The heady, pungent scent of some nearby high desert thunderstorm seeped into the cab of my SUV.

At twenty past eleven, the Long Creek Volunteer Ambulance sprinted by in the opposite direction, driving toward John Day. Its raging siren, combined with the Tahoe's, generated a piercing cacophony that reverberated from the crags on both sides of the highway.

"The siren's a good sign," I said after the ambulance passed. "It probably means Mark is still alive."

"Let's hope so. I'll call Ellie and let her know we met the ambulance heading to the hospital."

"Good idea."

Holly punched in her number and waited. "Is this Ellie? Oh, hi, Dorie. Hollis here. Let Ellie know we just passed the ambulance carrying Mark toward the hospital." He paused. "I'm not sure. Just a sec, I'll ask Maggie how soon she thinks they'll arrive."

"Thirty minutes tops. They're hauling ass," I called out.

There was another pause.

"Dorie says to quit your cussing," Hollis said, passing along her message to me.

I rolled my eyes. "The ambulance crew will likely be in contact with the hospital, too."

He made sure Dorie caught that last bit and ended the call. "Man, we're having luck with cell service today."

"Don't mention that to Dorie. She'll just attribute it to her and Ellie's bout of praying."

We rode in silence for the next several miles, across the immense basin of Fox Valley, through the town of Long Creek, past Sugar Loaf Mountain and Meadowbrook Summit.

I couldn't help but ruminate over the awful day nearly two years ago when Holly was seriously wounded during a bloody shootout with two bad guys. He might easily have died, and now Mark Taylor was facing death. I didn't like it. Not the fact of either incident or that both had occurred under my command.

Might've turned teary just then, but we had finally arrived in Dale, where we readily found the small trailer park. It was a little past eleven thirty, and the long shadows of mid-November draped across the forest and the petite roadside hamlet.

We found Charlie Archer's lodging at the end of the short row of mobile homes and knocked at Patti Hutchens's place next door.

"Sergeant Blackthorne?"

"Ms. Hutchens?"

"Please come on in. And you're welcome to call me Patti."

Although red-haired and taller, she reminded me of a younger Dorie—pleasant, warm, and friendly.

We stepped into her front room. "This is Senior Trooper Jones," I said.

"Nice to meet you both," she said and shook our hands.

Patti's small mobile home was sparkling and cozy, and judging by the décor, she had a fascination with dachshunds. They were depicted on pillows, as figurines or salt and pepper shakers, and in a multitude of photos and paintings.

"I used to breed shorthair miniatures," she explained, having noticed me gawking. "On the side, I should say. I was a nurse full-time."

"My family had a couple of dachshunds when I was growing up," Hollis said.

"I obviously have strong feelings for them. Unfortunately, the winters here are too cold for their liking," she said and turned to address me. "The door to Charlie's trailer is still wide open. With that crazy windstorm blowing every which way, I thought about shutting it. But decided maybe I shouldn't."

"Your instincts were right, Ms. Hutchens."

"Just Patti, okay?"

"Sure. Had you heard Mr. Archer being violent with the woman before?"

"Not violent. Just the usual couple stuff, if I heard anything at all."

I retrieved a small logbook from my hip pocket and flipped to the notes I'd made earlier. "I'd appreciate you describing exactly what you heard next door this afternoon, and why it compelled you to report a DV?"

"DV?"

"Sorry, cop lingo for domestic violence incident."

"Oh, of course. Charlie and the woman were inside the trailer house they were staying in, and I was outside feeding my pet goat. I heard him yelling really loudly, saying something like...he was using profanity, and he definitely called her a slut, a whore, and the B-word. She was screaming and crying, but he just kept hurling her into the walls, and I think punching her. But I know he was kicking her, Sergeant Blackthorne, because the woman kept telling him not to kick her there."

Patti was shaking, her eyes glistening with tears.

"Sorry to upset you. It's not that I doubted you, not at all."

"I didn't realize until now how much it had affected me. And then when the officer was shot and I realized he was Mark Taylor...As a nurse, I witnessed plenty of trauma, but it had never come this close to my own home."

I let her catch her breath before replying. "Trooper Jones was able to find a recent photo of Mr. Archer, but can you give us a description of the woman staying with him?"

"Not a really good one, I'm afraid."

"We'll take what you can give us," Hollis said in his deep, comforting voice.

"Very thin, hair dyed blond, dark roots. And petite like Sergeant Blackthorne."

"Short, you mean?" I asked.

"Well, not as tall as I am, let's say."

"How old do you think she is?"

"Younger than him by several years, I'd guess."

"I have just one more question, and then we'll get out of your hair. Did you write down the name of the person who came looking for Mr. Archer?"

"No, sorry. But he said he was the boss of some outfit thinning trees near Desolation Ridge, or maybe it was Desolation Creek. Close by in the Umatilla National Forest."

"Off of Road 10?"

"I believe so. It's been a while since I drove out there, but I go to Pendleton pretty often and pass the turnoff. I'm pretty sure the sign says Road 10."

"Thanks, you've been really helpful," I said.

"I sure hope Mark makes it," Patti added. "He and his family are beloved in our church."

Hollis and I moved next door to inspect Archer's trailer, located on the other side of Patti's small, fenced-in yard where a spotted goat lay in the short grass.

We reached the two-step landing leading to the open front door. After gloving up, we entered the mobile home and flicked on the lights. A disgusting and dizzying amount of fresh blood clung to the floor, walls, and ceiling of the combination living room, kitchen, and dinette.

"Jesus. Some brutal shit," I said.

"I've never seen anything like it. And I've responded to more than a few DVs."

I brought up my phone to contact our forensics guy just as it rang with an incoming call.

"Hi, Sherry Linn. What's the word?"

"My God, Maggie. Mark died in the ambulance on the way to the hospital."

2

MIDDAY, NOVEMBER 12

Sherry Linn cried softly on the other end of the line. Stunned, I turned to Hollis and shook my head.

He sighed deeply. "Mark?" he whispered.

I nodded. "Sherry Linn...I don't even know what to say. It's just terrible."

She exhaled. "Dorie said Ellie was in shock."

"I'm sure. But she's with Dorie, so in good hands."

"Would you like me to contact Doug?" Sherry Linn asked.

"One of us will do that. And you should close up shop for the day and go home."

"I don't think I can stand to go home," she said haltingly. "I'd prefer to stay, hold down the fort."

"Sure, if that's what you'd like. But if the press contacts the office about...about the incident, let them know an officer will follow up."

"Okay, Maggie. You two don't hesitate to let me know if you need anything."

"Absolutely. And take care of yourself," I said and ended the call.

Hollis and I were still standing inside Archer's blood-soaked living room.

"Let's get the hell out of here, Holly."

He followed me back to the landing and shook his head. "This is messed up."

"Yeah. I feel shitty about it."

He reached over and hugged me. "It's not your fault."

I indicated my agreement, but in my heart, I wasn't so sure.

Hollis pulled up the collar of his jacket. "Let's take cover in the Tahoe."

We stepped away from Archer's trailer and moved toward my rig. Once inside and relieved of nature's disruptive bluster, the world seemed momentarily calm.

"I can radio regional and Doug," Hollis offered.

I pulled up my smartphone and scrolled through my contact list. "I'm making a call to Harry Bratton first. I want him out here pronto."

I punched in the number, but it went to voicemail right away.

"Shit." I waited for his message to end. "Harry, Maggie Blackthorne here. One of the Fish and Wildlife guys in my outfit—you remember Mark Taylor—was shot out in Dale. He died in the ambulance on the way to the hospital. Anyway, you're still on contract with us for forensic work, and I'd like you to meet me at the scene ASAP. I'd appreciate you ringing me back right away."

I hung up and glanced at Hollis. "I should get ahold of Bach before you radio anybody," I said hoarsely.

Al Bach, a homicide detective stationed three hours away in Bend, had supervised our investigations of a spate of Grant County murders over the last couple of years. And despite being my opposite in every way—conventional, reverent, strict rule-follower—he and I got along pretty well. He'd even put up with my profanity a time or two.

"Would you like me to go speak with Ms. Hutchens while you're making the call?" Hollis asked.

"Nah, you already made the tough call to Ellie. I'll go see Patti after I talk to Al."

"And I'll get ahold of Doug."

"Sounds good."

When I reached Detective Bach, I learned he'd already heard about the shooting. Even knowing that Mark Taylor's demise had at least been a possibility, he was distressed by the news of his death. "I can't believe we've lost another member of the force to murder. And such a nice individual."

I choked back tears. "Yeah, it's a lot to take in."

"What were the circumstances?"

"Trooper Taylor was responding to a DV report."

"Always dangerous duty." Al sighed. "Did he have a family?"

"A wife and two kids."

"Oh, dear. I'll need to drop by with my condolences."

And offer to pray with Ellie, no doubt.

"He was shot just outside of the shooter's residence. Hollis and I are there right now."

"Unfortunately, I'm involved in another homicide case for pretty much the rest of the day. I could see about booking one of the state's Cessnas this evening if you need me to be there that soon."

"It might not be possible to get a flight anytime today. Much of eastern Oregon is experiencing heavy windstorms, and they're predicted to continue through most of tonight."

"Flying is really that precarious?"

"Afraid so. The woman who reported the shooting this morning initially tried to call out a Life Flight helicopter, first from Pendleton and then La Grande, but they were grounded in both places due to high wind gusts. And I've already called Harry Bratton and given him a heads-up. Had to leave a message, but I'm hoping to get him out here right away."

"Good you did that. It's better to have him collect samples right at the scene. I'll drive over first thing in the morning. In the meantime, you know the drill."

"Unfortunately, I've become a little too used to the drill, Al."

"I hear you. Is there a way to lock up the place before you leave for the day?"

"I'll come up with something," I assured him.

"Sounds good. And if you speak with Mrs. Taylor, please send her my regards."

Police academy had trained all of us in the finer points of informing next of kin regarding the death of a loved one. But in my experience, when you *are* the next of kin, there's some chance you end up experiencing a strange animosity toward the person who brings you the news, whoever it is. Patti Hutchens was not next of kin, but she had a vested interest in Mark's survival. When I gave her the word, she sank into her dachshund-pillowed davenport sad, exhausted, and clearly anxious for me to take my leave.

Moving from her tidy little place, my thoughts turned to Duncan. I needed to get in touch with him right away. News traveled fast in our county. If he heard about a cop being shot out here, he'd be sick with worry. Hollis must have been thinking the same about Lil; when I caught up with him, he was inside my police rig, talking to her on the phone.

I left him to finish his call and tucked myself behind a small shed, out of the tempest whipping through a stand of blue spruce, and dialed up McKay's Feed and Tack. Fortunately, Duncan hadn't yet heard about the shooting. Unfortunately, after letting him know Mark had been shot and killed, he was anxious for me to head back to John Day.

"I can't do that, Dun. I still have work to do out here."

"But this is a cop killer we're talking about, babe."

"And the cop was part of my team. I'm not letting anyone else go after his murderer."

"Then promise to come home as soon as you can. Please."

"I'll be okay. Hollis is with me. Besides, it's Ellie who's not doing so well."

Just as we ended our call, Harry Bratton rang to tell me he was on his way.

"I'm glad you can make it out here this afternoon. The killer's place is a bloody mess."

"As in blood everywhere?"

"You got it."

"Is that where the officer was killed?"

"No. Mark was shot outside the dude's trailer house, but he went there in the first place on a DV call."

"Yeah, I was just on the phone with Sherry Linn. So all the blood, it's from the DV victim?"

"I assume so, but that's where you come in."

"All right. I'm about an hour to an hour and a half out."

"Thanks, Harry. You can't miss the trailer court. It's not far from the lone country store and service station, and I'm parked beside the lime-green mobile home in question."

I clicked off and moved from the shed's shelter to open ground. On the short walk to my SUV, the wind strengthened, nearly wrenching away my grip on the handle when I opened the driver's side door. I managed to slide inside and shut it against the onslaught of weather.

I raked the windblown hair from my face and sighed. "Harry's on his way."

"Good."

"Did you talk to Doug?"

"He's pretty down," Hollis said.

"I expected that, I guess."

"Yeah, me too." He paused. "Doug also told me that by the time he met up with the timber thinners, the cougar had apparently taken off. But after interviewing the crewmembers, he's pretty certain the animal was stalking them."

"Christ. That shit gives me the creeps."

"Does me too a little. And it gave the thinning crew the creeps as well. Doug said they decided to call it a day earlier than usual."

"I can see why."

"Anyway, he plans to confer with a big game specialist about trapping the cougar. Oh, and he got the name of the boss of the timber thinning outfit." Hollis brought out his notes. "Lyndon Cummings. Lives up the highway in Ukiah."

"I know Lyndon. He's a second or third cousin of mine, I can't remember which. Didn't know he lived in Ukiah, though. Is there an address?"

"A phone number and a PO box. But apparently he told Doug his house is the only one across the street from Jacoby's Hardware Store on Main Street."

"Ukiah's got fewer than two hundred residents, right?"

"Something like that, I think."

"Makes John Day seem like a metropolis," I put in. "Anyway, it should be pretty easy to track down Cousin Lyndon. I want to ask him about Charlie Archer, assuming Lyndon's the guy Patti mentioned had come to the trailer court looking for the reprobate."

"Makes sense." Hollis turned toward the white Oregon State Police Ram 2500 parked across the road. "What about Mark's truck?"

"Why don't you check it out? It'd be against protocol, and not like the man, but he might've left it unlocked with the keys in the ignition. Otherwise, we'll have to have it towed."

He stepped out of the Tahoe and wrestled to balance himself against the whipsaw gusts. Through the front window, I watched a car pull into Blue Mountain Gas & Groceries next to 395. It was possible the attendant had seen Archer pull out onto the highway this morning, maybe noticed which direction he went.

"Mark's vehicle was locked," Hollis said as he rejoined me.

"Should've known Mark would never leave it unlocked."

"And I reached out to Whitey Kern. We got lucky. He'd already been called out to Fox Valley, some rancher needing his tractor pulled up out of the mud, so he'll be here relatively soon with his tow truck."

A skiff of sugar snow danced in small pinwheels across the roadway and up the hill behind the trailer park.

I felt a chill. "I should've been nicer to Mark. He had a great heart. And I let his—I guess I'd call it his goofiness—get to me sometimes. The worst thing is, I think he knew what a butt I was to him, but bless his heart, he kept trying to get into my good graces."

"You were a lot more tolerant of him these past six months or so, and it showed."

"Awfully big of me, wasn't it? Anyway, what I want now more than anything is to find his killer. Let's head back inside Archer's place, check out cupboards, drawers, et cetera. Harry's on his way, so we should hold off on any sampling and dusting for prints, save all that for him. Especially given the quantity of blood splatter."

We stepped back outside and shuffled quickly to the green Fleetwood.

"I'll search the other rooms in back while you're going through the front," Hollis offered once we were back inside the trailer house.

"Sounds good. Let's keep an eye out for any photos of the woman."

My inspection of the combination kitchenette/dining/living room area took little time. And other than the requisite cooking accouterments—dishware, pots, pans, utensils, spices, some dry goods, and tinned soup and sauces—I didn't find much of interest in the cupboards. The small refrigerator was well stocked by comparison and included several packages of frozen venison dating back to last month's state-sanctioned hunting season. A few bills, a calendar and matchbook from a café in Long Creek, and an Extension Service bulletin titled, "Trees to Know in Oregon" composed the collection of items stashed in the two small drawers.

Hollis emerged from the rear of the mobile home. "Nothing much to see back there, and besides aspirin, there's zip in the bathroom's medicine cabinet. But I did find a photo." He handed it to me. "It was the only thing on the dresser. The guy is definitely Archer, and I assume the woman is this morning's DV victim."

"Dyed blond hair, dark roots, younger than him. That's gotta be her." She looked familiar, but I couldn't place the name. "This gal's really young, don't you think?"

"Yep. I'll snap a shot of the photo and send it off to regional dispatch."

"Before you do that, I'd like you to go next door and see if Patti Hutchens confirms this is the woman who lives with Archer. In the meantime, I'm going to try and find some means to lock up the trailer in case they come back tonight."

I trudged back to the Tahoe and searched the rear cargo hold and the front storage compartment for something to secure the place, only to come up empty. I was about ready to call Judge Campbell and beg him to let me tow the old Fleetwood trailer to John Day, when Hollis returned with a padlock and chain all still in the original packaging.

"Ms. Hutchens said she was happy to lend this to us if we needed it," he said.

"Thank God. I wasn't looking forward to rousting Judge Campbell from his courtroom just so I could get permission to haul it away as evidence."

"Yeah, that might've been interesting."

"And a pain in the ass all the way around." I thumbed toward Patti's home. "How's she doing, by the way?"

"She was emotional, but I think she was pleased we were planning to lock the trailer. She's worried Archer might come back, so she plans to stay with her sister in Mt. Vernon for a few days. Oh, and the woman in the photo is definitely the one who's been living with him."

"Okay, ship the photo to regional and to me. I'm going to lock up Archer's trailer, and once Whitey gets here, I'm thinking you should get a ride back to the station with him. I'll stay until Harry arrives, then I plan to pay a visit to Cousin Lyndon in Ukiah."

"Can't that visit wait until tomorrow?"

"Apparently not."

Whitey Kern arrived at the trailer park shortly before two in the afternoon. By the look of his tow truck, extracting the rancher's tractor from the mud had been a bit of an ordeal. I'd always known the man to be serious, kind, and meticulous about keeping his rigs spick-and-span at all times, so I decided not to razz him about the mess he'd made of his usually shiny red truck. I wasn't in that kind of a mood, anyway.

"Maggie, Hollis," Whitey said, tipping his hat. "I'm sorry to hear the news about Trooper Taylor. He was good people."

"Yeah, it's a shock, all right," I said.

"Sorry my truck's such a mess."

"We don't care about that, Whitey," Hollis put in. "We're just glad you were able to make it here so quickly."

Whitey blushed, fiddled with his hat, and gazed over at Mark Taylor's police vehicle. "Let's get her loaded up, if you don't mind helping."

"Happy to. And we'd appreciate you giving Hollis a ride back to the station."

"Sure, no problem. I promise the interior's clear of mud."

Hollis smiled. "I'm good either way. A little mud never hurt anyone."

Whitey and Hollis headed out with Mark's OSP-issued Ram 2500 lashed to the back of the tow truck. The battering wind had prompted Whitey to take extra precautions in securing the vehicle. And as they pulled away from the trailer court, I momentarily panicked watching them drive through Dale proper and turn south on 395. It would not do to lose three kind citizens in one day.

Closing my eyes, I willed that worry from my head just as Harry Bratton pulled up behind my Tahoe. I hopped out, and we greeted one another with a handshake.

"Thanks for taking the time," I said.

"Think I'm getting paid for it. Besides, Sherry Linn was pretty upset. I don't like to see that."

I'd suspected they had become sweet on one another over the last three or four months, but even his sentiment just now didn't confirm it.

Harry gathered up his equipment, and I led him to Archer's trailer house and opened the padlock I'd attached to the front door. Once inside, I again wondered where Archer had taken the woman and whether she was still conscious or whether she was dead.

"Jesus H. Christ," Harry exclaimed, perusing the walls. "Who would do this to another human being?"

"A fucking bully."

"And don't forget, a cop killer." He sighed and attended to his equipment. "This will take me a while, Maggie. And I want to get it done by nightfall."

"Is there anything I can do to help?"

"You can find the asshole who did this."

"I'm on it."

3

LATE AFTERNOON, NOVEMBER 12

I left Harry to conduct his work and pulled up at Blue Mountain Gas & Groceries before leaving Dale. The service station out front offered two pumps, one with diesel and one with gasoline. There weren't any cars waiting to fuel up or parked in the vicinity of the place, for that matter. It seemed a good time to inquire whether an employee or possibly a customer had noticed which direction Charlie Archer had driven when he sped onto Highway 395 this morning.

As I stepped out of my rig, I battled nature some but managed to make my way inside the semi-darkened building. The space was close to steamy, what with the furnace on high, the collection of preserved animal heads jutting from the walls, and the stuffed, glass-eyed bear standing watch. It was both a hothouse and a taxidermist's dream.

The floorboards creaked as I stepped toward the checkstand where the short, wiry clerk greeted me with a cheerful nod and scratched his scruff of silver whiskers.

"Can you believe this wind?" he asked. "Been livin' here a thousand years and never seen such a thing."

I must have looked rattled because he paused before going on.

"What can I do you for, officer?"

"Sorry, I didn't catch your name."

"Hi, I'm Hi." He laughed at his little joke and stuck his arm out. "It's short for Hiram. Hiram Appleby."

I shook his veiny hand. "Sergeant Blackthorne, Oregon State Police. I'm assuming you know about the shooting this morning?"

"Oh, yeah. Even helped Patti get that other police officer into a down sleeping bag and under a bit of cover."

"Unfortunately, he didn't make it."

"Oh, hell. Sorry to hear that. You should know, though, Patti and I did the best we could under the circumstances to keep the guy alive."

"Of course. I appreciate all you both did."

I couldn't gauge his response exactly, but I needed to get to the meat of why I'd dropped by in the first place.

"I'm hoping you might have noticed Patti's neighbor as he was leaving Dale earlier today," I said. "Maybe you saw which direction he took off in?"

"That guy with the old orange Scout who shot the officer? No, sorry to say. But Daddy might've."

It took quite a bit of forbearance to refrain from showing my astonishment. I figured Hi to be at least in his mid-seventies, so Daddy had to be quite a bit older. But I decided Daddy would have to do under the circumstances. Besides, Hi was already hollering for him to come to the front counter.

"Daddy," he yelled again. "There's a police officer here to see you."

"For shit's sake," Daddy, I assumed, bellowed as he ambled to the counter, "quit your caterwauling, Hiram."

I bent forward and shook hands with the frail, shrunken fellow. "Mr. Appleby, I'm Sergeant Blackthorne, Oregon State Police."

"I ain't an Appleby," he said, his gray, bloodshot eyes staring through me. "Last name's Ponder. Married Hiram's mother when he was a kid. Now, what do you wanna talk to me for?"

A chap who got straight to the point. Just my kind of guy.

"A neighbor in the trailer park beat up a woman and killed a police officer this morning, then he escaped with the woman in his 1980 orange International Scout. The only way out of Dale is Highway 395, and if you saw him leave, I hope you can tell me which direction he drove."

"North," he said. "And he gunned it. Didn't see who or how many was in the rig, just seen it was that orange hog of a thing."

"Thank you, Mr. Ponder. I'll also need your first name for my report."

"Zeke's the first name. Alfonso's the middle. Need my date of birth, too?"

I wanted to say yes just to satisfy my curiosity about his age. "No, thank you, sir. That won't be necessary."

"So, are we done here?"

Not only did he get straight to the point, but he also appeared to be another crotchety old man who didn't like cops.

"Yep, we're done. For now, that is."

He bobbed his head dismissively and sauntered to the back of the building.

I thanked Hi and drove the fifty feet or so to the junction with 395. North could take me all the way to the Canadian border. North also took me past Road 10 just up the way, which led to Desolation Ridge and the worksite where the cougar had been spotted this morning. And if I kept going a little further north beyond Road 10, I'd get to Ukiah, where I could find Lyndon Cummings and ask him what he knew about Charlie Archer.

The Canadian border was mildly tempting, but the chances of that being a fruitful venture were nil to none. I needed more to go on before heading up Road 10 toward Desolation Ridge, so a trip to Cousin Lyndon's was clearly next on my agenda.

I pulled out onto Highway 395 and began the twenty-one mile trek to Ukiah. Designated as a scenic corridor, it was a narrow and serpentine stretch of roadway that wound upward another four hundred feet in elevation. The continual bluster made the trip more treacherous than usual but failed to take away from the grace of bluebunch wheatgrass, now golden in the waning sun and buffeted by a fast breeze.

Turning east on State Route 244, I rumbled along for a mile or so and arrived in Ukiah, Oregon, proper. Finding Jacoby's Hardware Store was relatively easy, as was locating Lyndon's house directly across the street. It helped that a large, battered crew cab pickup was parked outside with signage on the door panel indicating the truck was the property of Cummings Forest Maintenance.

Lyndon opened the front door as I traipsed up the walkway. I couldn't exactly remember the last time I'd seen him, but I would've recognized him anywhere, despite the signs of a slight beer gut and his graying hair. We hadn't been all that close back in the day, but in truth, I'd expected a friendlier greeting than it seemed I was about to receive.

"You need something, officer?"

"You don't recognize me, do you?"

"No. Except you're not the same state cop who drove out to my worksite today."

"Trooper Doug Vaughn. He and I work together. Are you the guy who called in the cougar sighting this morning?"

"Yeah. My crew was pretty anxious. Is there some kind of problem?"

"Not at all, but I wanted to speak to you about another matter." I stepped closer to the porch. "I'm Sergeant Maggie Blackthorne."

He eyed my name tag. "Maggie Blackthorne? My second cousin?"

"Yep."

"You must not be on Facebook."

"I definitely avoid all that crap."

He smiled. "Come on in. It's cold as hell out there."

He opened the door wider, and I took the steps up to the porch and moved inside.

Some fool had covered the walls of his warm, comfortable front room with fake wood paneling back in the sixties or seventies. But mostly, it was a lovely home, nicely decorated with antiques and tasteful historic paintings and photographs. No shots of a wife and kids, though.

"Please, sit wherever," he said.

I seated myself in the lovely Mission-style rocker near his potbelly woodstove and across from the chair he'd taken.

"This doesn't seem like a social call. Because I can't remember the last time I saw you or knew what you were up to. I thought you'd moved to the Willamette Valley or something."

"I lived there for a while, ended up becoming a State Police officer. A little over four years ago I was promoted to sergeant, and I asked to be stationed in John Day."

"You've been back in eastern Oregon that long? Man, I need to pay more attention."

"Well, I could've also reached out with a howdy."

We sat silently after that. It seemed our bit of back-and-forth had reached its conclusion, as will happen when you run into a long-lost relative or friend after a couple of decades or so.

"Actually, Lyndon," I began. "I'm here to ask you about one of your workers."

He glanced at me suspiciously. "Which of my crew did you wanna ask me about?"

"Charles Archer. You probably know him as Charlie."

"I fired the idiot over a week ago. But how'd you know he'd worked for me?"

"We received a call this morning—his neighbor reporting a disturbance occurring inside Archer's residence. The neighbor told us you had recently stopped by her place in an effort to locate the guy."

"Yeah, so I could fire the jerk. He was always late or absent and/or drunk or high, I never knew which."

"Was he ever violent?"

"Not that I ever saw, but that doesn't mean he wasn't. He was often mouthy or unfriendly, but I didn't care about that. I have lots of people working for me who are one or both of those things, but as long as they do their jobs and I can count on them to show up on time, I don't give a care about their nasty personalities."

"One more thing I'd like to ask you. The woman who lives with Mr. Archer? Do you happen to know her name?"

"Jenna Rhinehart's been staying with him." Lyndon was now alarmed. "You said disturbance, what kind of disturbance?"

"The neighbor was concerned it was a domestic violence situation, so I sent an officer out to investigate."

"Why didn't Jenna call me?"

I let that sit a moment. "Is she a relative of yours?"

"No, but I've known her since she was born."

"Maybe Jenna wasn't able to call anyone."

His eyes widened. "My God, where did he take her?"

"That's what I'm hoping you can help me with."

"I...don't. I got no damned idea." Lyndon shrugged. "Maybe out where he goes mudding in that Scout of his?"

"Where's that?"

"Somewhere around Desolation Ridge, near my worksite."

The man was distressed, so I paused, gave him some time to let it all sink in.

"Is Jenna related to former sheriff Dirk Rhinehart?" I finally asked.

"His daughter. And my godchild, I guess you'd say. She's the only reason I gave that asshole a job."

I knew the *asshole* reference was directed at Charlie Archer, but Dirk Rhinehart was the epitome of asshole.

"Are you a friend of her father's?"

"God, no. He was married to my pal Anita for a while, but Jenna's been estranged from Dirk since she was very young. Her mother and I are close —not a couple, mind you—just good friends, and I love Jenna like she's my own kid."

"Where did she grow up?"

"Anita and Jenna lived in Dayville for a few years when the girl was really young, and then her mother moved them to John Day. Jenna graduated from Grant Union High School last year. Was planning to go to college in La Grande but somehow hooked up with Archer. I'll fucking kill that shithead if—"

"Lyndon, you need to calm down, stay out of this, and let us do our job. But I'll be straight with you. There's not much doubt that Archer physically abused a woman—Jenna, in all likelihood—in his mobile home this morning. But we haven't officially identified her as the victim."

He nodded reluctantly and pulled his wallet out of his hip pocket. "Just remembered, I got a recent picture with me. Her high school graduation photo."

I took it from him. "Thank you. I'll make sure this gets back to you."

"I want you to make sure Jenna gets back. Alive and well."

"I completely agree," I said and glimpsed at the photo. No big surprise, but Jenna was a match to the woman in the framed shot Hollis had found, only not with bleached-blond hair and a body too scrawny for words.

Lyndon sank back in his chair. "I want to know whatever you find out as soon as you find it out. If that's okay."

"A statewide search has already been ordered, and I'll let you know when I learn something concrete."

"Appreciate that, Maggie."

Lyndon reminded me of other aging bachelors I'd known. Shy, with few friends who were often women they relied on for safe kinship, camaraderie, and a certain kind of love that came without the entanglement of sex.

"There is one more thing, Lyndon. The OSP trooper who responded to the report of a domestic violence incident inside Archer's place was shot shortly after he arrived. He didn't survive, and we suspect Charlie Archer killed him."

"Then what in the hell are you doing sitting in my living room? Get out there and find him. And find my Jenna."

I took Lyndon's point about finding Jenna and raised myself from his rocker. "You're right. Do you have any sense about where Archer may have fled to?"

"I wish I did."

"Okay, I'll send someone to speak to Jenna's mother."

"I'll do that. She'll take it better from me."

"Afraid that's not how this works," I said, handing him my card. "I need Anita's contact information, and is her last name Rhinehart?"

"Yeah, she still goes by Rhinehart." He pulled out his company business card and jotted something down. "I put Anita's number and address on the back."

"Thanks," I said and took the card. "I'll be in touch."

Shortly after pulling away from Lyndon's house, I hit the Bluetooth connection and called Hollis's office phone.

"Maggie? You on your way back to John Day?"

"Just leaving Ukiah, and I was hoping you're up for a visit with a citizen before heading home."

"If that's what you need me to do, I am."

"Unfortunately, it's what I need you to do."

I relayed the highlights of my conversation with Lyndon Cummings and read off Anita Rhinehart's info.

"Got it. I'll also drop by Sheriff Rhinehart's place afterward. But before you hang up, Maggie, you should talk to Doug. He has some news to share."

"Is he still at work?"

"Yeah. I'll send you over to his desk phone."

Doug picked up right away. "Evening, Maggie."

"You should go on home, Doug. It's been a long day."

"And for you too. Anyway, I wanted to talk to you because Hollis told me all about Archer. I realized I might've seen a truck like his on my way back from interviewing the thinning crew. I didn't catch the plate number or get a look at the driver, unfortunately, but how many of those old Internationals can there be out there? Plus it was definitely orange."

"Where'd you spot it?"

"I was traveling west on Road 10 heading back to Highway 395 when I saw it turn up the gravel track that goes to Desolation Ridge."

"Had to be Archer. You didn't notice a female passenger, by any chance?"

"No, but I wasn't paying attention."

"I'm nearing Road 10 right now. How far from the entrance do you think you were when you noticed the Scout moving toward Desolation Ridge?"

"I'd estimate around fifteen miles."

"I'm going to drive up 10 at least that far, see what I can see."

"Be careful out there. It's a pretty rough road part of the way."

"I will. How're you doing, by the way?"

"I'll be okay," he said.

"Glad to hear that, now go on home."

"No disrespect, but you should do the same."

"See you tomorrow, Doug."

Continuing south on 395, I brooded about Archer and his orange International Scout. Patti had described it as having caked mud on the truck's body. And Lyndon hadn't seemed to be aware the activity was illegal when he mentioned Archer fancied driving out to Desolation Ridge to go mudding. Those facts, combined with the truck's vanity plate—M-U-D R-U-N—likely meant he often went there for that purpose.

I envisioned the scofflaw loser squealing around the forest, tearing up threatened watershed and vegetation, and pulled off the highway and onto Road 10. Enormous, wet drops began to fall, whipped and swirling in the crosswind, and pelted the hood and roof of the Tahoe. Within a few miles of travel, I realized how asinine it was to be driving on flood-damaged pavement on a rainy night and in an area with which I had little recent familiarity.

As a kid, we'd camped near here late one summer. Zoey, my mother, had spent the days gathering wildflowers and singing all the old hymns she'd abandoned to her childhood. My father, Tate, had chopped up downed tree limbs to use for firewood and built a pit for bonfires. We stayed until a Forest Service worker let us know it was wildfire season and not safe, or really legal, for us to be lighting fires. The outing had lasted a couple of weeks and was one of my fondest memories. Not long after that, my parents' miseries, for years a shadowy presence, took hold of them for good.

I'd driven a good while in the growing darkness listening to k.d. lang singing a duet with Tony Bennett, and I had no idea if I'd traveled five or fifteen miles, having not checked mileage when I turned down Road 10.

"You're an idiot, Blackthorne."

A moment after chastising myself, a vacillating pine tree appeared in my headlights, heaved its roots from the sodden earth, and crashed thunderously across the roadway. I pumped the brakes and slid to a stop.

"Goddamn it!" I screamed. A futile, profane rebuke of Mother Nature.

I backed up slightly, figuring to turn around and return to Highway 395, but as I moved the steering wheel, my tires spun wildly, stuck in a hollow of deep mud. In a fit of driver's remorse, I shifted into four-wheel drive, moved the truck slightly forward, then slightly backward, attempting to rock my way out of what I assumed to be a large sludge-filled pothole. Meanwhile, a downpour began to fall in great, heavy sheets.

Suddenly hungry and slightly delirious, I put the Tahoe in park and fished around in my pack for a piece of fruit or a bag of cashews, snacks I occasionally remembered to toss inside. Toward the bottom of the pack, I wrenched up an overly ripe banana, scarfed it down. Grabbed my half-full water bottle and drank a portion of its contents.

I knew I should call Duncan, or at least reach out to Whitey Kern again, but I sat in the dark feeling sorry for myself and having an internal argument about whether to get out of the rig and build a branch-laden pathway leading out of the hole I was stuck in.

Looking out across a swath of darkened forest partially lit by my headlights, the eyes of some animal shone in the distance. The summer Zoey, Tate, and I stayed out here, we had watched deer and elk grazing near our encampment, and once a lone bull moose foraged in the distance. The critter peering in the direction of my SUV wasn't a deer or elk, and certainly not a moose. But it was larger than a raccoon and most other nocturnal animals I'd ever observed.

Before I had an opportunity to speculate about the creature and its searching eyes, it moved rapidly into full view. A large cougar stood six feet from my Tahoe. It had to be the animal Cousin Lyndon had reported stalking the timber thinning crew earlier today.

My shaking hands grasped the steering wheel tightly as I gunned the engine and jerked forward out of the pothole. I turned around in the roadway and sped back toward Highway 395, the big cat bounding after.

4

NIGHT, NOVEMBER 12

What the hell had I been thinking, pulling onto a forest road at nightfall and during the onset of a torrential downpour? Even worse, momentarily stranded and spurred on by an overactive imagination, I'd convinced myself the prowling cougar from this morning had pursued me as I sped away in my three-ton vehicle.

My trek over the washboard surface of Road 10 had been an act of stupidity. One that would only serve as fodder for future nightmares. In retreat, I plied the gas and checked the rearview mirror, relieved to see nothing but the churn of mud shining in the taillights.

Once Highway 395 came into view, I parked on the road shoulder and punched in Duncan's number. He picked up on the first ring.

"On my way home, Dun."

"Do you know what time it is?"

"Yeah. That's why I pulled over to call you."

He sighed. "Are you hungry?"

"Starving."

"I made your favorite."

Didn't know I had a favorite. "Great. I hope you made enough for you too."

"Har har."

"I'm getting back on the road now."

"Drive carefully, babe."

I was damned exhausted, and it would take me more than an hour to get there. I retrieved my bottle of water, took a couple of swigs, and searched the satellite channels. Landing on an Americana music station, I listened to Joseph, a trio of sisters from Portland, as they sang "SOS (Overboard)." Perfect. I obviously needed some kind of help.

From the pathway leading to the front door, I could smell chicken frying. Duncan had been struggling to perfect my mother's recipe, a craving left over from my childhood. He hadn't quite gotten Zoey's method down yet, even with my coaching via memory. And certain I'd over-spice, undercook, or burn the bird, I'd never actually attempted to tackle the recipe myself.

I slipped inside the house, and like every day since my aged tabby left this world, I paused at his cat pillow still sitting in its place near the front entrance. "Ah, Louie. I miss you, old boy."

I removed my coat and holster, hung both inside the front closet, and turned to find Duncan standing behind me holding a fork. He wore the chef's apron I had made as a birthday present. It was the first and last time I used the sewing machine I had long ago inherited from Zoey. I'd ripped out seams and started from the beginning three or four times, and I never quite got the hang of hemming the thing. But Dun's reaction when he received my handmade gift—surprised, thrilled, emotional—was worth every frustrating hour I'd put in.

"Supper smells fantastic," I said.

"Yeah, well, you look fantastic." He wrapped me in his bull-rider arms.

"Watch the fork there, dude."

He loosened his grip but continued to hold me close. "You want to shower first, or eat first?"

I kissed him. "You're too damn nice to me. So to return the favor, I'll go clean up before chowing down."

After my shower, I easily could have trundled off to bed and fallen into a deep sleep, but Duncan deserved more than that. Plus, as it turned out, he had mastered my mother's fried chicken recipe.

"Delicious. Zoey would be proud." I brought up my glass of milk, Duncan lifted his beer mug, and we toasted.

"We might need to postpone the wedding," he suggested.

I momentarily found the suggestion surprising. "Oh, because of Mark's funeral."

"Well, I'm assuming the family won't wait that long. But I meant the murder investigation."

"I called Al right after I learned Mark had died. He's arriving tomorrow, and the investigation shouldn't take too long since we know who we're looking for. Unless we can't locate the shooter right away, of course."

"How dangerous is this guy? I assume it's a guy, anyway. Does he have a history of violence?"

I took his hand. "Please, Dun. It's been a terrible day. Let's not go there, okay?"

He acquiesced, and we concentrated on the meal, chitchatted about his day at work for a while, and by the time we'd finished eating, my tired, pregnant body had regained some energy.

"I talked to Dorie on the drive home tonight," I said. "She and some of the other church ladies were already gathered at Mark and Ellie's house."

"Personally, I'd hate that. And I know you would too."

"We could try to nix that possibility by leaving instructions in our wills, but this is Dorie we're talking about. I'm as close to her as a daughter, and by extension, you're about to become her unofficial son-in-law. She'd just ignore our wishes."

"It's the cross we've got to bear."

"Oh, good one."

He sent me a wry smile. "Yeah, I've been practicing up lately."

"Dorie also told me Mark and Ellie wrote each other a last letter every few years or so."

"What's a last letter?"

"In advance of your own death, you leave a note for someone to read after you're gone. Anyway, Ellie fetched his most recent letter from their family Bible, and it seemed to bring her a bit of comfort, I guess."

Duncan puzzled over that for a time. As for myself, I wasn't sure a last letter would bring me anything but more heartbreak.

"Let's toss everything in the dishwasher and hit the hay," I said.

"As long as I can hold you for a while."

"I'd like that."

Waking next to Duncan's warm body, I was certain snow had fallen nearby. The surrounding higher, white-capped peaks had hinted at nature's reset a few weeks before, and this morning, I finally caught the scent of the approaching season. I usually welcomed the ripe-apple essence of autumn shifting toward the winter's dry juniper berry crispness, but today had begun with a feeling of dread. Where had Jenna Rhinehart spent the night?

Hollis had radioed me while I was on the road back to John Day last night to let me know he'd spoken with Jenna's mother in person. His visit with an emotional Anita Rhinehart hadn't gone well, and she'd taken her fear and grief out on Holly.

Anita's ex-husband, Dirk, hadn't taken the news much better. He'd also rattled on about my law enforcement skills, claiming that if he had still been sheriff of Grant County, he would've amassed a search party and combed the entirety of the Umatilla Forest and not stopped until his daughter was found.

In terms of police work, yesterday had been a shitty day all the way around.

"You're awake," Duncan said in his hoarse morning voice.

"I forgot to tell you. I spotted a cougar lurking in the woods last night."

"You dreamed about a cougar again?"

"No, I saw one. Out in the Umatilla Forest."

"You were out in the Umatilla Forest last night?"

"Well, nighttime comes on pretty early these days."

"I'm glad you didn't tell me this before."

I moved closer to his bare chest and pressed my nakedness against his. "What would you have done if I had told you? Gone out there with your shotgun?"

"Oh, you're witty this morning."

"Fuck you, I'm witty every morning."

He propped himself on his elbow. "There were some days early in your pregnancy when you weren't witty at all."

I shoved him playfully, and he pulled me close.

"I love you, babe."

I passed a finger over his daybreak whiskers, and we kissed.

"I need to get a move on," I said, rolled out of bed, and reached for my robe.

He sat up. "I don't know if I should tell you this, but this is the first time I've noticed. Your body has changed just slightly."

I checked out my image in his full-length mirror. A bit of a tummy bump and slightly darker nipples.

"Well, what did you expect? I'm expecting."

"I like the look."

"You damn well better. This is all your doing."

I made it to the office early and before everyone else, which didn't surprise me given the events of yesterday. It was hard enough coming to terms with a coworker passing away, but when we're talking about a friend who happens to also be a colleague and the victim of cold-blooded murder, that's very different emotional calculus.

Walking through the quiet modular, I paused at Mark Taylor's desk. Decorated with family photos, most depicting their trip to Disneyland last year, I momentarily pondered what it must be like to live that kind of life. Marriage, children, and church the priority, career secondary to all that. Didn't mean individuals couldn't prioritize exactly that way and still be good at their jobs. Lots of people had managed it, including Mark.

Religion wasn't a concern of mine, but I did wonder about the place order of Duncan and our child in relation to my cop life.

"Maggie?" Sherry Linn had arrived. Her attire was far more conservative than I'd ever known her to dress. All of her usual bangles, scarves, and colorful frilly outfits were a welcome contrast when compared to the drab and uniform uniforms that were required of the rest of us. I always got a kick out of her reaction to office visitors who seemingly assumed she was an airhead based on her appearance. On several such occasions, she had artfully disabused folks of that notion with a few well-placed ten-dollar words.

"How are you this morning?" I asked her.

"I don't really know." She sighed. "In disbelief, I guess. Mark was such a nice man."

"He was."

While Sherry Linn delivered her sack lunch to the small refrigerator stationed near the storage room in back, I leaned against the front counter, momentarily paralyzed by an old sorrow.

The office door opened behind me, and I heard Hollis hang up his coat and hat. Next, he plunked his massive forearms on the counter beside mine.

"Don't think I've asked you lately, Holly. How's Lil doing?"

"Doing pretty well with the chemo and feeling stronger every day."

"That's good."

"But *I* feel like shit."

Hollis cussed occasionally, but I'd never heard him say anything about being unwell.

"Sorry to hear you're under the weather. What's going on?"

"I'm sick of people being murdered in our district."

"I was just thinking something similar."

Sherry Linn joined us at the counter. "This is what, the third murder in three months?"

"Seems worse when put that way," I said.

"Tense times everywhere these days, seems to me. Lots of anger and distrust," Hollis added.

"That's no excuse."

"None of us think it is, Maggie," he said forcefully.

"I know that, Holly."

He moved abruptly to his desk.

Hollis was rarely annoyed, and never with me. I told myself this wasn't really about being irritated. I knew he carried a particular anxiety with him always, even without the shadow of a murdered colleague. He was a Black man living in the rural American West with his Paiute wife and their son and among a population that didn't always respond well to change and difference. He had reason to be anxious.

The office was unnaturally quiet. Hollis, Doug Vaughn, and I sat at our desks typing up our formal reports regarding yesterday's events. Meanwhile Sherry Linn busied herself with the tasks that had transformed our office into an organized and more professional police station.

Shortly before nine, Doug mentioned he planned to patrol the Strawberry Wilderness Area this morning after he stopped by to visit Mark's wife, Ellie. The mere mention of her name was guilt inducing. I hadn't yet called to see how she was faring.

After Doug took off, Hollis paused his rapid-fire typing. "Before I left Anita Rhinehart's place yesterday, she called a friend—your cousin Lyndon. I gathered he was planning to drive over and spend the night."

"Lyndon's pretty worried about her daughter," I put in.

"Yeah, I got that."

"Oh, here's one for the books. Last night after Doug told me he thought he'd spotted Archer's vehicle turning up the gravel road to Desolation Ridge, I stupidly attempted to go out there and hunt for Archer and the woman myself. It was pouring rain, and I just about got the Tahoe stuck after a tree fell across the road in front of me."

"And are we going to try and travel out there this morning?"

I drove the image of that damn cougar out of my head. "I am. But because of that downed tree, I might have to figure out a different route. I'd like you to come along, but I understand if you—"

"Stop. Please. I was out of sorts earlier, and I took it out on you. I apologize."

"Not necessary."

"When do you want to leave?"

"I checked the weather report, and the rain out in the Umatilla Forest is supposedly subsiding around ten this morning."

"Assuming the forecast is accurate, if we left now, we'd be landing at about the right time to begin a search of the area."

"All right. Let's roll, but we'll take both of our rigs this time."

"Sounds like a plan."

———

We checked in with Sherry Linn before taking off. She was planning to visit Ellie Taylor during her lunch break. When Hollis and I heard that, we eyed one another.

"We're on our way to Ellie's now," I said. "After that, we're headed out to Desolation Ridge to search for Archer and Jenna Rhinehart."

"Is that the woman's name?" Sherry Linn asked.

"She's a kid, really. Graduated from high school this past June."

"Is she related to the former sheriff?"

"His daughter."

"Will that complicate things?"

"Not if I can help it," I said and put on my coat.

"Be careful out there," she said as we took our leave.

"One of us will call from the road later this afternoon."

We hopped in our look-alike Tahoes and drove toward Ellie and Mark's home. On the way, we passed her driving the family's minivan in the opposite direction. Her mother and her children were also seated in the car. I radioed Hollis.

"Looks like Ellie was on her way somewhere," he said, picking up.

"Sam Damon's mortuary is my guess."

"We keep driving?"

"We keep driving."

We signed off our radio call, but Hollis phoned me back immediately.

"Is there a problem, Holly?"

"No, it's just, I don't think I've told you this, but I like the idea of you getting married on Thanksgiving Day."

I hadn't expected that, but it was a sign he was back to his normal self.

"Me too," I answered. "Someone else will do all the cooking, and all I have to do is show up, say *I do*, and pig out."

"And all I have to do is show up in a suit and tie and pretend to give you away."

That reminded me of something I'd been meaning to ask. "Would you be willing to wear the African-print jacket you wore to your wedding? You know, instead of wearing a suit and tie."

"Dang. That was supposed to be a surprise. Don't let on to Lil. She's been planning it all for a while."

Hearing that almost gave rise to some waterworks on my part. "Is she wearing the Paiute wedding dress she wore when you two got married?"

"She is, and wait till you see the outfit she's conjured up for your ring bearer. A mix of Black and American Indian traditions, so she tells me."

"Well, that clinches it. Makes the whole damn rigmarole worth it."

"I thought you'd like that. Talk to you when we get to Desolation Ridge."

"Yep."

5

MORNING, NOVEMBER 13

On the drive out to the Umatilla National Forest, I attempted to contact Al Bach. Assuming he was on the road himself and driving toward John Day, I left a message on his smartphone. But as the old adage went, *never assume.*

Shortly after leaving the voicemail, Corporal McIntyre, the district commander in Bend, radioed me. I'd met him the one time last summer. He wasn't particularly friendly, but speaking of old adages, he clearly didn't suffer fools lightly. Out of respect for that alone, I put on my serious, professional police officer voice.

"Sir, how can I help you this morning?"

"Find the criminal who murdered Trooper Mark Taylor."

"On my way to the location where the killer was reportedly seen." Speaking of assuming, I was. And hoping Doug Vaughn was correct, that he'd actually spotted Archer's old orange International Scout turning up the road to Desolation Ridge.

"I have other unfortunate news," he interjected ominously. "Detective Bach appears to have suffered a heart attack last night. He's stabilized and in the hospital, but I've assigned a different detective to work with you on the case."

I was shocked. Al Bach was about the fittest law enforcement officer I'd ever known. I wasn't sure of his age, but I knew he'd been a member of the force for going on three decades, so in his fifties at least. And not a person I would have seen as heart attack prone.

"I'm sorry to hear that about Detective Bach. He's an inspiring mentor."

"Yes, he is, and he'll be back in action in no time. I'm sure of it."

Somehow Corporal McIntyre didn't sound very sure of it.

"Anyway," he continued. "Detective Bryce Horne has been assigned to the case. He'll be reaching out to you later today."

"I appreciate you alerting me. Please pass along my best wishes to Detective Bach."

"Will do."

After signing off, I considered reaching out to Ray Gattis, the medical examiner who had accompanied Al Bach to the scene of too many murders in my county over the last couple of years. It had been a few months since the two of us had communicated, but last I knew, she and Al were still trying and failing to end their affair.

The drive to northeastern Grant County was only in its second day and already tiresome. Beautiful country, stark and luminous all at once, but the distance we needed to travel in search of a violent killer and the eighteen-year-old victim of his brutality was taking its toll on this expectant mother's stamina.

My phone rang. In the mindset of avoiding a discussion with Detective Bryce Horne for as long as I could, I made sure I knew who it was before answering.

"Ray, I was just thinking about you."

"That must mean you've heard the news about Al."

"Afraid so. Corporal McIntyre put in a call about ten minutes ago. How are you holding up?"

"Numb. Sad. Guilty."

"Guilty?"

"We were together when it happened. Working a case, but on our way back to my place."

She began to quietly cry.

"I'm so sorry, Ray."

She took a jagged breath. "Thanks. I'm sorry too and driving your way to meet up with Sam Damon at his mortuary."

"Mark Taylor's autopsy?"

"Yeah. I don't remember meeting the officer. Just that other trooper, name's Hollis, I think."

"That's right. Hollis Jones."

She sighed. "Who is McIntyre sending to cover for Al?"

"Um, a guy named Bryce Horne."

"Fuck. That shithead?"

"Great. And here I thought I wouldn't be coming across any more male shitheads in my life."

"Well, that will never happen. This one reminds me of your ex-husband, or I should say, second ex-husband. Speaking of husbands, how's the Duncan guy?"

"You and I haven't touched base for a while, have we?"

"No. What's new?"

"Duncan and I are getting married on Thanksgiving."

"I don't believe you."

I laughed. "It's true. And are you sitting down?"

"Uh-huh, and driving the ugliest state-owned, American-made car I've ever been in."

"Well, don't go into shock and wreck the thing, but I'm four months pregnant."

"How in God's name did that happen?"

"Oh, divine intervention, I suspect."

"Yeah, more like not being mindful of the calendar."

"Something like that."

"Well, last I knew, Oregon wasn't even close to limiting a woman's right to choose."

"Oh, I've chosen not to in the past, and I made a choice this time too."

"Then congratulations are in order."

I definitely wasn't completely confident about my parenting skills, but from the moment I knew I was expecting, there was no question about having this child. I also knew that to be true in part because I was taking this journey with Duncan. Made all the difference in the world.

"Thanks, Ray. Are you planning on staying in John Day tonight?"

"I haven't decided. I couldn't bear to go to the hospital and find Al surrounded by his wife and family. But if I drive back to Bend later, I wouldn't be able to stop myself from going there to see him."

"If you're still in town this evening, let's get together."

"I'd like that, Maggie."

Just north of Dale, which was really more of a pit stop than a village, I'd decided, I turned onto Forest Road 10. I pulled over to the road shoulder and idled the engine, waiting for Hollis to catch up. He soon pulled up next to my rig and rolled down the front passenger-side window of his vehicle. I followed suit with my driver's-side window.

"How far do we figure?" he asked me.

"I brought an atlas with me, but I also checked it before we left. It's about fifteen miles to the single-track road leading to Desolation Ridge, near as I can figure. Then another slow-going twenty-mile climb over unimproved roadway."

"Where to after we get out there?"

"Let's figure that out when we get there, assuming we can get there, given the tree that fell across the road last night."

Hollis started to roll up the window.

"Wait, I got some other news on the way out here. Al Bach apparently had a heart attack last night. Another homicide detective's been assigned to the case."

"Is Detective Bach going to be all right?"

"Don't know about that, really, but I'm sending good thoughts his way."

"I'll do the same."

I moved out, and Holly followed me up the road. I put in an old Suzanne Vega CD, listened to her sing "Left of Center," and let the rest of the album play out. The high winds of yesterday had skedaddled, along with last night's downpour, and despite my earlier premonition, it didn't appear snow had fallen. I took all that as a hopeful sign that if Jenna Rhinehart spent the night out here in Archer's Scout, at least she didn't freeze to death.

We drove along a crystal-clear creek past a vibrant patch of lodgepole pine and an ancient copse of old-growth fir, surrounded by the ever-present Blue Mountain Range and the North Fork Wilderness. I'd forgotten how thick and verdant the Umatilla Forest could be. Traveling through stunning landscape was the payoff for the long drive to get here.

Coming upon the tree that had fallen and blocked my Tahoe during last night's deluge, I spotted a relatively simple pathway around it. It required four-wheel drive, but that was exactly why rural Oregon state cops drove heavy-duty vehicles of the type. I wasn't sure why OSP officers in the metropolitan areas had to be outfitted with them, but this was a philosophical question I wasn't going to explore.

Arriving at the single-track road—number 1010, it turned out—that wound toward Desolation Ridge, which now towered above us just to the southeast, we began the literal slog up the muddy, unpaved byway. Last night's rain had taken care of any tire tracks that may have been left before the storm, and none were present this morning.

We passed over a last rough patch of unimproved road, stopped, and got out of our rigs. Before I had gone to the office this morning, Duncan had insisted I take along the quartered apple, thermos of milk, and peanut butter and jelly sandwich he'd packed for me. I brought out the brown paper sack he'd stashed my snack/lunch in and pulled out the plastic container of apple chunks.

"I see your mom is making sure you're eating healthy," Hollis said.

"Yep, he is. No more greasy Prairie Maid burgers for me."

"I don't believe that."

"All right, no more greasy burgers until next week, then." I offered up a piece of the fruit.

"Nah. Thanks, though." He gazed up at the fat, rocky ridge in front of us.

I continued chewing a piece of apple.

"Where to next?"

I shrugged. "They could be anywhere out here, don't you think?"

"Definitely. Those old four-wheel-drive Scouts, like the one Archer owns, could travel about anywhere out here."

"Yeah, that's what I was afraid of."

Hollis pointed to a sign marking a trailhead. "He might've been able to drive on the trail, at least partway."

"That's illegal, right?"

"Oh, you're hilarious. And in rare form this morning, aren't you?"

"Not so rare, I'd say. Anyway, let's take a look at the topographical atlas."

We stepped to my Tahoe, and I drew the atlas out of my pack, spread it out on the hood.

"Here's where we are," I said, pointing to the spot we had driven to. "Using the mileage guide on the legend, you can see the trail goes on for a ways. The north loop continues into the wilderness area. The south loop ends up at Desolation Guard Station, a forest ranger cabin no longer in use."

"Looks like you can take the other fork into the wilderness area like you said, and then it seems to eventually meet up with a paved road."

"Saw that. All those roads through the forest could eventually get you to a highway. But you'd have to have a map or really know your way around."

"What's your theory?" he asked.

"Let's say the woman is seriously injured, but not enough to need a doctor, at least in Archer's estimation. But they left in a hurry and probably didn't take food or water with them. The guy comes out here to go mudding, is my thinking, so he's probably got a backcountry map that would show every path in, through, and out to civilization and sustenance. But he knows he shot a cop, maybe killed the guy, so he's got to be picky about where he travels."

"Okay. Good so far, and then what?"

"These mountains held gold at one time, and that sprouted a few mining towns."

"I've heard about that."

"One's called Greenhorn, another's Robinsonville. There's also Sumpter, Granite, and Susanville. Some other G-named town too. Oh, and something called Cracker City."

"No, you're making that up."

I showed him the atlas page. "See for yourself. And there were other mining towns in the hills and hollers, as my father used to say. Old logging towns, too."

"I know Sumpter's populated, but the others?"

"Granite's got a small population. One of its citizens was actually murdered there years ago."

"Really?"

"Back in the early eighties, I think. The guy killed was a deputy county sheriff and also the mayor of Granite. Anyway, my point is, there would be places Archer and the woman could go, buy groceries, gas, and supplies, and basically never leave the forest."

"Unless they run out of money."

"Unless they run out of money. And my guess is they don't have much of that. And I really don't want to think about what Archer might do when that happens."

"One reason they need to be found."

"Yeah. Let's snag our canteens and binoculars and start walking the shorter trail, the one that circles back to Road 10."

As we began our hike, I reminded myself about the cougar but also recalled that cougars tend to hunt early in the morning and at dusk. Or in the case of last night's big cat, not long after sundown.

Still, I couldn't help but bring it up as we began to walk down the hiking trail. "I saw a cougar last night. Back there where that tree fell."

"That's a ways away from here, so I don't think you should worry."

"Too late."

"We're armed, Maggie."

"I know, but that didn't help me at all last night."

"You freaked?"

"Yeah, and I was sitting inside the Tahoe."

"Well, it's good to know you're afraid of something."

"You don't know the half of it."

"All I know is you weren't afraid to return fire when John Vickers started shooting at us."

"Well, if we'd been trained to fight off wild animals at the Academy, I might not be afraid of a cougar either."

"Good point. Maybe one of us should make that suggestion."

The trail wound through dense forest and grew narrower as we made our way down. Wide enough for hikers and possibly pack mules and horses to get through, but not for anything as large as Archer's Scout, or one of our vehicles, for that matter. It was cooler walking through the stand of old-growth fir, and we each slipped on winter gloves as we crunched across the remains of recent snowfall.

We'd gone about two miles when we arrived at Desolation Guard Station. Having never been there before, and probably because I was comparing it to the Murderers Creek Guard Station, but the place looked like shit. And that was saying a lot, since the last time I was out in the vicinity of Murderers Creek, I was investigating the gruesome stabbing death of one of my ex-husbands.

The roof of the so-called guard station appeared to be in relatively good shape, but the overgrown surroundings, peeling paint, and lack of general services—no electricity or water in the cabin and no vault toilet outside—was evident without performing a detailed inspection. Still, and obviously, we took a look inside, even though it required climbing through one of its broken windows.

The place was relatively clean, all things considered, but there were signs of recent entry. A sleeping bag rolled out on the floor, a lantern, a cracked dish full of cigarette butts, a bloody rag. Clouds had begun to gather outside, and without light, the interior of the cabin was quite dark. I retrieved my Maglite from my utility belt, and Hollis followed suit.

"I'll check the back half of the place. You get the front," I said.

There wasn't much to either half of the building. The one bedroom I explored was empty of furniture, and the bathroom had been relieved of all of its fixtures, except for a stained shower pan and toilet. The back door was locked fast, but someone had successfully rammed a good-sized hole through it, probably trying to get at the lock.

"Maggie!" Hollis barked behind me.

When I turned and took in his expression, I knew he'd found something god- awful.

"The woman?" I whispered.

"No. It's Archer. Shot to death."

"Christ."

"That's not all. Looks like some animal got to him first."

6

AFTERNOON, NOVEMBER 13

Hollis led me back through the living room to the kitchen and storage closet where he'd found Charlie Archer's body, his head and torso inside the closet and his legs sprawled out on the kitchen floor.

"Know you don't like it when I get all chivalrous, but I don't think you should see this," Holly said unapologetically.

"Are you prepared to take photographs of the body as you found it?"

He hadn't thought of that.

"You look like you need some air, so why don't you walk back to Desolation Ridge, get your Tahoe, and call it in. I'll take the photographs, and we'll leave prints, et cetera, to Harry."

Could see I was right about Holly needing some air from his drawn expression alone, and it lined up with his history of being squeamish about dead bodies. Plus, he could get back to where we'd parked our vehicles and radio dispatch faster than I could, but he wasn't going to point that out, of course.

I pulled out my cell phone and was surprised to see I had full service out in the middle of the forest. "It looks like I can call it in from here. I'll track down Sam Damon and Ray Gattis, too."

"She's the ME assigned to Mark's case?"

"Yeah. She also phoned on our way out here and might've arrived at Sam's mortuary by now."

"Dr. Gattis is worried about Detective Bach, I bet."

"Yep. Also turns out she's not a fan of the detective McIntyre assigned to the case, either."

"Crap, we don't need to get stuck with some jerk." Anxious, or nauseous, I couldn't tell which, he looked back down at the body on the closet floor. "I'll be back quick as I can. Give me your keys, and I'll bring the rest of your lunch to you."

"Thanks, but I've lost my appetite."

I contacted Sam Damon, the county undertaker, at his place of business in John Day—the fancily named Juniper Chapel Mortuary and Crematorium. He answered in his nasally voice, pronouncing every other syllable of his establishment in the countrified lilt spoken by many locals.

"Sam, Maggie Blackthorne here."

"Sergeant Blackthorne, what can I do for you?"

Stop calling me *Sergeant Blackthorne*, I wanted to say. I had been his babysitter when he was a kid, and the formality he used with me now that I was a cop often got on my nerves.

"We've had another killing out in the Umatilla Forest."

"Oh, heavens. Two days in a row."

"Yeah, sorry to say. I'd like you out here as soon as possible, if that can be arranged. I'd also like Dr. Gattis out here, too, that is if she's arrived at your mortuary yet and is available to come with you."

"She arrived a while ago, Sergeant. I'll need the directions to your location."

The route to Desolation Guard Station itself was fairly straightforward —Highway 395 north to Forest Road 10, and then south on 10 for fifteen miles or so.

"There is one hiccup, Sam," I said after listing off the directions. "A tree was blown down last night during the windstorm, and it blocks Road 10 in one spot. We were able to make our way around since we were in our four-wheel-drive vehicles. I seem to recall you used an all-wheel-drive hearse when we brought bodies out of a canyon up Aldrich Mountain this past August."

"That's right. I finally bought one of those 'bout a year ago. It's just a necessity sometimes."

"This would be one of those times, but if you have any trouble bypassing the tree, you should give me a call. Anyway, you can't miss the abandoned building at the old guard station. For one thing, there's a sign identifying the place, and the greenish-yellow paint on the exterior is peeling off."

"I assume you want the ME to examine the body before I remove it."

"Yes, that's right."

"Okay, I'll see if she can speak with you now."

"She has my number. I'd appreciate you asking her to call me as soon as it's convenient. Oh, and Sam, this information is not to be shared with anyone else for the time being."

"Why, of course, Sergeant," he said rather indignantly before hanging up.

Everyone knew Sam Damon was a gossiping fool, so I wasn't impressed with the little snit he'd ended with just now.

I photographed Charlie Archer's dead body. He'd landed on his back after being gut shot, and it appeared to be from close range. I saw what Hollis meant about it looking like some animal had gotten to his remains before us.

After reporting Archer's death to regional dispatch, I contacted Harry Bratton. His forensics lab was located on his property in Silvies, near the southernmost tip of the county, ninety-seven miles from Dale. This would be the second day in a row I'd called for his services near the northernmost tip of the county. That amounted to a trip across a long stretch of high desert, through the John Day River Valley, and up and down several mountains. So it was a good sign when Harry responded pragmatically to my request that he drive back up this way.

"Exactly why my contract includes that exorbitant fee for gas and mileage. Anyway, I've got a couple of things to do first, plus I'm traveling from my place today, so it might take me a while."

"It takes as long as it takes, I guess."

"That could easily be Grant County's motto."

"See you when you get here."

"One more thing, Maggie. All that blood inside Archer's trailer? It belongs to two different people."

"You think the woman was fighting back?"

"That's how I would see it, but I can't make that call officially. All I can do is ID the two different blood types."

"Conveniently, I guess Archer's happens to be readily available."

I walked the guard station property, which didn't amount to too much more than the cabin, several tall Ponderosa and lodgepole pine trees, some new-growth fir trees, and a patch of willows. The day had gotten warmer, but November could be tricky out here, and warmer could turn cold and snowy with little warning.

Shortly after sitting down on the cabin's frail front steps, Ray Gattis got back to me, the road noise in the background making it difficult to hear her.

"Maggie, I wanted you to know that Sam and I are not terribly far from the location where you found the cadaver. Also wanted to let you know I heard from Al."

"He's feeling well enough to talk to you?"

"Uh-huh, and he's doing better than expected. He'll likely go home in a day or two. He said to tell you hello, and to not take Detective Horne too seriously. Al thinks the secret to success with the guy is to nod your head and then do what you think is best."

"Al Bach said that?"

"Yeah. Made me laugh."

"Tell Al I said that's what I usually do when I work with him."

"Ha!"

"You sound a lot more chipper, Ray."

"I am, but I'm staying in town tonight at Mack's Motel."

"Depending on how long we're out here this afternoon, maybe you and I can get together for a while this evening."

She paused before speaking in a whisper, "You're probably not drinking alcohol, are you?"

"No, but I happen to know you can drink enough for the two of us."

"Oh, I know I can too, but that doesn't mean I will. I'd like to wrap things up and drive back to Bend sometime tomorrow." Whispering again, she added, "A hangover would make all that less likely."

After we hung up, I wondered how long the relationship between Al and Ray could possibly continue. He was a practicing member of the Church of Latter-day Saints. Maybe he just needed to do some more practicing, because where Ray Gattis was concerned, he definitely wasn't a saint.

Hollis returned with his vehicle, and we sat in the front seat waiting for Doc Gattis and Sam Damon to arrive. His walk back up the trail to retrieve his rig seemed to have revived his usual spunk, leaving room for normal conversation.

"I'm glad Lil's feeling better," I said.

"Hank's stopped running her ragged, and that's been a big help. How are you feeling these days?"

I shrugged. "I've noticed I have a lot more energy."

"You're four months along, right?"

"Yeah."

"Are you excited yet?"

I shrugged. "Duncan's excited enough for both of us."

"Ah, come on, Maggie. The birth of a child is one of life's great experiences."

He sounded like he'd been the one who gave birth to Hank, but I let that go.

"I hope you're right about that, Holly. All I know is, I'll be a forty-two-year-old sergeant in the Oregon State Police when the kid is born."

"And you're with Duncan McKay, a great guy who loves you and who'll love this child."

"I know. But I'm just not thrilled about becoming a mother, not yet, anyway."

"Now that Lil's feeling stronger, you should talk with her about all of this. She wasn't thrilled about the prospect of motherhood early in her pregnancy, either."

"Really?"

"Yeah. And now she's hoping we'll eventually be able to make Hank a big brother."

"Wow, she *is* feeling better."

"Her oncologist was all smiles and good news during her last visit."

"All right, I'll take your advice and set up a get-together with her sometime after the wedding."

"She'll like that."

Our conversation languished for a few minutes, Hollis fiddling with his radio while I took in more of our surroundings. The wind had picked up and clouds had gathered in the south, blocking views of the Greenhorn Mountains. The scent of a nearby downpour of rain filled the cab of the truck. I watched the branches of a broad stand of mixed evergreens sway in the fast breeze, their needles trembling gracefully.

"I wonder why the area's called *Desolation*," I mused. "Because I've been to a lot more desolate and isolated places out here in God's country."

Hollis shrugged. "Maybe whoever named it hadn't."

I pulled up my cell phone and searched the internet for an answer. "Looks like it has something to do with all the gold mining in the 1860s, but that's about all it says."

"Are you getting bored or something?"

"Nah, just antsy. What I'd like to be doing right now is cruising the area looking for Jenna Rhinehart instead of standing guard over Charlie Archer's dead body. In fact, I think I'm going to hike back up the trail and rescue my Tahoe."

"At the risk of becoming the victim of one of your caustic remarks, why don't you let me hike up and retrieve your vehicle?"

"Victim? Caustic? How would you like to be the victim of a caustic demotion?"

He put up his hands in surrender.

"The water's off inside the building, but I noticed an old hydrant at the back of the property. Because of the threat of forest fires, I'm betting it's still connected to the water supply," I said. "Anyway, I'm hoping I can fill my canteen before leaving."

"Thank you for not demoting me."

"If it makes you feel better, I'll call you when I make it to my rig."

"Yeah, that would make me feel better."

"Huh, and you called Duncan my mom for putting together my sack lunch this morning?"

"See you in about an hour. And just be careful, okay?"

<hr>

Officially exhausted when I reached the trailhead overlooking Desolation Ridge, I was also officially relieved I'd been able to refill my canteen before starting out, and for completing the hike without once reminding myself there was a cougar on the prowl. I hopped in my Tahoe and radioed Hollis.

"On your way back down?"

"Yep. Doc Gattis and Sam might be there by the time I get back."

"Hope so. I'm also getting tired of standing guard over Charlie Archer's dead body."

We signed off, and I began backtracking toward Road 10. Coming around a rather treacherous bend, I peered over the edge into a deep and thickly forested canyon below. It brought to mind the long drives of my childhood through backwoods and mountains on similarly winding, narrow, and fear-inducing rides with my mother and father. Until we arrived and set up our little tent and all the magpies, jays, and meadowlarks gathered nearby hoping for treats.

The macadam leveled out some, but the forest remained dense, primordial, and possibly untouched by a chainsaw. Then I saw it, stopped, and pulled up my binoculars.

"Archer's Scout," I said aloud.

The orange beast, as Holly had dubbed it, sat abandoned. I pulled to the curb, got out, and walked to the unlocked vehicle. The back passenger-side door was wide open, as was the rear hatch. A heavy-duty safe took up much of the cargo hold. Up front, both seats were smeared with blood, and bloody handprints covered the passenger window.

I gloved up and began inspecting the interior, finding a small handgun on the floor under the driver's seat and retrieving several backcountry maps of the Umatilla National Forest and the adjoining Wallowa-Whitman National Forest from the glove compartment.

It was hard to tell, but it looked like Jenna Rhinehart might've stayed the night in the Scout or had planned to, anyway. A sleeping bag matching the one we found at the guard station was stretched across the bench seat in back. Whatever the situation had been between her and Archer after their bloody encounter wasn't discernable, other than this fact—one, or perhaps both, had a key to the vehicle, and neither was around.

I moved to the cargo area and found the safe to be also unlocked but loaded with the remainder of Archer's stockpile of handguns and an ammunition storage container. Some of the weapons were antiques, the kind typically purchased by collectors or gun aficionados, but the majority was of the cheap sort or ghost guns.

After bagging and labeling the handguns—fifteen in all—along with the ammo box, maps, and sleeping bag, I stored them in the evidence locker in the cargo hold of my SUV and began driving back toward Desolation Guard Station. In the event the doc and Sam had arrived and Hollis was inside with them, I phoned him with the rundown.

"The maps remind me a little of the investigation into J.T. Lake's murder back in August," Hollis said.

"Yeah. There's a lot of forested backcountry in our district."

"A lot of homicides in our district over the last few years, too."

"Like you said this morning, a lot of angry and distrusting people around."

"And like you said this morning, that's no excuse."

"Not much is, I guess," I said.

"Not even self-defense?"

I thought about the instances when J.T. Lake had knocked me around.

Not until he slammed me into a hot woodstove, leaving me with an ugly burn scar on my shoulder, did I pull out a gun. I didn't shoot the bastard, but call it destiny, karma, or bad luck, a stranger did stab him to death years later.

"Self-defense speaks to state of mind. I can imagine a young woman being beaten senseless might believe Archer was trying to kill her. I also could imagine her defending herself however she could. When I called Harry earlier, he said the blood in the trailer house came from two individuals."

"So the speculation is that she was fighting back?"

"Could've been. Or he could've been, I guess."

"You think that tiny woman was the aggressor?"

"Well, I guess we won't know anything more until we ask her. But I think I've told you before, J.T. liked to use me as a punching bag on occasion, and I came really close to firing my weapon at the son of a bitch once."

"I remember. My guess is you weren't the only person who ever got close to killing J.T. Lake."

"No, probably not."

"Want me to contact Whitey?"

"It would be pitch-black in the forest by the time he made it out here. And even though his towing business is a twenty-four-hour operation, the orange beast's going nowhere."

"Okay, I'll give him a heads-up we'll need his services tomorrow."

"Thanks."

"Hey, Dr. Gattis and Sam Damon just drove up."

"Great. I'm only about ten minutes from the guard station, maybe less, so you can go on home if you want."

"No, I don't want to give up on finding the woman today. Not just yet, anyway."

"I hear you."

7

LATE AFTERNOON, NOVEMBER 13

Meeting back up with Road 10, I bumped up the speed. It was nearing four o'clock, and the sun would begin setting soon, meaning we could easily be searching for Jenna Rhinehart in darkness. I was beginning to regret our lack of strategy today going back to the decision to drive out here in separate vehicles. We'd had but the one clue about where Archer and the woman had gone, and I supposed that had panned out by some measure, just not for the dead man.

About half a mile from the guard station, the source of my pessimistic musings stepped from the forest and into the roadway. And she was carrying a gun.

"Shit." I slammed on the brakes.

Jenna Rhinehart broke into a run and raced toward me still holding the weapon. She was barefoot, wore a purse strapped over one shoulder, was understandably disheveled and possibly in shock.

I picked up the radio mic, routed the amplification through the siren system, and called for her to stop and put down the weapon. She complied, so I drove forward slowly and pulled to the side of the road. When I reached her, she appeared to be saying something. I got out, snapped open my holster.

"He shot somebody," she said numbly.

She clearly wasn't a threat to me, so I refastened the holster to my Glock. "Your name's Jenna, right?"

She nodded.

"Would you care for some water?"

"Yes, please."

I opened my canteen and handed it to her. She sipped and swallowed.

"He shot somebody," she repeated, this time louder.

"Who was shot, Jenna?" I asked when she passed the canteen back to me.

"I don't know his name. Charlie shot him."

"Why would Charlie shoot him?"

"He doesn't like cops."

"Where is Charlie now?"

"He went to find food."

"When was that?"

"Yesterday, I think."

"I have a peanut butter and jelly sandwich in my truck, along with a thermos of cold milk."

The look on her face could not have been blanker.

"I brought that for you." A fib, of course, but she needed sustenance more than I did.

"Thank you."

I walked her to the passenger-side door. "You're welcome to sit inside the vehicle."

Jenna climbed in, and I walked to the driver's side, retrieved my lunch, and handed it across to her. She tore open the bag and began to scarf down the sandwich.

"Can I have the pieces of apple too?"

I hadn't eaten them all earlier. "Everything's for you."

While Jenna focused all of her attention on the food, I quickly wiped my prints from the thermos and placed it on the seat near her. She passed me a smile, and that's when I noticed the rock band *Thundermother* depicted on her tattered black T-shirt.

"The gun you were carrying? Is it yours?"

She was initially perplexed by my question. "Oh, it's one Charlie kept in his safe."

"I'm going to make a phone call, all right? But I'll be right outside."

The young woman stared at me almost as if she didn't understand why I was telling her what I was doing next, why anyone would tell her what they were doing next.

I rang Hollis, and he answered instantaneously. "I was getting worried."

"I'm parked a mile or so north of the guard station on Road 10, and I'm with Jenna Rhinehart."

"I'll be right there."

"Bring Dr. Gattis with you."

After ending the call, I slipped on a glove and picked up the gun Jenna had been carrying. I bagged and labeled it, walked to the rear of the Tahoe, and stowed it in the evidence locker separately from the weapons I'd collected from Archer's Scout. By then Hollis and Ray had arrived.

"Maggie, good to see you," Ray said. "You wanted me to take a look at the DV victim from yesterday?"

"Yeah, she's finishing up my lunch, and that might make a difference, but she seems pretty traumatized."

"Well, of course."

"Thing is, she was also packing heat when I found her wandering out of the woods, or maybe that was when she found me."

"What's her first name?"

"Jenna."

"All right, I have my kit with me, so let's go talk to her."

The doc got out of Holly's Tahoe, and I led her to the front passenger side of my police vehicle and opened the door. "Jenna, this is Dr. Gattis."

"There's doctors out in the forest?"

"Well, she happened to be nearby, and I asked her to see about your injuries."

"Okay."

"Jenna, that's such a sweet name," Ray said.

"Thank you."

"Would you mind if I sat in the driver's seat while I ask you a few questions about how you're feeling? It's getting a little cold outside."

"I'm fine with you being in the front seat with me, ma'am."

I knew from experience Ray did not like being called *ma'am*, and I also knew she wasn't going to bring that up here. She walked to the driver's-side door and got in beside Jenna.

"One more thing," I said to Jenna. "I'd like permission to go through your purse."

"Ain't much in there."

"It's just one of the police rules I have to follow."

"Okay," she said and handed me her purse.

I toddled over to Holly's rig and climbed in.

"I think Sam's pretty anxious to get on the road," he said.

"Is Ray through over there?"

"Yeah, she told him she'd finish up in the morning at his mortuary. I said I'd come back as soon as I could and help him load the body bag in his hearse."

"Why don't you go back and do that, and then call it a day."

"I was pretty relieved when you called to tell me you found the woman and that she was alive."

"Me too. She's already scarfed down my lunch."

"I've got a banana and a piece of Lil's cornbread in the glove compartment. I'm afraid I already ate my sandwich, though."

"Thanks, Holly. I'll take the cornbread for sure."

"Eat the banana too, please."

I smiled and pulled the remainder of his lunch out of the glove compartment.

"I don't mind waiting for Harry, then you and Dr. Gattis can take Jenna home or to the hospital, whatever the doctor decides is best."

"Waiting for Harry would be a big help."

"I've become pretty good at waiting today. And I can start setting up some lighting. He's going to need it soon."

I finished off the cornbread and raised the banana in salute. "See you Monday morning if I take off before you do."

I stepped out of Holly's police vehicle, walked to mine, and opened the hatch. I spread out the contents of Jenna's purse. She was right; there wasn't much in there.

Harry Bratton pulled up behind my rig and idled his truck.

I closed the hatch and moved to his driver's-side window, which he'd already lowered.

"What's going on?" he asked.

"Found the Rhinehart woman wandering through the woods carrying a Colt .45. Ray Gattis, the ME on our murder case, is giving her a checkup right now."

"I know Ray. She's a pistol," he said without any irony.

"Yep, we've become friends over the last couple of years."

"Is she still having a fling with Al Bach?"

"Not that I know of."

"Tell her howdy for me."

"I will. In the meantime, I have a buttload of weaponry, already bagged and labeled, in the evidence locker in my Tahoe. I'd like to send all of it along with you so you can do your ballistics magic, see what turns up. Dust for prints, too, of course."

"What's a buttload?"

"Sixteen handguns, including the one the young gal had with her." I indicated Jenna. "Plus a large ammunition container."

"Holy crap."

"Yeah, she took the .45 from the safe in Archer's Scout. That's where I found fourteen of the other fifteen this afternoon. He kept another one under the front seat."

"You've got one hell of a case going on here, Maggie."

"Tell me about it."

Didn't know if Jenna had noticed me retrieving the Colt .45 that she'd been carrying or if she saw me store it in the back of my vehicle, but I doubted it. And if she eventually inquired about the gun, I'd claim I was following another pesky police rule requiring me to confiscate it for the time being.

Harry stepped out of his truck carrying a large Sirchie evidence bag. "Let's get this over with."

"And let's try not to attract Jenna's attention."

"Got it."

We walked to my truck, and I quietly lifted the hatch. The evidence locker was already open, so Harry took a quick look inside.

"All of them unloaded?" he whispered as we put on gloves.

"They are."

We quickly placed each individually bagged gun inside Harry's larger evidence bag. He also grabbed the ammo box, and I nabbed Jenna's purse and closed the hatch.

"I'll get back to you about the weapons as soon as I can," he said.

"I nearly forgot to tell you. Hollis drove back to the guard station earlier to set up some lighting for you."

"That'll be a big help. Talk to you later, Maggie."

I moved to the driver's-side window of my Tahoe. Ray rolled it down.

"I just wanted to check on you and Jenna, Dr. Gattis," I said.

"We're getting on okay, don't you think, Jenna?"

"Yes, ma'am."

"Jenna has agreed to stay in the hospital for a few days."

I looked over at the younger woman, and she acknowledged her willingness.

"Have you talked to your parents? They've both been pretty worried."

"I lost my cell phone somewhere, so Dr. Gattis loaned me hers to call my mom."

"How about your dad?"

"Nah. He'd just start yelling and saying stuff about Charlie. Mom said she'd let him know."

"Can I ask you one more question, Jenna?" I peered over at Ray just in case she had an objection.

"I think Jenna's good for another question. After that, I'm going to suggest that she rest in the back seat while we drive her to the hospital."

"Sounds like a plan. First, you can have your purse back, Jenna." I passed it to Ray, who handed it to the young woman. "You said Charlie had gone to get some food yesterday. He was on foot, right?"

"Yeah, after he hid the truck—Mud Runner's what he calls it. Anyway, I woke up in the middle of the night. Charlie still wasn't back, and I was cold 'cause he'd taken the keys and I couldn't run the heater. I was scared too, so I got one of the pistols. Don't even know if it's loaded."

Sam Damon had passed by just as I was about to turn the Tahoe around and drive back north toward Highway 395. He bobbed his head and gave me the traditional backcountry greeting as he moved on by. The gesture of raising a thumb was how many locals chose to acknowledge one another, strangers too, and occasionally the odd animal lingering near the road.

We motored in the dwindling twilight, Jenna Rhinehart sleeping restlessly but bundled in the blanket I'd pulled from the cargo area. When we arrived at Blue Mountain Hospital, Jenna's mother, Anita, and my cousin Lyndon were sitting as far away as they could get from her father, Dirk.

Both Anita and Dirk stood and hugged Jenna, but her parents were soon at each other's throats. Their daughter glumly refereed the ruckus until the head nurse intervened and escorted the young woman to an exam room, Ray tagging along after.

No one asked about Charlie Archer, not even Jenna, and so I saw no need to pass along word of his death just yet.

Back inside the Tahoe afterward, Ray made a tiny scream and shook her head. "Fucking save me from family dramas."

"I assume you're talking about the Rhineharts. I understand Anita divorced Dirk the dick a long time ago, so I'll give her some credit for that. Where Jenna's concerned, I just don't know what to think. And between you and me, there are still a few unanswered questions, so I can't rule her out as a murder suspect just yet."

"No, I wouldn't if I were you. There was something off about her behavior, and it was more than shock. But I'm not a psychologist, so there you go."

"Is there anything you can tell me about your initial exam of Archer's body?"

"Not much. I'd say he's been there since early this morning, but I'll need more time and better lighting to nail down time of death. And it'll probably turn out to be within a range."

"Hollis was under the impression an animal had gotten to the body first."

"No, but I can see why Hollis might've thought that. The lesions on the body were the result of Jenna Rhinehart clawing the deceased during their fight, I'm fairly certain. I sampled the skin under her fingernails while we were chatting inside your police car, so I'll be able to tell you more later."

"That was smart, but she didn't object to you doing that?"

"Sampling the skin under her fingernails? No. I explained I knew she was a victim of domestic violence the day before. Told her it was standard practice. I also suggested to the nurse at the hospital they might want to conduct a sexual assault forensic exam."

"A rape kit?"

"I prefer the term forensic kit, but yes. Not for evidence against the Archer guy, obviously, but medically it's a prudent thing to do."

"Could also speak to her state of mind."

"Yeah, rape is a demeaning and demoralizing act for any victim. Hell, I read recently that one in ten women are raped by an intimate partner."

"So I'm in good company, then."

That silenced Ray for a moment. "I'm sorry to hear that, Maggie. It shouldn't happen to anyone."

"No, it should not."

For a long minute, we were both quiet.

"I don't know if you saw," I said. "But Harry Bratton passed by while you were with Jenna Rhinehart. We've contracted with him to do forensics work, and he was on his way to the murder scene. Did you ever work with him before he retired from the State Police?"

"No, sorry to say, but I've met him a few times, and he has a good reputation."

"He's an interesting guy to work with. And I'm damn glad he retired here in Grant County."

"I'll bet, since the state labs are a hell of a drive from here."

"Hey. Change of subject, but would you like to come to my house for a home-cooked meal?"

"You cook?"

"God, no. Duncan is an amazing cook, though. Makes a mean gin martini, too."

"I don't know, Maggie. I don't want to intrude."

"Listen, I'll give him a call, see how his day went, and ask him about having you over. If he says we need to take a rain check, you and I will go to the Blue Mountain Lounge, have dinner, and catch up."

"It's a deal. But call him while I'm not sitting in your vehicle, so he really can say no if he wants to."

I dropped Ray off at Sam's mortuary where she'd left her car and told her I'd let her know about dinner right away. We were both starving, but I needed to store the maps and sleeping bag I'd found in Archer's rig in the office. That and my thermos; I wanted Harry to get us a clean set of Jenna's fingerprints without raising her suspicions.

The place was empty and strangely quiet when I arrived, except for the rattling refrigerator and the *tick, tick, tick* of the schoolhouse clock on the wall. After securing the sundry items in the evidence locker, I called Duncan.

"Hey, babe," he answered. "What's the word?"

"Another long day, another dead body. How 'bout you?"

"No dead bodies, but a long day. I'm over at Mom and Dad's right now helping them put together some new shelves. My reward was a bowl of homemade chili and cornbread."

"Funny, I scored a piece of cornbread today, too."

"It was a cornbread kind of day, I guess. So the second body, does it have anything to do with Mark Taylor's death?"

"Keep it under your hat, but in all likelihood."

"Lips are sealed. But I'm afraid you'll have to fend for yourself dinner-wise."

"Well, that's what I was calling about. Ray Gattis and I are going to have supper at the BM Lounge."

"She's the ME I met one time, right?"

"Yeah, we're kind of carved from the same cloth."

"You mean *cut* from the same cloth?"

"You're correcting my idioms now?"

"It's my husbandly duty."

"Getting a little ahead of yourself, aren't you?"

"I am. Have a good time at the BM."

"I always do. Say hi to your mom and dad. See you later, Dun."

After hanging up, I considered this man I was about to marry. He'd turned all that tumult and hurt from long ago—my mother's suicide when I was a girl, my father's alcoholism and early death, and my two failed marriages—into past history. The misery and fucked-up state of mind I'd been left in had become a distant memory of madness and grief.

8

NIGHT, NOVEMBER 13

Ray was waiting for me in a corner booth when I stepped inside the Blue Mountain Lounge. She had already ordered a glass of white wine for herself and a basket of warm French bread for us to share. I scooted into the seat opposite her, drew a slice of bread from the basket, and buttered it.

"Delicious," I whispered.

"Especially the butter, right?"

"Oh yeah."

Our server, the daughter of a guy I'd gone to high school with, fluttered to our table shortly after I sat down.

"Have you decided?" she asked, filling a water glass and placing it on the table beside me.

As usual, I spaced on her name and had to check the tag she wore. "Not quite, Willow. How's your dad?"

"Oh, he's fine, Sergeant Blackthorne," she said and turned to Ray.

"You, ma'am?"

"Last time I was here, I had the fried chicken dinner. But I don't see it on the menu tonight."

"Oh, it's always available. This here's just a list of tonight's specials."

"Great. I'll have the fried chicken dinner, then."

"And I'll have my usual, but with salad and ranch dressing instead of fries," I said.

"So, the burger, cooked rare, and salad with ranch dressing?" Willow asked.

"And a chocolate peanut butter shake, please."

"Comin' right up." Willow whirled around and marched to the kitchen.

I took a sip of water.

"A chocolate *and* peanut butter shake?"

I learned early on to not take Doc Gattis's snark seriously.

"It's delish. And I'm famished."

"And pregnant."

"Pregnant has nothing to do with ordering a chocolate peanut butter shake."

"Well, if you order a second one, my point about your condition will've been confirmed."

"So be it."

She smiled. "Speaking of your condition, are you excited?"

I shrugged. "I'll get there."

"I never wanted children, but you're someone I would've pegged as being very excited."

I had been pregnant and excited about it once, and then Morgan dropped his bombshell. He'd figured out he was gay and decided we should divorce.

"It's funny, but Hollis asked me the same question earlier today. Suggested I talk to his wife about her experience. I guess she wasn't all that thrilled about the prospect of motherhood early in her pregnancy, either. And now they have an adorable and much-loved toddler."

"His wife. What's her name again?"

"Lillian Two Moons. Well, Lil."

"Didn't you tell me recently she had some kind of cancer?"

"Ovarian."

"Yeesh."

"They removed an ovary, and she's in treatment. Holly says she's feeling stronger every day."

"Holly? Is that what you call him?"

"It's my nickname for him. We're pretty tight pals."

"And that's never been a problem for Lil?"

"I don't believe so. She and Hollis are really close."

"How about for Duncan?"

"No. For the same reason."

She nodded and let out a sigh of exhaustion. "Today's been a long, strange day."

"You must experience that often."

Ray laughed. "You have no fucking idea."

"It doesn't help that getting to places in this damn county often takes forever. Poor Harry Bratton had to drive close to a hundred and twenty miles to get to the Desolation Guard Station today."

"Jesus."

"And I forgot, but he asked me to tell you howdy."

"That's sweet."

"He also called you a pistol."

"I think that's supposed to be a compliment."

"I know I'd take it that way. He also asked me if you were still having a fling with Al Bach."

"And you said?"

"*Not that I know of.* Figured if I just said no, it would sound like the straight-out lie it would've been."

"Thank you for that. Not that Harry would probably care."

Willow brought round my milkshake and placed it on the table. "There you go, Sergeant."

As I slurped down a bit of my delicious shake, Ray gave me the eye.

"You know the last time we were here, you gave me shit about ordering a rare burger," I said after placing my milkshake back on the tabletop.

"Yes, I remember."

I noted she had barely touched her drink. "How's the wine?"

"Disgusting."

Nearly spitting out the mouthful of chocolate peanut butter heaven I'd just drawn from my straw, I picked up her empty water glass, poured in a bit of my creamy drink, and handed the glass back to her.

"See if you like this any better than the wine."

She took a swig. "God, that's fabulous."

Fortunately, Willow was nearby, or Ray might've chased the girl down and tackled her. Instead, the good doctor politely raised a hand and ordered her own chocolate peanut butter shake.

"You definitely know what you're talking about when it comes to milkshakes, Maggie, but I'm still dubious about you eating rare hamburger."

"Tell me, does all your skepticism come from being a medical examiner?"

"No, dear. I was born with that gift."

<hr>

After we finished our meal, Ray and I shared another chocolate peanut butter milkshake. I was completely stuffed after that and feeling gluttonous and ready for a night's sleep.

"Let me drive you back to your motel," I said as we were leaving the Blue Mountain Lounge.

"The walk will do me good," the doc said, patting her tummy.

"It's cold and dark."

"So, I'll walk faster."

"Nah. Let me give you a ride."

"All right."

We were quiet on the short drive to Mack's Motel. Once there, I idled my rig in front of her room.

"There is one thing about the two bodies I neglected to mention, Maggie," Ray said rather darkly.

"Oh?"

"In my opinion, the fatal wounds to both men were caused by handguns."

"So not a shotgun or hunting rifle?"

"I don't believe so, but autopsies and ballistics should get us to an answer."

"Good night, Ray."

"Sweet dreams, Maggie."

I woke to a chilly morning. The temperature in our bedroom felt as frigid as I'd experienced in a long while. Winter was officially more than a month away, but the high winds of two days ago and the raw cold of today were a sure hint of its oncoming.

Reluctantly, I withdrew from Duncan's warmth and wrapped my nakedness in the robe draped over my nightstand. His mother had given it to me as a birthday gift, so there was not one thing sexy about it.

"Come over here," he said as I stepped onto the carpet.

"What's in it for me?"

"A surprise."

"You don't surprise me anymore," I said, moving quietly to his side of the bed and yanking back the covers.

"No fair!" Duncan howled.

"Oh," I whispered and slid off the robe. "I take it back. You're full of surprises this morning."

I climbed in beside him and brought up the covers. He pulled me close, kissed me lightly down the length of my neck, and cupped my breasts in his broad hands.

"Your changing body is damn beautiful."

"I'm so happy to be with you, Dun. To be a part of you."

"Ah, babe. I want you so bad."

"You have me."

Our lovemaking had been fierce and tender at once, as passionate and new as it had ever been. And afterward, we lay entwined, warm, hearts still pounding.

Then my phone's sharp ring broke through the sweet calm. It was only seven a.m. And on a Saturday morning.

"Crap," I whispered.

"Don't answer it, maybe?"

"Nah, afraid not."

I rose from the bed and carried the robe with me, putting it back on as I answered the call. "Sergeant Blackthorne speaking."

"Good morning, Sergeant."

I might have recognized the voice but wasn't certain.

He continued. "This is Dr. Hilliard, director of Blue Mountain Hospital."

"Good morning, Dr. Hilliard. How can I help you?"

"I apologize for calling so early, but I wanted to let you know that Jenna Rhinehart left the hospital earlier this morning. She didn't let anyone know she was leaving, and no one noticed until she was already gone, I'm afraid."

"There's nothing illegal about her leaving, I suppose."

"No. However, I was asked to pass along the word to Dr. Gattis. She had a conversation with Ms. Rhinehart's doctor yesterday. But all he knew about Dr. Gattis was that she's a medical examiner working on a case with you."

"I appreciate you letting me know."

"I toyed with the idea of just leaving a message at your office. But I decided since it's the weekend and you had given me your cell phone number a few months ago, it might be more prudent if you and Dr. Gattis knew about this right away."

"You made the right move, Dr. Hilliard."

"I'll let you go, then."

"Before you do that, did you notify the parents?"

"Jenna Rhinehart is an adult, officially."

Meaning no, Anita and Dirk hadn't been notified.

"All right. Again, thank you, Dr. Hilliard."

Duncan was sitting up in the bed and lying back on a pile of pillows when the call ended. "Your day's starting early, then?"

"Yep."

"Then mine is too." He threw off the covers and rose from the bed. "You go take your shower, and I'll make breakfast."

"Come here first," I said.

I held open my robe, and he encircled my waist with his muscular arms. We rocked back and forth a few moments.

"You mean everything to me, Dun."

He kissed the top of my head. "Sweet love. Go take your shower."

After my shower and breakfast, I rang Ray Gattis and passed on the word about Jenna leaving the hospital, apparently of her own volition and without bothering to let any hospital official know.

"Fuck," she said rather sleepily. "Have you contacted the parents?"

"No, I thought I would take a little drive to her mother's place this morning. From what I've heard, that's likely who Jenna turned to."

"You don't want to just call and ask her?"

"I assume the mother knows. If Jenna's there, I want to make sure she gets the message there's a murder investigation underway, that she's, thus far, our primary witness and I need to know where and how to contact her. I also want to see her reaction when she learns Charlie Archer is dead. And I want to do that before I hear from Detective what's-his-face, who, by the way, was supposed to contact me yesterday."

"That's the other thing about Detective Horne. He's a flake."

"Is he someone's nephew or something?"

"As a matter of fact."

"Please tell me it's not Corporal McIntyre."

"No, someone higher up."

"Shit."

"Maybe you'll solve the thing before he bothers to get his ass over here. Speaking of which, did Hollis drop by the office last night with the items I removed from the body?"

"I'm still at home, but if he said he was going to do that, you can count on it. Did you find anything interesting besides a wallet?"

"A set of keys and two smartphones."

"Jenna said she'd lost her phone somewhere."

"Well, maybe she didn't realize he'd taken it."

"Maybe."

"Or maybe he had two phones for some reason. Although one of them is pink. And sparkly."

"I'll drop by the station and check out the phones. If Jenna's is one of them, it might come in handy when I meet up with her."

"I'm on my way to Sam's mortuary soon."

"If I don't see you before you leave for Bend, drive carefully."

"I will. Hey, when's your wedding?"

"On Thanksgiving day."

"That's soon."

"We're having a small service and leaving for a short honeymoon the next day."

"Where to?"

"Bend."

"Whoa, you know how to live it up. Give me a call while you're there, and I'll buy you dinner as a wedding gift."

"It's a deal."

"Take it easy, Maggie. If I find anything interesting during the autopsy, I'll let you know right away."

The office was cold as hell, and of course no one else was around given it was the weekend. I fired up the tiny heater I kept beside my desk, opened my computer, and checked for any bulletins from regional dispatch. The only thing of note was a wordy alert relaying news of the two murders in my police district. It was my guess that part of the motivation for lumping the two incidents together was to let Mark Taylor's statewide cop brethren know his presumed killer was now dead himself. An effort to prevent any possibility of OSP vigilantes taking it upon themselves to go after Mark's assassin.

From the evidence locker, I gathered the bags containing the two smart-phones, wallet, and set of keys Doc Gattis had removed from Charlie Archer's body. The pink phone had to belong to Jenna, and it was possible she might know the passcode to Archer's. Not that either device had any connection to the two homicides, but there might be something of interest buried inside.

I slapped on a pair of latex gloves and pulled Archer's wallet from the baggie Ray had stuffed it in. It held a couple of five-dollar bills, credit cards, and a condom. His out-of-date driver's license and a few other items were tucked inside the wallet's transparent inner compartment. I lifted out the license and what was stuffed in behind it.

He'd actually carried three licenses. The one from the Department of Motor Vehicles identified him as Charles Sean Archer. The first fake ID called him Archie Sean Charles, and in the second he was named John Charles Archibald.

9

MORNING, NOVEMBER 14

"Thought I'd find you here," Hollis said, wandering into the alcove and placing his pack on the floor beside his desk.

"It's Saturday, dude."

"Is it?"

"You should be home with your family."

"I should. And so should you." He opened his computer. "I see you found the stuff Dr. Gattis took from Archer's pockets. I decided not to go through it all last night."

"These were in his wallet." I held up the fake driver's licenses.

"Same photo, different names?"

"Yep." I stood and placed the DMV knockoffs on his desk. "See what you can turn up on Archie Sean Charles and John Charles Archibald, will you? In the meantime, I'm going to pay a visit to Anita Rhinehart. Jenna left the hospital without checking out."

"That's interesting. No one noticed?"

"Nope. I was planning on taking the two cell phones with me, but I think I've changed my mind. At least until after I have a conversation with her."

"So, you're assuming Jenna is at her mother's house?"

"I am."

"And if she's not there?"

"I'll call on Dirk and put up with his insults. And if she's not there, I'll drive to Ukiah and have a conversation with Cousin Lyndon. I have to head back north, anyway."

"Ah, you have to lead Whitey Kern to Archer's Scout."

"Uh-huh."

"I'll go with you."

"Why would you want to do that on a Saturday if you didn't have to?"

"Just like you, this case is personal, and I have a vested interest in the outcome."

"Speaking of Mark, I'd like to drop by and see Ellie and the kids."

"Yeah, that's a good idea."

"So, we'll do that right after I get back from my visit to Anita. And Dirk, if it comes to that."

"In the meantime, I'll check out Archer's aliases and start putting together our report regarding yesterday."

"Sounds good. This shouldn't take too long." I stood to leave. "Oh, did Harry find anything interesting?"

"He mostly dusted for prints and collected evidence from the closet, including a bullet slug from the back wall. He plans to send us an initial report tomorrow."

———

I pulled up to Anita Rhinehart's place. She lived in a small cottage on Hillcrest Drive, not far from our police station. The remains of a large vegetable garden took up much of the yard on the east side of the structure, and a small silver car was parked in the driveway. I popped out of my Tahoe, stepped to her porch, and knocked.

After a few minutes, I knocked again. It occurred to me that she might have been at work or walked to one of the stores a few blocks away, when she suddenly opened the door.

"Morning, Sergeant Blackthorne," she said.

"May I come in, Ms. Rhinehart?"

"Well, I was about to leave, but come on in."

She opened the door, and I slipped inside her spare but neat and tidy home.

"You're welcome to have a seat."

"Thank you, but I'm hoping to talk to Jenna."

"Oh."

"You did know she left the hospital, right?"

"Yes, but she's not here."

"Where can I find her?"

"I don't think she wants to be found."

"This is a homicide investigation, Ms. Rhinehart, and Jenna's a witness."

"Please, Sergeant. She just needs to rest and get to feeling better."

"Where is she?"

"I'm right here," Jenna said, stepping into the room.

Except for the bleach-blond hair, the bruises painted over with foundation, and the *Thundermother* T-shirt she'd been wearing yesterday, Jenna had nearly transformed back into the young woman I'd seen in the photograph Lyndon Cummings provided me.

"You look like you're feeling better," I said. "Folks at the hospital were worried about you."

"It was too noisy there. People crying and in pain. Bells and buzzers going off everywhere."

"So, you called your mother and had her come get you."

"Don't have a phone, remember? Ain't that far, so I just walked."

"All right, but now that you're feeling better, I need to remind you that we're investigating a murder. You're a witness, and you need to be available for questioning."

"She just didn't want to stay in the hospital anymore," Anita put in.

"And it doesn't help matters for you to not be truthful about her whereabouts, Ms. Rhinehart."

Anita's face reddened. "It's just, I wasn't expecting to see you, and I, well, I panicked."

As far as I knew, she didn't really have a reason to panic, but now wasn't the time to go into all of that.

I turned to the woman's daughter. "Jenna, let's sit down."

The room was sparsely furnished and decorated, as though Anita was prepared to light out of there at a moment's notice. Jenna sat down on one side of the small arm-rolled settee and plopped her legs and feet across the length of it. I pulled up a chair tucked into the nearby dining table, and her mother claimed the rocker.

"What happened to your cell phone?"

"I told you, I lost it."

"Lost it, or did Charlie take it away from you?"

She gave that question some thought. "He could've, I guess. I was scared, and in shock, I think. And there's stuff I ain't remembering."

"Did you have a key to Charlie's Scout?"

"Nobody else was allowed to drive Mud Runner," she said.

"I located Charlie's vehicle shortly before coming upon you yesterday." She shrugged.

"Jenna, how come you haven't asked about Charlie?"

"Whaddaya mean?"

"You haven't asked if we arrested him or if he got away—or anything, for that matter."

"She's been through a lot because of that man, Sergeant Blackthorne. Beaten, left to freeze in that truck of his. Maybe she doesn't care what happened to him," Anita said.

"Is that true?" I asked Jenna.

"Don't really know how I feel. He probably got away, I think."

"How?"

"He's got friends from Lyndon's crew."

"He didn't get away, Jenna."

"You arrest him?"

"No. Someone killed him."

That registered in her eyes only. She sat stock still.

"Dead?" she whispered.

I leaned forward slightly. "Yes."

"Are you all right, honey?" Anita asked her daughter.

Jenna ignored her. "Does his sister know?"

"I didn't know he had a sister."

"Yeah, up in Seattle. Never met her, though. And I don't think they were close."

"Do you know her name?"

She thought about that. "Pammy something."

"Parents?"

"Died in a car wreck when he was sixteen."

Her face was now drawn, her eyes slightly glazed over, reminding me of her flat affect of the previous day.

"Mom, I need some water."

Anita hastened toward the kitchen.

"Did Charlie have other siblings?" I continued, and without a sense of where I was going.

"Not that I knew about."

"Tell me about your missing phone."

"What do you mean?"

"What brand?"

"I can answer that question." Anita had returned with a tumbler of water for Jenna. "I got her a Samsung Galaxy as a graduation gift."

I directed my attention to her daughter. "Does it have a case? And if it does, what color is it?"

"Did you find it?" she asked.

"Charlie had two smartphones in his pocket."

"Mine's got a pink case. Pink's my favorite color."

She was wearing fuzzy pink slippers as if to prove it.

"Then I believe your phone may have been found."

She suddenly became more animated. "Password's *joy, asterisk, luck, dash,* and the number eighteen. *Joy* and *luck* are capitalized—named after a book we read at school last year. Anyway, if that opens it, doesn't it prove it's mine?"

"It does, I believe."

"Can I get it back?"

"Yes, but it may be a few days before I can release it to you." I fully intended to peruse the phone's data inside now that she had conveniently given me the password.

"Do you want Charlie's, too?"

"His password?"

"Yeah."

Had Archer shared that with her but not a key to his vehicle?

"He thought I was pretty stupid, plus he said I was getting fat. Called me *lard ass* all the time."

"I'm sorry that happened to you, Jenna. Is that what started the fight between you the other day?"

"I don't wanna talk about that."

"We'll have to talk about it sometime. But I promise, not today."

"I'm not as stupid as Charlie thought." Her expression darkened. "I figured out his password. It's *orange scout*, all one word, and all caps."

"That's helpful, Jenna. And Charlie didn't give you a key to the Scout, in case of an emergency?"

"I would've used it to warm it up if I'd had it."

Which didn't mean she hadn't traipsed to the guard station early the next morning and killed Archer.

"I have one other question," I said. "Did you know Charlie carried two fake driver's licenses?"

She looked puzzled. "Nah, but that might explain why he got stuff forwarded to his mailbox with different names."

"And you never asked?"

She ran fingertips faintly across a set of her facial bruises. "He didn't like me to ask too many questions."

"There is one other thing I need you to know. In the matter of Charlie Archer's death, you're considered a suspect until we determine you're not."

"What are you saying?" Anita broke in.

"Jenna had motive, and until I have proof to the contrary that she didn't kill Archer, she is not to leave the county."

Anita put an arm around her daughter. "That's ridiculous, Sergeant Blackthorne."

"Thank you for your time, Jenna," I said.

I stood and fixed my gaze on the young woman. There was something not quite square about her, something besides being abused by a bully.

"I'll get your phone back to you as soon as I can," I told her.

"She just spit out her password?" Hollis was dumbfounded.

"Well, let's see."

Once I'd driven a few blocks from Anita Rhinehart's house, I'd pulled over and jotted down both passwords in the notes function on my cell phone before I forgot them. Archer's was basically simple and easier to remember, but as for inspecting the content of their apps, calls, email, and shit, Jenna's was more complicated and interesting. Interesting, too, that she had read Amy Tan's *The Joy Luck Club*.

After putting on gloves, I picked up the baggie containing the pink phone and brought out the device. I entered *Joy*Luck-18*, and the phone opened to a photo of Jenna and Charlie Archer.

"I'm in."

"I get why she might give you the password to his phone, but I don't understand why she gave you hers."

I shrugged. "Maybe because she knows there's nothing incriminating there. Or could be there's no way to unlock anything that may be incriminating without an additional password."

"Even so, seems not too bright of her."

"She's pretty sensitive about being perceived as not very bright. Sounded like Archer hit a nerve on that score."

"Enough so that she killed him?"

"That's one possibility, and add that to the beating he handed her," I said, retrieving Archer's phone.

I thumbed in *ORANGESCOUT*, and a shot of the man standing in front of his large vehicle appeared.

"Jackpot!" I called out. "And speaking of jackpots, I forgot to tell you, I turned over the fifteen guns I found inside the Scout to Harry yesterday. He'd stopped and chatted with me a bit before meeting up with you at the guard station."

"Good move, Sarge. So while you're driving us back to Desolation Ridge today, I'll peruse the phones, assuming we keep having the luck we've been having cell service–wise."

"Sounds like a plan. Before we head out, did you find anything on the aliases?"

"Not yet. No jail or prison time in Oregon for anyone with either name. I'll take a look at the western states fingerprint databank tomorrow."

"Not tomorrow. Monday. You deserve a day off this weekend."

He gave me one of his fake salutes.

"Now let's pack up and be on our way. We'll call Whitey after we pay our respects to Ellie Taylor and the kids."

———

Ellie had sat quietly during our visit, and although her usual pleasant self, she was caught up in grief. Dorie and a couple of the other church ladies were tending to the boys and making fried ham and pancakes for breakfast. The intense odor of the sizzling meat and maple syrup triggered a return to all-day-long morning sickness, a phase I thought had passed weeks ago. But I knew I needed to buck up, say all the fitting words of condolence and sorrow. Not only say them but mean them.

The visit was made easier by the presence of Sherry Linn Perkins, who had volunteered to assist Ellie in going through family photograph albums and picking out a variety of shots to put on display at Mark's funeral planned for Wednesday of next week. Occasionally, Ellie would laugh about a particularly goofy picture of her husband or weep if she happened on an especially meaningful one.

Nigh on to eleven o'clock, Ellie let us know she needed to take a short nap, and Sherry Linn, Hollis, and I took our leave and gathered beside my rig. It remained cold, but the sky was cloudless and deep ultramarine in color, gracing the John Day Valley with another shimmering autumn day before winter finally set in.

"Your timing was perfect," Sherry Linn said. "Right before you arrived, Ellie asked me when I thought you two would stop by. I don't believe she understands that you two are investigating Mark's murder."

"And so far, without the assistance of a homicide detective," Hollis said.

"I didn't know that."

"Yeah, and we're driving back out there now. Mostly to recover the second victim's truck," I said. "And we should probably get going."

"See you Monday morning, then."

"Enjoy the rest of your weekend, Sherry Linn."

She smiled. "Thanks, boss."

We watched her get in her old MG and drive away.

"She's such a good person," Hollis said.

"She is. Great person, tolerant and talented. Just wish we could pay her more."

I climbed in behind the wheel of the Tahoe, and Hollis traipsed to the passenger side.

"Holly, would you call Whitey and see how soon he can drive out to Forest Road 10. Let him know we'll meet him at the junction of 10 and Highway 395?"

"Sure."

"I need to get the tank filled before we drive out there."

I pulled away from the curb and headed to the only gas station in town that accepted the government per diem rate for fuel.

10

___

MIDDAY, NOVEMBER 14

We were about to head out of town on our way back to Desolation Ridge, when I had the brilliant idea of stopping off at Prairie Maid and picking up vittles. Whitey Kern had agreed to meet us at the junction of Highway 395 and Forest Road 10 around one thirty, so a stop at our favorite lunch spot before the long drive was deemed doable. After I parked next to the squat little building, we got out and stepped to the service counter.

Angie Dennis slid open the order window. "Howdy, you two. Just your usual today?"

"Think I'll change it up some," I answered. "How about the chicken sandwich with coleslaw."

"I'll have my usual, with chips, and a large cola," Hollis said.

"Add a small chocolate dip cone to my order, please," I put in.

"Everything's to go, right?" Angie asked.

We both nodded.

"All right, coming right up." Angie slid the window shut, and we got back in my Tahoe to wait for our order.

I tuned in KJDY, the local AM station, and we listened to some old-timey country music, that is until George Strait belted out "All My Ex's Live in Texas."

"That's enough of that," I said and clicked it off.

"Oh, come on, that's a classic."

"More like classic crap."

"Kind of like the dessert you ordered. I don't see how you can eat that crap."

"You don't like chocolate?"

"I love chocolate, but the ice cream's not even ice cream."

"Tastes like ice cream to me. Besides, who cares?"

"I'd want to know what kind of chemicals go into that stuff."

"Says the man who just ordered a large cola."

Angie opened the service window and indicated our orders were ready.

"It's on me today," he said and climbed out.

Hollis paid for our lunch and carried it all back to my side of the vehicle, where he handed over my chocolate dip ice-cream cone and the bag containing my sandwich. He got in on the passenger side, and I made a show of chowing down my tasty dessert before pulling out of the parking lot.

In spite of the day's chill, the sky was deeply blue and cloudless. Shadows fell across the dense patches of willow and the scattering of mountain mahogany that grew along Beech Creek. All of which became obscured from view as 395 rose higher and we came to the broad basin of Fox Valley and its latticework of brooks and springs.

Hollis had busied himself poring over the phones found on Archer's body for much of the trip while I listened to Patty Griffin's latest album, *Before Sunrise*. The music was an interesting mix of folk and country songs she had recorded live back in 1992, less studio-perfect, but edgier in some way.

"I forgot to ask, are you okay with the music?"

"Better than that junk you had on earlier."

"That doesn't really answer my question."

"I don't mind it. Even liked her version of 'Crazy.'"

"I dug 'I Write the Book.'"

"Groovy."

"What are you finding on the phones?"

"Not much. Lots of photos of the orange Scout on Archer's phone, many showing off a copious amount of mud spray on the truck body. Neither one had a whole lot of contacts listed."

"Did you notice someone named Pammy on his contact list?"

"No. What's that about?"

"Supposedly he has a sister in Seattle named Pammy."

"Did that come from Jenna Rhinehart?"

"Yeah."

"Well, I don't know what this means, but Archer had several calls and texts back and forth with someone named Tess Slater recently. A John Day prefix. She tried to reach him after he'd been killed, too."

"Interesting. I know Tess's parents, but I don't know much about the girl. Although now that I think about it, I'm pretty sure she and Jenna are close to the same age."

"I don't know her at all, which likely means I've never pulled her over for anything."

"Well, she doesn't seem like someone who would fall for Charlie Archer, but I guess you never know."

The highway continued to climb toward the town of Long Creek, then gradually descended eight hundred and fifty feet until we passed by Dale once again and met up with Road 10. We pulled over to the curb and waited for Whitey. I idled there and kept the heater going but opened my window a crack. The scent of western juniper, Ponderosa pine, and western larch drifted into the cab of the Tahoe.

"The smell of eastern Oregon forest land is worth every bit of hassle that might be tied to living over here," Hollis said.

"I hear you, dude."

"There's Whitey now, Mags."

He had pulled up behind us and was flashing his headlights, an indication he was ready to follow me to our intended destination. I moved onto the macadam, and we drove in tandem up Forest Road 10, advancing around the fallen tree, and up the dirt road toward Desolation Ridge. I turned off the roadway and parked near the heavily forested tract where I'd spotted Archer's orange Scout yesterday.

I reached into my pack and brought up the binoculars. "Fuck."

"It's not there?"

"No, the damn thing's been moved."

"Someone had the key or hot-wired it."

"Or they towed it somehow. Let's ask Whitey to come along with us to that thicket of pines and give us his opinion."

"Good thought."

"Oh, I'm a genius, all right."

"Well, Maggie, my opinion don't mean a lot." As per usual, Whitey Kern was humbly directing his gaze at the earth under his feet.

"I could explore all forty-five hundred square miles of our county and not find one person who knows as much about towing vehicles as you do."

His face reddened. "See them tracks?" He pointed to the slightly smaller set of tire tracks in the layer of mud created by the downpour two nights ago.

"Yeah."

"Probably a one-ton vehicle pulling the heavier International Scout. How old is it again?"

I turned to Hollis, who had pulled that info off the net.

"It's a 1980 model," he replied.

"Oh yeah." Whitey smiled at his shoes. "Them old things was heavy. Some makes are bigger these days, but it's got to be two tons at least."

"Your giant wrecker could've picked it up pretty easily," I said.

"Yep. That's why I got it."

"So, how would somebody be able to tow it out of here?"

"Well, they didn't have nothin' like my wrecker, but they was probably equipped with a heavy-duty tow chain and a winch. Lots of farmers and ranchers have 'em, logging outfits too. Use 'em to move equipment, vehicles, felled trees, what have you."

He walked to where Archer's Scout had been parked, and Hollis and I followed.

"See all that churned-up mud? Whoever moved it had to put up quite a fight to get the Scout to budge."

"Thank you, Whitey. That helps us quite a bit."

He turned red-faced again. "I reckon it's my duty to help if I can and then keep what I know under my hat."

"Knew I could count on you. Be sure to send us a bill for your services even though you're leaving empty-handed."

He tipped his worn cap. "Maggie. Hollis."

We watched him saunter back to his wrecker.

"So, now we interview every farmer, rancher, and logger in the area?" Hollis asked.

"I think it'd be more effective to put out flyers all over Dale and Ukiah and on every rock and tree between here and Mt. Vernon."

"I see what you mean. You're a dang genius, all right."

"Thanks for your support."

<hr>

At the junction of Highway 395 and Forest Road 10, I turned south and drove the short distance to Dale. I had decided we should check to see if anyone had dropped by Blue Mountain Gas & Groceries with Archer's orange Scout in tow or possibly driving it after hot-wiring the thing. We pulled up next to the tiny establishment and parked.

"I'll join you inside shortly. I need to visit the facilities," Hollis said, referring to the public restrooms on the south side of the building.

I nodded and proceeded inside to chat with my buddy, Hi Appleby, assuming his daddy wasn't in charge of the front counter today.

"Sergeant, you're back," Hi said as I approached the counter.

"How are you today, Hi?"

"Can't complain, can't complain. Well, as a matter of fact, my back is givin' me fits."

"Sorry to hear that."

"What can I do for you?"

"I'm afraid it's about that orange International Scout."

"But I heard you found the guy dead."

"That's true, Hi. But the Scout was stolen from where he'd parked it."

"Don't mean to sound unfriendly about your police work, Sergeant, but if yuh knew where it was parked, why didn't you move it afore it got stole?"

"You've got a good point there, Hi. And I don't want to sound defensive or anything, but there are only two of us in the whole county working on the case, so we're a mite shorthanded."

He wagged his head. "I see. You're higher-ups should get you some help."

Hiram Appleby didn't know the half of it.

"Anyway, Hi," I began. "Did you happen to see that old Scout in the last few days?"

"Why, heavens, you're a Black man, and a Black police officer to boot."

Hollis had pulled up beside me. "Why, yes, I am," he said to Hi. "You've got a problem with that?"

"No sir, no sir. Is there something I can help you find?"

"Nope, I'd just like you to answer Sergeant Blackthorne's question."

"Oh, sure. I ain't seen that orange Scout since it lit out of Dale on Thursday."

"Thanks, Hi. Appreciate your help," I said.

"Why don't yuh tack up some flyers asking people to report it if they seen it?"

"Yeah, we thought of that, but we'll have to wait until we get back to our office in John Day."

"Shoot, Daddy's got all the equipment you need in his back office."

"A computer, printer, and copier?"

"Yep, we're far enough into the twenty-first century to need that kind of stuff around for customers. Business folks out here during huntin' season, loggers passing through, folks living down there in the trailer court."

"How much would you charge us to use your equipment to make twenty copies or so?"

"Well, Daddy won't like it, but I'll let you do it for nothin'."

"We don't mind paying for it."

"I want you to catch that killer sooner than later, so I ain't chargin' you nothin'."

"Well, Trooper Jones here is the technology expert in my office, and I bet he could put together a poster in only minutes."

"Well, why don't you come with me, Trooper Jones. You're a big guy, so I don't think Daddy will give you much guff."

"Appreciate your help, Mr. Appleby," Hollis said.

"I'm sorry if I made you feel unwelcome or anything like that when yuh first come in. It's just, I never seen a Black person around here before."

"I'm pretty used to that in Grant County. Well, much of the state, really."

"Well, it ain't a nice way to act around a person, no matter what. Now, let's go wrestle with Daddy."

Hollis had fetched Charlie Archer's phone to use one of the deceased man's photos of the Scout before he and Hi dealt with Zeke Ponder, Hi's so-called daddy. Turns out I had misjudged old Zeke, who was surprisingly a law-and-order guy first and foremost, so there were barely any histrionics in his exchange with Hollis.

We left Blue Mountain Gas & Groceries and Dale about three o'clock and hot-footed it to Ukiah, where we tacked up the newly minted posters at the various businesses around town. That attracted quite a bit of attention, and really, why wouldn't it? Ukiah was an isolated community of two hundred or so out in the middle of nowhere, Oregon.

Other than the stunning views of the Blue Mountains to the east and the surrounding Umatilla National Forest, Ukiah was long on country flavor and short on industry, except for logging, which tended not to be a year-round endeavor, and possibly ranching. And during a winter cold snap in 1933, Ukiah and Seneca, near the southern end of Grant County, tied for having the lowest temperature ever recorded in our state—a crisp fifty-four degrees below zero.

I shared that last bit of trivia with Cousin Lyndon Cummings when Hollis and I were seated in the living room of his home in Ukiah.

"Yes, everyone in town knows that. They're all pretty pissed that Seneca holds the record, though."

"What?"

"Yeah. Ukiah was that temp the day before, so because Seneca was the same temperature the next day, the Weather Service has Seneca on books as having the coldest on record in Oregon."

"Such an injustice."

"Talk to the old-timers about it, they'll give you an earful."

"Speaking of injustice, I assume you heard about Charlie Archer's death," I said.

"Anita told me. You think that was an injustice, huh?"

"Even more of one if we don't catch his killer."

"Can I get you two anything to drink? Water, juice, a beer?" Lyndon asked.

"Nah," I answered.

"No, thanks," Hollis said.

"If you don't mind, I'm going to get myself a beer."

I shrugged. "Go right ahead."

While Lyndon stepped out, Hollis turned to me.

"Where'd you get that piece of trivia about the 1933 cold snap?"

"I'd like to tell you I remembered it from the Oregon history notebook I put together in eighth grade, but it's wrong for a person to lie. I spotted it on the web a while ago."

"Huh."

Lyndon rejoined us and drew a slug of beer from his can of Fort George IPA.

"What is it you wanted to ask me about, Maggie?"

"I'm curious why Jenna Rhinehart hooked up with someone like Archer in the first place."

"Don't really know. She had a couple of boyfriends in high school, but nothing very serious, that is if you can actually have a serious relationship in high school."

"I remember I thought I was having serious relationships in high school a couple of times," I countered.

"That's my point, Maggie. You *thought* you were having serious relationships."

"But the thing with Archer," Hollis began. "His capacity for violence must have been obvious early on."

"I'm sure it was too, but Jenna's not smart that way. Thinks it's her fault when somebody gets mad."

"I had that delusion about an ex-husband once, so I get it," I said.

"Did she ever talk to you about it?" Hollis asked.

"No, but every time I saw her while she was with him, which wasn't often in their short time together, she had a dull, frightened look about her."

Lyndon drew out some more of his IPA and continued, "It hurt to see her like that."

"Did you talk to Anita about it?"

"Yep. Just about ruined our friendship, Maggie."

"Why?"

"Nobody says anything negative about her Jenna."

"But you were asking out of concern, not trying to knock Jenna."

"That wasn't how Anita took it. Not at first, anyway. But we made it through that rough patch."

"I spoke to Jenna's mother the evening after we learned Archer had fled with Jenna. After he had killed Trooper Mark Taylor. She was really upset," Hollis said.

"Of course she was. Jenna's her only kid."

"Do you think she was upset enough to go after them to try and get her daughter away from Archer?" I asked.

"She wouldn't have the foggiest notion where he'd gone with Jenna." Lyndon's temperament was changing with each long pull on his beer can.

"Who would?"

"I have no idea, Maggie."

"I think you might."

"What are you saying?"

"I'm saying you might know where he would've gone to hide out. Or maybe one of the guys on your crew had a run-in with him and figured out where to find him."

"How would I, or anyone else on my crew, know?"

"You tell me."

He lunged from his chair and carried his empty can of beer back to the kitchen, where he retrieved another. When Lyndon returned, I glanced over at Hollis, who promptly crossed his eyes. I nearly burst out laughing at that.

"Maggie, I apologize for getting so upset. I've had a terrible last few days," Lyndon said upon returning.

"I hear you. We lost a friend to murder, and your goddaughter was beaten severely by her boyfriend. But, to do our jobs, we have to ask you some painful questions."

He sat down. "There are a couple of guys on the crew he had run-ins with. I mean, there are always people on work crews who have dust-ups. So, it might not mean anything."

"Names and addresses, please."

Lyndon placed his beer on his coffee table. "I'll get their info from the office."

"Are you thinking what I'm thinking?" Hollis quietly asked as Lyndon padded down the hallway toward his office.

"Sadly, I believe I am."

Lyndon returned and placed two completed job applications next to his beer.

"Brad Slater and Calvin James. They live together in that same trailer park in Dale, and they couldn't stand Archer."

"Which mobile home?" I asked.

"Don't know, Maggie. Sorry."

"It won't be too hard to figure out. Is there anything else you want to tell us?"

He undertook a sustained pull on his beer can. "Dirk Rhinehart hated Archer."

"Enough to kill him?"

"You'll need to ask Dirk that question yourself."

Back in my Tahoe, I pulled away from Lyndon's place and headed out of Ukiah.

"Holly, what do you think about that whole discussion?"

"I'd say we're ready to start the murder board, and there's already a list of several possible suspects."

"Yep. Including Cousin Lyndon."

11

———

LATE AFTERNOON, NOVEMBER 14

As we drove back into Dale, we could see that Hi and Daddy had tacked up one of our posters on the bulletin board outside of Blue Mountain Gas & Groceries. They'd even laminated it first, and before we left them to their various shopkeeping duties, they promised to also post one inside their store.

"Those two could turn out to be our best north county friends," Holly said.

"Well, Hi could. Don't think his daddy is the 'being a friend' kind of guy."

"You're probably right," he said after a pause. "So, who else is a possible suspect in your view?"

"Jenna Rhinehart, for one. Maybe her father, but I don't think we could be that lucky."

"Man, you really dislike that guy, don't you?"

"Um, let me think for a second. Yeah, I really dislike him."

"That can't be healthy, Maggie."

"Didn't he call you *boy* once?"

"Uh-huh, but he's just an ignorant ass."

"Don't forget a racist bully."

"Okay, you're right. He's pretty unlikable."

We turned into the trailer park. The lights were on at Patti Hutchens's place, so I decided to pay a visit and possibly see what she knew about Brad Slater and Calvin James.

We knocked at her door and could hear footsteps moving from the back of the small mobile home.

"Who is it?" she asked from the other side of the door.

"It's Sergeant Maggie Blackthorne, Ms. Hutchens."

She opened the door. "Just Patti, remember? Come on in."

"How's it going?" I asked.

"I'm doing fine. It's been a sad time for Ellie, though."

"Yeah, Hollis and I stopped by and visited with her this morning."

"Please, have a seat, you two. Can I offer you some coffee or tea?"

"Not for me, thank you."

Hollis shook his head. "But I appreciate the offer."

We sat down among the dachshund pillows on her couch, and she sat in a rocker by the gas fireplace.

"Had you heard the news that Mr. Archer, your neighbor, was found murdered the day after Mark Taylor's killing?" I asked her.

"Oh, dear. I hadn't heard that. And the woman?"

"She's alive, and safe."

"Thank goodness."

"We wanted to stop in and check on you, and also ask you about a couple of your other neighbors."

"Do I need to find another place to live?"

"I don't believe so, Patti."

"I certainly hope not. I've really enjoyed living here. The beautiful countryside, our delightful country store just a short walk away."

"I'm sure everything is fine. The men I'm looking to speak to knew Mr. Archer because they worked together, at least until he was fired. I'm just trying to get some background information, but unfortunately, I don't know which mobile home they live in."

"Oh, are you talking about Brad and Calvin?"

"That's their first names, all right."

"Charming boys. Cousins, I think. Don't know their last names, but they live in the silver Airstream three trailers over."

"Thank you, Patti. That's very helpful."

"I'm glad to be of help. Anything else?"

"Not today, anyway."

"Well, you know where I am if you need me."

I nodded, and Hollis and I stood to leave.

"I'll see you both at Mark's memorial service next Wednesday, right?"

"Yes, definitely. Take care."

We left my rig parked near Patti's place, sauntered over to the Airstream, and knocked on its metal door. Since no one answered after the second knock, we decided to head on back to John Day, but we were waylaid by the next-door trailer park neighbor.

"You might try the tavern in Long Creek, officers. These boys are fans of the female servers there."

"That so, Mr....?" I said.

"Ulanowicz. Max Ulanowicz. I work at Jacoby's Hardware Store in Ukiah. Where you put up that sign about the missing truck today."

"Yeah, I remember you now. And you live out here in Dale?"

"You've been to Ukiah, right?"

I didn't want to go into comparing different dinky small towns and dinkier villages, so I punted. "I see your point. A lot more trees out here."

"Fewer nosy neighbors too."

I suspected Max was nosy in his own right, but I let that go.

"What can you tell me and my partner about the guys who live here, other than they like the female servers at the tavern in Long Creek."

"Are they in trouble?"

"No, just looking for character witnesses, I'd say."

"You probably need to look somewheres else, then."

The Ulanowicz guy was tall and gangly, somewhere between fifty and sixty, and he had an edge to his attitude. Like somebody with a chip on his shoulder, but shrewd enough to whip everyone's ass in a game of poker.

"Anything you could share with us would be helpful," Holly put in. His deep, calm voice always came in handy.

"All right. They're a couple of assholes. Pardon my French."

"I think your French is pretty clear, Mr. Ulanowicz," Hollis said.

"Anything else?" I asked.

"You could accidentally check the stash behind that propane tank of theirs."

"Thanks for your help, Mr. Ulanowicz."

"Anytime Sergeant, uh, Blackthorne?"

"Yeah, Maggie Blackthorne. And this is Senior Trooper Hollis Jones."

"Blackthorne and Jones. Sounds like the name of some TV cop show."

"That's us, all right. Have a nice evening."

Ulanowicz strode to his dinky trailer house, stooped slightly under the top of the doorframe, and folded himself inside.

"Interesting guy," Hollis said.

"Let's check the stash behind the charming boys' propane tank."

We walked to the back of the mobile home where the tank was situated. I gloved up and squatted to the ground. Reaching behind the tank, I pulled out a blue bag with *Crown Royal* embroidered on the outside.

"Doesn't seem like there's anything in it," I said and opened the bag. Inside was a single sheet of paper folded in half. I pulled out the paper and unfolded it. I handed it to Hollis.

He smiled and read it aloud. "Go to hell, old man."

"A little message to Mr. Ulanowicz, I believe."

"Yeah, I'd say so."

I refolded the note, put it back into the Crown Royal bag, and returned it to its hiding place.

"All right, let's get the hell out of here. We might even make it back to John Day right at suppertime," I said.

"I'm up for that."

As we walked back toward the Tahoe parked near Patti Hutchens's place, an older station wagon drove past us and parked next to the silver Airstream. Two young men—likely the subjects of our present visit to Dale —and we hailed them down as they got out of their vehicle.

They walked toward us slowly, and it occurred to me they might turn around and take off in a dead sprint, but they stopped and let us catch up with them. They appeared to be not only really young but also not used to being questioned by the cops.

Slightly out of breath, I made our introductions. "We were hoping to talk to Brad Slater and Calvin James."

"That's us," one of them said.

"Would you mind showing me some identification?"

"No, ma'am. I mean, sure, we can do that," the talker said, handing me his driver's license.

"Thank you, Mr. Slater," I said after spotting his name. He had just turned twenty-one. "This says your address is in John Day."

"Yes, ma'am. My cousin and I are renting the mobile home temporarily while we're working for Cummings Forest Maintenance. At least until the weather closes us down."

I handed back his license and proceeded to take a look at the other guy's. Calvin James was a few weeks older than Brad Slater but shared the same John Day address.

"We'd like to ask you a few questions. Shall we all go inside your trailer?"

"Oh, ma'am, it's a mess," said Brad, the apparent spokesperson for the duo.

"We don't care about that."

They whipped around in unison and began walking to the Airstream. Hollis and I followed, and the four of us crowded into the combination kitchen/dining/living room and took up all the available seating.

"Just curious, you two share an address in John Day?"

"Yes, ma'am," Brad said again. "My mom and dad live there, and so does my younger sister. Cal and me are cousins, but he's lived with us since he was a little kid."

"You guys must be close."

"Yeah, I guess."

"Trooper Jones and I want to ask you about Charlie Archer."

The two young guys were like synchronized swimmers: sitting down and placing their elbows on their knees at precisely the same moment and now turning ashen simultaneously.

"You have heard that he was found dead yesterday? Shot to death."

"Yes, ma'am. Lyndon sent out word to the whole crew."

"Oh, he didn't mention that. But he did mention that the two of you weren't very fond of Archer."

"Nobody was."

Those were the first words Calvin James had uttered.

"Why would Lyndon pick you two out in particular to talk to?"

Those were the first words Hollis had uttered since we caught up with Brad and Calvin.

The two young men looked at one another.

"Archer and I had a fight, like a physical fight," Brad said. "He beat the hell out of me."

I noticed that bit of news registered with Hollis.

"What was the fight about?" he asked.

"He had the hots for my little sister," Brad answered. "I couldn't stand by and let that happen."

"How was it any of your business?"

Brad's face reddened. "He was a disgusting bum, a dirty old man in every way. And he was already shacked up with someone Tess had gone to school with. And he was just a fucking slimeball."

Brad ran his fingers through his full head of dishwater-blond hair, barely holding back the tears welled up in his very brown eyes.

"Sorry, ma'am."

An apology for his use of bad language, I presumed. "That's okay, Brad. I use that term all the time. Just ask Trooper Jones."

That made him laugh, which gave Calvin the all-clear to join him in chuckling at my very funny lady cop joke.

"I do have another question for the two of you," I said.

They both came to attention.

"When did Lyndon send out word that Charlie Archer had been killed?"

"I don't know when he sent the email, but I didn't read it until this morning," Brad said, turning to Calvin.

"Me neither, but let me check my phone." Calvin opened his email app and faced his phone my direction. "He sent it last night around eleven."

"I see that, thanks."

"Why'd you need to know that, ma'am?" Brad asked me.

"Because I'm a cop investigating a murder."

"Oh yeah, of course."

———

Dusk had hit by the time we got back in my rig and were driving back through Dale. I came around the one bend in the road and abruptly stopped.

"What the hell?" Hollis said, uncharacteristically.

"See him?"

"Who?"

"The cougar. He's camouflaged in the brush, but he's there." I rolled down the window and turned on my spotlight. It picked up the glint of the big cat's eyes, which prompted the animal to lope across the roadway in front of the Tahoe and bound up the hill into a burst of giant pines.

"What are you now, the cougar whisperer?" Hollis teased.

"About the last thing I'd ever want to be."

"Yes, I know. That was a wild cat, and you're a fraidy-cat."

"Shut up."

"Yes, ma'am."

That made me laugh. "God, Brad needs to get that stupid term out of his vocabulary."

"I almost think he was using it to get your goat. At least in the beginning. I felt the need to ask some questions, just to get him to knock it off."

"It all worked out pretty well in the end."

"Unless they're a couple of liars."

"Always a possibility."

The remainder of the drive back to John Day was relatively quiet, except for the Sade channel, which Holly had selected, playing in the background.

When we arrived at the station, Lil and Hank were sitting in their old Vanagon waiting to drive Hollis home. I slipped out of the Tahoe and climbed in the back seat of their van where Hank was sitting in his toddler seat.

"Aunt Maybe. Where were you and Daddy?"

"A kiss first, and then I'll tell you."

He kissed my cheek, and I kissed his.

"We went to the mountains to find a cougar."

"What's that?"

"A great big kitty."

"Bigger than Louie was?"

"Oh, yeah, but not as nice."

"Were you going to take it to your house?"

His father hooted at that.

"No, this kitty is way too big for Uncle Duncan's place."

"Oh."

"Okay, I'll see you soon, guy," I said and gave him another peck on the cheek. I got out and stood at the driver's-side window.

"Let me take a look at you," Lil said.

I turned and gave her a side view of my tummy in the light of the open back door.

"Oh my, you really are pregnant. Do they make maternity wear for OSP sergeants?"

"I don't know, but maybe I can start a trend."

She smiled broadly, but even that didn't take away from the dark circles under her eyes. "If anyone can start a trend in the Oregon State Police organization, it's you."

"Good night, everybody. Don't come to work tomorrow, Holly. That's an order."

He gave me one of his fake salutes, and I unlocked the office door and placed my pack on the floor by my desk. The phone was blinking madly, and I toyed with the idea to wait and check voicemail tomorrow.

"Damn it," I said and listened to the first message.

"Maggie, it's Al Bach. I'm out of the hospital and actually back at work. Long story, but supervision of your investigations has been turned back over to me. I hope to make it to John Day in the next day or two. You have my cell phone number, so call me sometime Sunday afternoon, if you can. Or, for that matter, any time you need to reach me."

His voice sounded, well, like someone who had just had a heart attack, but I was thrilled to be working with him again instead of some guy who would likely make the effort to boss me around and give me shit rather than work collaboratively with me.

Hell, maybe things were turning a corner, and we'd identify Archer's killer sooner than it seemed we might. With that bit of positivity, I listened to the second voicemail.

12

———————

NIGHT, NOVEMBER 14

The second voicemail was from Dr. Randall Croft, Jenna Rhinehart's physician concerned about her whereabouts and looking to talk to me about her physical health, which I considered odd since the medical establishment's usual inclination was to take doctor/patient privacy beyond what might even be best for their patients.

The third voicemail was from an emotional and frightened Anita Rhinehart. She had come home from shopping and found the door to Jenna's bedroom shut. Assuming her daughter was napping, she didn't check on Jenna until around two o'clock. The young woman was gone, and the only things Anita could tell that she had taken with her were her purse and a coat.

Assuming Anita's call had been a cry for help, I decided I'd drop by her place on my way home. I pulled up in front of her little house, and by the time I'd gotten out of the Tahoe and shut the door, Anita was walking down her lighted front steps toward me.

"Did you find her, Sergeant Blackthorne?"

"I was out of the office most of the day and just now got to your voicemail."

"I know she's an adult, but it worries me. She's not herself right now."

"Did you check with her friends?"

"She doesn't have any friends, Sergeant."

"I'll put out an alert that she's wanted for questioning, which is technically true. She wasn't in a good state of mind this morning, or I would've questioned her then."

"It was bad enough you told her she was a murder suspect."

I could appreciate Anita's position as her daughter's number one defender and protector, but Jenna Rhinehart was indeed a murder suspect.

"What's going on now?"

Jenna had returned.

Anita stepped quickly toward the girl and hugged her. "I was so worried, baby."

"I'm all right, Mom. I needed to go for a walk and clear my head." She wrenched herself from her mother's grip. "I'm ready to talk to you now, Sergeant Blackthorne."

"Not without an attorney, Jenna," her mother said.

"I don't need an attorney. And I just want to get this over with."

"Are you sure, Jenna?" I asked.

"Yes."

"Let me get the recorder from my vehicle." I paced back to the Tahoe while the two women moved inside the house. I fetched my pack, then strode to the house and up the steps. The door had been left ajar, so I went inside.

"Mom would like to be here while you're questioning me."

"That's fine."

The three of us sat around the small dining table, and I placed my recorder on the shiny vinyl covering decorated with pink and purple peonies. I turned on the recorder and read Jenna her Miranda rights. She acknowledged that she understood and signed and dated a waiver form.

"Wow, just like on TV," Jenna said.

"Jenna, let's go back to this past Thursday morning, November twelfth," I began. "What started the fight between you and Charlie?"

"The fight started the night before. He'd been carrying on with that bitch Tess Slater, and I wanted it to stop."

"How did he react to your demands?"

"I think you seen how he reacted."

"I need you to describe it in detail."

"He beat me off and on for a few hours. Whenever I fell asleep on the couch, he'd wake me up and start in all over again."

"Did you fight back?"

"Fuckin' right I fought back, but he was a lot bigger than me, and he kept punching me in my... Mom, I need some water."

Anita left us to draw some water for her daughter.

Jenna continued, "He kept punching me in my groin area."

"How did you know he was seeing Tess Slater?"

"Just like you probably did. I snuck into his phone. But I knew somethin' was up before that 'cause I could smell that fuckin' bitch on him."

Anita returned with the water, and Jenna chugged the glassful.

"Tell me about the shooting of the State Police officer."

She closed her eyes. "Charlie had me down on the floor with the gun to my head," she said and touched her bruised temple.

"Would you like to stop for a minute?"

She shook her head. "The cop was knocking, saying it was the police. Charlie stood and screamed for me to get up. He opened the door, shot the cop, and pulled me by my hair and threw me into the front seat of the Scout."

"When did you grab your purse?"

She thought about that question. "It was hanging on the door handle. My phone was inside of it, and I didn't want to lose track of my phone."

"When did Charlie remove the phone from your purse?"

Again, she mulled over the question. "I don't know."

"When did you realize the phone was missing?"

"After he went looking for food. And like I said yesterday, I was so scared when I woke up in the middle of the night, I got that gun out of the back. Got even more afraid early the next morning 'cause some snarling animal was pacing around the Scout."

That damn cougar, no doubt.

Jenna sighed and kneaded her temple. "I'm so dang tired."

"Just one more question. Where did you go this afternoon?"

Jenna closed her eyes again. "I went to Tess Slater's house. I wanted to tell her myself that somebody had killed Charlie. I wanted to see the look on her face."

"Did you tell her that Charlie was dead?"

"Yeah." Jenna teared up. "She just shrugged, said everybody knew that already."

"All right. I think we're finished for now. But I may have more questions at some point."

"Okay."

I shut off the recorder. "I'll bring your cell phone to you tomorrow so next time you decide to go for a walk, you can let your mother know."

"Thank you, Sergeant Blackthorne. Don't know what would've happened if you hadn't been out near Desolation Ridge yesterday."

"I think we both got lucky."

"Tell that nice lady doctor thank you for me."

"Her name's Dr. Ray Gattis. I'll give her your regards."

I was welcomed home by the smell of something delicious. I stashed my pack in the coat closet beside the front door. That's when it occurred to me Louie's cat bed had been moved from its place near the closet where it had sat since he'd gone to his final resting place. I stared at the spot, not sure how I felt about its absence.

"We have a visitor," Duncan said.

I turned around. In his arms he carried the most beautiful orange tabby cat I had ever seen.

"What's our visitor's name?"

"Raleigh, like Sir Walter."

"And where is Raleigh visiting from?"

"A customer's barn. He has three brothers, and the customers, Errol and Judy Brown, are hoping to find Raleigh here and maybe one of his brothers a new home. He's about a year old, and he's already neutered."

"He's gorgeous, too. I say Louie would approve; I know I do. But unless Errol and Judy can't find anyone to take in the brother, I'd say Raleigh's enough."

Duncan handed Raleigh over to me. "Yeah, especially with a little one coming in the near future. And I hope you don't mind, but I brought home a new cat bed."

"Nah, I don't mind. I've probably mourned Louie's passing long enough."

"We'll always miss him."

"Yep."

"Here, give me Raleigh, and you go take a quick shower. Then you can tell me all about your day."

I scratched Raleigh under his chin, then handed him back to Duncan. "Catch me up on your day, too."

"Well, it started out with a roll in the hay."

"God, was that only this morning?"

He kissed me on the cheek. "Yep. Now go take your shower."

Awakened by Raleigh's thrumming purr coming from the corner of our bedroom where he lay in his new cat bed, I shivered and opened my eyes. Yesterday's weather forecast had predicted thirty-two degrees overnight and a high of forty today. I felt a deep chill, pulled the down duvet closer, and lay there thinking about our murder case. Not a good way to start off a Sunday morning.

I closed my eyes and attempted to empty my thoughts of anything having to do with murder. In the quiet, Raleigh purring, Duncan snoring lightly, I felt a brief fluttering within my womb. I lay still, and after several minutes, decided it was my imagination, until the brief quaver occurred a second time.

I climbed slowly out of bed, then dressed inside the clothes closet, making every effort to avoid waking Duncan. I needed to think. Not about the fucking homicide case but about what might be happening in my pregnancy.

I tiptoed downstairs and moved to the back deck, taking a seat in one of the lounge chairs. My gloved hands were freezing in no time, so I pulled my down jacket over my hands. The snow-covered Strawberry Mountain and

Wildlife Area were blocked by a band of thick gray-black clouds, inspiring me to an even more somber mood. Fearful that I'd gone too far in putting my job before my pregnancy, my future child, and my life with Duncan, I looked up the number of my OBGYN in Pendleton.

It wasn't even seven yet, and it might take hours to hear back from the doctor, who already wasn't particularly friendly. But Dorie Phillips would be up readying herself for church. She had never married or given birth, but she had cared and prayed for many a pregnant woman, and she sure as hell knew a lot more about being with child than I did.

Listening to Dorie's number ringing over and over, I decided she was probably in charge of setting up something for today's services at the Church of the Nazarene. Being a serious church lady, she had likely already taken off for the morning. I clicked off and suddenly remembered the stack of pamphlets my OBGYN had given me during my first visit. They contained information about the phases, or whatever they were called, of pregnancy.

I took my cold body back into the house and dug through the items in the file box I kept in Duncan's small, pristine office. I pulled out a pamphlet titled "The Forty Weeks of Pregnancy." Reading through it, I came to a section titled "Quickening." There was my answer in plain, simple English. It explained that quickening—or the first movements in utero—began to occur at around twenty weeks or so. The description of how it feels to most pregnant women matched what I'd felt. I was relieved, happy to discover those tiny flutters were a normal part of the whole damn experience. And if I'd bothered to read the information earlier, I would've known and expected it.

Here was the best news to my secret self. I cared more than I'd realized about this baby. I was almost tempted to call Dorie again to let her know I'd finally embraced motherhood.

My phone rang, but I didn't recognize the number. I picked up anyway. "Good morning, Maggie Blackthorne here."

"Good morning, this is Yolanda Young."

Somehow, I knew that name. One of Dorie's church lady pals?

"Dorie Phillips asked me to call you. I'm sorry to say she's had a mild stroke, and she's in the hospital."

Christ. This could not happen now. Dorie was the reason I'd made it through untold shit, and she had to be at my wedding. Dorie had to know my child and be a part of its life.

"I'll be right there," I said.

"Dorie's in Bend. St. Charles Hospital has the specialists she needs."

"When did all of this happen?"

"Yesterday evening. I drove her over here."

"You're there with her at the hospital?"

"Yes, well, I'm in the waiting room making calls while she's asleep."

"When can I talk to her?"

"I'm afraid I don't know."

I began to cry. "Please tell her I love her."

"Oh, she knows that, sugar. That's why you were the first name on her list of folks to contact."

I was still weeping when Duncan found me sitting on the daybed in the so-called great room.

"What's happened, babe?" he asked and sat down. "Is it the baby?"

I dried my eyes and took a deep breath. "No, it's Dorie. She had a mild stroke and has been hospitalized in Bend."

"St. Charles is a great hospital. I'm sure she's getting really good care."

"I know, I'm just feeling emotional is all."

"You have a right to be emotional. You could be that way more often, I'd say."

"What kind of tough cop would that make me?"

"A tough cop with a good heart. Which you already are. Who let you know?"

"A woman named Yolanda Young. Someone from her church, I think."

I took in a sudden breath and put one of his hands on my belly. "This is the third time this morning I've felt little flutters. It's something called quickening. The fetus's first movements."

"I can't feel anything."

"Well, I guess movement increases as you get further along in your pregnancy, and we'll not only be able to feel it, we'll also be able to see it move."

"Nice," he said. "I've been meaning to tell you, I hope it's a girl."

"Really? I don't care, I guess. I just hope it has your red hair."

"Not me. I hope she has your dark hair."

"Will you be disappointed if it's a boy?"

"Of course not. Do you want to know the gender before it's born? However they do that these days."

"No. I don't want to make a thing out of it being either. Because someday the kid might decide they're not."

"Will Dorie be okay with letting the kid decide?"

"She'll have to be. Besides, I think Dorie's more interested in what the last name's going to be. She already poo-pooed Blackthorne or Blackthorne-McKay."

"Oh, I like the Blackthorne-McKay idea. Makes us sound modern or something."

"Well, we'll let Dorie get over her stroke before we tell her."

"Let's call a florist in Bend and have flowers sent."

"How sweet, Dun. I should've thought of that. After all, she's *my* surrogate mother."

"You're too hard on yourself sometimes."

"And not hard enough other times."

Around eleven o'clock, I hopped in the black Subaru Crosstrek I'd traded in my ancient Volkswagen Jetta for and drove into John Day to shop for maternity clothes. Where, though, was the question—not the one department store or the two dress boutiques, I discovered. Since I was traveling to Bend for my honeymoon in eleven days, I decided my shopping spree could wait until then.

I had promised Duncan the only work I would do today was call Al Bach this afternoon as he'd asked me to. So, on the way back home after my unsuccessful search for duds to wear during my upcoming body transmogrification, I stopped off at the office and made the call.

It worried me that Al didn't answer given his recent health scare, but perhaps he was still doing his thing at the LDS temple. While attempting to reach the detective, a call came in on my desk phone. Caller ID indicated the phone call was from Anita Rhinehart, and now the voicemail light had come on. I watched it blink for half a minute, and against my better judgment, played the message.

"Sergeant Blackthorne, this is Jenna Rhinehart. Tess Slater came to the house looking for me, but my mom told her I wasn't home. Now she's sittin' in a truck down the street, waitin' for me to come out of the house or come back from wherever I mighta gone, I guess. She ain't alone either. There's five other gals waitin' with her in a white crew cab pickup. Anyway, I just thought you might wanna know."

Jenna had used her mother's phone because we still had hers housed in our evidence locker. And yesterday I had promised to get it back to her today, so I retrieved it and got back in my Crosstrek and drove toward Anita's house. I parked next door and got out.

I recognized Tess Slater as the driver, and since I was in street clothes and not driving my OSP Tahoe, Tess and the other girls were chatting it up and laughing inside the crew cab pickup and didn't pay any heed to my presence—that is, until I rapped my fist on the driver's window.

Tess rolled it down. "Can I help you?"

"I'm Sergeant Maggie Blackthorne, Oregon State Police." I showed her my ID and badge. "Several people in the neighborhood here have called complaining about a gaggle of young women drinking and partying it up in a white crew cab truck. Everyone here twenty-one?"

"No. But we're not drinking anything but water." A few held up their clear plastic bottles of water.

"It could be laced with vodka."

Tess giggled. "You're welcome to smell them all."

"Or I could ask all of you to dump out your drinks, and also search your truck."

The peppy blonde in the back seat spoke up and insisted on using a tone of self-righteous sophistication and privilege. "None of us drink alcohol, officer."

"How about weed? Do you smoke it?"

"God, no," Tess said.

It appeared that I'd insulted her, so to salt that wound a little, I took an exaggerated whiff and gathered in nothing but the offensive fragrance of cheap perfume. Weed would've made for a better aroma.

"All right, I'm not going to cite anyone. But I don't want to hear about the six of you hanging out in a vehicle in any more neighborhoods so you can have one of your little gossip parties again."

"My father is a town police officer here, and I'm going to ask him if it's illegal to park here and talk." It was the sophisticated blonde in the back again.

"Go right ahead. Uh, what's your name?"

"Claire. Claire Nolan."

"Say hi to your dad for me. In the meantime, who wants to tell me why the six of you chose this spot to park at? There's no view, especially with all of those dark clouds today, but there would be nothing much to look at even if it wasn't cloudy."

"Um, we're waiting for some guys we know."

"Well, you'll need to text them and tell 'em to meet you at the park or one of your homes, anywhere but here."

"Are we free to go now?" Tess fired back.

"You are."

I stood in the middle of the road and watched them drive away. It still bugged me that Tess had turned up with a truckload of backup. Were they planning a six-to-one showdown, a shaming session, or worse?

13

MIDDAY, NOVEMBER 15

Jenna Rhinehart answered the door after I knocked. She seemed frightened, not the wild-animal bearing of two days ago, but I sensed an underlying foreboding.

"Would you like to come in?" she asked.

"Now that Tess Slater and friends have moved along, I should take off as well."

"I watched the whole thing. Did you tell them I called you?"

"I said several neighbors complained."

"Did they believe that?"

"I doubt it."

She nodded. "I wouldn't think so neither. Was Claire Nolan with Tess?"

"I didn't take down any names." True, but Claire Nolan was the tall gal in the back seat who mildly challenged me. "Why are you asking about a Claire Nolan?"

"She's a bully. Hates me. Always brings up her dad being a city cop. What's the big deal? I mean, Shay Baker's dad used to be a cop, and now he's in the state pen."

I pulled her cell phone from my hip pocket. "Remember I said I was going to bring this to you today?"

"Oh, thank you, Sergeant Blackthorne."

"You're welcome. I'll be in touch."

I drove back to the station and tried again to reach Detective Bach. When he still didn't pick up, I left a long voicemail for him and let him know Hollis and I would put together a full report of what we knew about the Archer shooting tomorrow. I felt tired just thinking about it.

Checking in with Harry before going home crossed my mind, as did starting our murder board. But I had promised Duncan the only work-related activity I'd engage in today was making a quick call to Al. Of course, I'd already broken that vow when I responded to Jenna's message, but hell, no one's perfect.

On the way out of town, just past Prairie Maid and the high school, the white crew cab pickup pulled out onto Highway 395 less than a quarter of a mile in front of me. When it reached Canyon City, the driver turned left onto East Road, and I followed. The truck was moving at a relatively fast pace, up the hill and past the cemetery, until making a right down Dog Creek Road.

It occurred to me there was no real reason to pursue Tess Slater and her friends, if that was even who I was following. And if it was them, perhaps one of the young women lived on Dog Creek Road, and Tess was taking her home. I turned around and drove back toward the cemetery.

After a couple of miles, I pulled over for a peek at the view. The sun had finally burned through the day's thick layer of clouds and now lit up the thick swatch of juniper on a hillock at the base of Canyon Mountain. The eight-thousand-foot peak and its smaller sister, Little Canyon Mountain, were formed by the intrusion of peridotite from deep within the Earth. I only knew this because Doug Vaughn was an amateur geologist and a bit of a nerdy rock hound, and he often expounded on the geologic wonders of our county. And occasionally I actually listened to what he had to say and then happened to remember it. In this case, I'd retained that detail because I treasured the one thing I had inherited from my mother—a ring with a setting of sparkling peridot gemstones. Didn't know if or how peridotite and peridot were related, but I'd decided they must be.

The crew cab passed by my Crosstrek where I'd parked on the road shoulder, and Tess Slater was indeed at the wheel. She was chatting with Claire Nolan, her only passenger, and they appeared not to notice me. For good measure, I jotted down the plate number, something I'd neglected to do earlier. But once again, I wasn't sure what any of it had to do with Charlie Archer's death. In fact, I wasn't sure where any of the threads of this case were taking us, and I had the feeling that more than ever, Hollis and I needed Al Bach's help homing in on the killer.

Duncan had invited his mom and dad to an early dinner. They were pleasant people, of course, but I always imagined I was being judged in some way. Their son and I weren't married yet, but we were expecting a child in five months. Worse yet, or at least somewhat unorthodox, Duncan did most of the cooking in our household. And I didn't think his mother was particularly pleased I was a police officer. Had no idea if I was right about any of that, but Greta and Scotty McKay were straightlaced and conservative; about that there was little doubt.

I reminded myself they had raised Duncan, so that spoke volumes about his parents' character and generosity. Of course, they had also raised Duncan's sister, Kat, who was about as friendly as a porcupine.

When they arrived, I received a kiss on the cheek from both, and I returned the gesture. They had never greeted me so warmly, and I immediately regretted any unkind thoughts I'd had about them.

I had set the table and placed a bouquet of red roses I'd picked up at Chester's Market in the center.

"So lovely. And they're still fragrant," Greta said.

"Would you like anything to drink? Sparkling water, beer, wine?" I asked.

"Just tap water for me, thanks," Greta answered and picked at her fingernails.

"You want ice with that?"

"No, thank you."

"What's the beer you have on offer?" Scotty asked.

"Um, let's see," I said, opening the refrigerator. "We have a Terminal Gravity IPA and a growler of amber ale from 1188 Brewing in town."

"No Budweiser or nothin'?"

"Come on, Dad," Duncan chimed in. "Try the amber ale. It's good. And you'll be showing your support for a local business."

"All right, guess I'll have a small glass of that."

Duncan retrieved the growler, and ignoring his father's request for a small glass, filled two beer pint glasses with the amber ale. He handed one to his dad. While he did so, I fetched tap water for his mother and me, and we all took a seat around the table.

The salad bowls had been filled with a mix of greens and veggies beforehand, and Duncan invited us to all dig in.

"What about the blessing, son?" Scotty asked.

"Okay, here goes. I'm blessed to have loving parents and a loving partner who is soon going to bless us all with a child. Amen."

I didn't laugh, but I did join in. "And I'm blessed to have a loving partner, and together, we'll raise our child to be kind, loving, and open-minded. Oh, amen."

Greta also joined in. "We'll soon be blessed with another grandchild, thank you, Lord."

It was quiet for a beat, and then Scotty had his say. "You're right, the beer's pretty good."

"That was nice," I said to Duncan once dinner was over and Greta and Scotty had driven away in their old pickup.

He shrugged. "I guess."

"What's up?

"Those people we just had dinner with are not my mom and dad."

"You're saying that because they're afraid of pissing me off, and so they're tiptoeing around a couple of things like, uh, like me being a cop who intends to keep being a cop after we're married and after the baby comes?"

"Yes. And they need to hear that from you because no one else can make it as absolutely clear as you can. And once you straighten them out about all that in the way only you can, they'll truly understand what's what and move on."

"Oh, I see. If I clarify in Blackthorne-speak, your mom and dad will leave you the fuck alone."

He pulled me into his chest and held me. "Yeah, that should do the trick."

"I'll get right on that."

Monday morning broke dark and cloudy. A high desert fog had fallen over the land, its fine mist obscuring the prairie of bunch grass and sage brush. A thin slant of sunlight fell across the small stand of Ponderosa pines to the east of us.

Raleigh Cat, as I'd taken to calling our new orange tabby, and I were taking it slow. But Duncan had gotten up early and headed to McKay's Feed and Tack. Today was the first day of the store's big Autumn Jubilee. His nephew, Rain, was a sophomore at Oregon State University in Corvallis, Frankie Jacoby no longer worked at the store, and Duncan hadn't replaced either worker. Hell, thirty to forty customers might pop in for the sale, which today included some early bird specials.

After I finally crawled out of bed, showered, and dressed, I called Yolanda Young to get a Dorie update before heading to the office. Her phone rang several times before she picked up.

"Good morning, Maggie," she said breathily.

"How are you holding up, Ms. Young?"

"Wonderfully. And all the prayers coming Dorie's way have really done the trick. She might even be released from the hospital today."

"I'm so happy to hear that."

"And that beautiful bouquet of roses from you and your fiancé. Oh my, did her face light up when she saw that."

"Are you at the hospital?"

"I'm heading there soon."

"She's lucky to have such a good friend."

"Well, I think you would agree that we're lucky she's still with us."

"Couldn't agree more."

"One of us will let you know if she's being released today."

"Thank you so much, Ms. Young."

"Oh heavens, Yolanda, please. I'll let you go now, Maggie. I know you have your hands full these days."

Once the call ended, I made my way to our sad-looking modular cop shop. It was just before eight when I parked in front, and Hollis and Doug Vaughn pulled up right after. But like most days, Sherry Linn had arrived before any of the rest of us and had the coffee and tea water ready for everyone.

We all gathered at the front counter, Sherry Linn's official workstation and everyone's unofficial gathering spot.

"How are you doing this morning?" I asked her, even though she seemed like she was back to being the Sherry Linn the rest of us had come to appreciate and count on—witty, charming, hardworking, smart as a whip, and a fashionista with her own eclectic style.

"I'm doing a lot better, Maggie. Thanks for asking. How about you?"

"I'm doing okay. I took most of yesterday off, but there's a shitload of info to sort through before our investigation gets its legs."

"Speaking of that, Detective Bach called. He's leaving Bend as soon as he can. And he asked me to send along his apologies for not getting back to you yesterday."

"What happened to that other detective, something Horne, I think it was?" Hollis asked.

"I don't know what happened to Detective Horne. Al had left a voice-mail when I got back here on Saturday night telling me he was out of the hospital and back on the case. I called him twice yesterday but got nothing but crickets."

Hollis gave me a look. "Where did that saying come from, anyway?"

"A woman I worked with for a while. One of the funniest people I ever met."

"Crickets, huh?"

"I like that saying," Sherry Linn put in and played with the set of silver bracelets dangling from her wrist. "I used it last week after I left a voicemail for my mom, but I heard nary a peep back from her."

"Okay, I'll add it to my repertoire of goofy sayings," Holly said.

"That's the spirit. And before we get to it, I wanted to let you know Dorie Phillips had a minor stroke on Saturday. She's at St. Charles Hospital in Bend, and I learned this morning she may be released today."

"Dorie was so helpful with Ellie Taylor and the kids. Speaking of Ellie, I checked in with her yesterday. She had a house full of visitors and sounded worn out."

"Yeah, I dropped by early last evening," Doug added. "Her mother answered the door and told me Ellie had already gone to bed."

I shrugged slightly. "Sleep is probably a good thing right now."

We stood in uncomfortable silence for a beat.

Hollis turned to me. "Murder board or incident reports, Sarge?"

"Murder board."

"And I plan to drive back out to Desolation Ridge this afternoon and see if I can spot that cougar. Unless you have another assignment for me," Doug added.

"No, that works great. And be on the lookout for Archer's orange Scout, will you? Someone towed it away before Whitey Kern was able to. Also, we might've seen that cougar in Dale on Saturday evening."

"Could've been him, all right. I'm a little rusty when it comes to the habits of large wild felines. So over the weekend, I did some research and learned that a cougar's hunting territory can range over three hundred fifty square miles."

"Jesus. Including across a highway?"

For a moment he gazed at me as if wondering whether I was attempting to make a joke. "Uh, animals cross highways all the time."

I smiled. "Of course they do, Blackthorne. I even managed to talk a black Angus bull out of standing in the middle of the highway one night a while back. But I guess I like starting out some mornings with a dumb question. Anyway, let's get to work, gang."

I moved to my desk and stashed my pack on the floor next to it. Hollis and Doug had followed me back to our circle of desks but paused at Mark's desk. It still held several photos of Mark with his wife, along with several shots of their kids.

"I can't believe he's gone," Doug said solemnly before taking a seat.

"Yeah, it's a deal, all right," I added.

Hollis picked up the photo of Mark's young boys. "That's why we need to do right by his death."

"To that end, I'll fetch a chart pack and markers, then let's get started with our murder board."

"And I'll set up my laptop in the alcove," Hollis answered.

"Don't be getting all twenty-first century on me, now."

"I know how much you love to have it all out in front of us on the bulletin board."

"It's the American way."

I moved back to the front counter and opened the supply cabinet. Sherry Linn had organized all of the markers by color and stacked the chart packs so they were precisely aligned with one another, similar to how a member of the military might make a bed. I retrieved enough supplies to get us started and carted it all to the alcove, where we held meetings and ate our lunch. Hollis was already waiting for me.

After tacking up a couple of large sheets of paper, we began filling out the murder board. _Day One:_ *Thursday 11/12 @ 9:30 a.m. Patti Hutchens, Dale resident, reports DV at her neighbor's mobile home. *Trooper Taylor redirected from separate call to respond to DV report (DV assailant = Charles Sean Archer; victim later ID'd by Lyndon Cummings, Ukiah resident, as Jenna Rhinehart).

*Sgt. Blackthorne & Senior Trooper Jones leave for Dale as backup for Taylor, and Trooper Vaughn responds to cougar sighting near Desolation Ridge. *@ 10:30 a.m. Sherry Linn Perkins reports that Hutchens informed her Taylor had been shot.

"Was that only four days ago?" Hollis said.

"Yep."

I continued writing: *Jones reports shooting to regional dispatch + Archer fled in an orange 1980 International Scout, Oregon vanity plates = M-U-D R-U-N. *@ 11:30 a.m., Blackthorne & Jones arrive in Dale and meet briefly with Hutchens.

Finally, I listed off the most relevant fact thus far: *@ 12:00 p.m., Perkins *reports to Blackthorne that Taylor expired in the ambulance on the way to the hospital.*

I sat down at the flimsy card table across from Hollis. We both stared at that last bullet point.

Holly sighed deeply. "You're right, that last bullet point calls out a deal."

"A fucked-up situation, all right," I said, translating the cop-talk meaning of "a deal."

We continued on, spending most of the morning putting together the rest of the murder board, and afterward, we listened to Saturday's interview of Jenna Rhinehart.

"She sounds pretty lucid there."

"Yeah, she had even asked me to interview her so she could get it over with. But out of an abundance of caution, her name goes on the suspect list for both homicides."

Hollis stood and tacked up two more sheets from the chart pack. At the top of the first, he wrote *Suspects: Taylor Homicide*, and at the top of the second, he wrote

Suspects: Archer Homicide. He then wrote Archer's and Jenna's names under the first heading and listed Jenna under the second heading.

Hollis turned to me. "We haven't heard from Harry yet regarding the weapons used in either case, have we?"

"No. I expect we might hear something today, but given the fifteen handguns I found in the Scout and the one Jenna was packing when we found her, we might have to wait a little longer."

"Did Dr. Gattis have any thoughts about the murder weapons?"

"She suspected they were handguns."

Sherry Linn appeared in the alcove. "Maggie, someone named..." She looked at the slip of paper where she'd apparently written the caller's name. "Um, a Mr. Ulanowicz—I believe I'm pronouncing that correctly— would like to speak with you."

"Is he here?"

"No, but this is the third time he's called. And I've explained you were unavailable, but he won't leave a message."

"Go ahead and patch him through to my desk phone."

"All right. And I'm taking my lunch after that unless you need me to stay."

"Nope, we're good."

"See you later, then." She turned and flounced from the alcove, her heels click-clacking on the cement flooring.

Back at my desk, I answered the buzzing phone. "Sergeant Blackthorne here. Is this Mr. Ulanowicz?"

"Yeah. Wanted you to know I spotted that old orange Scout driving through town about an hour ago. Had the same plate number on that poster you put up in Jacoby's Hardware Store."

"Did you notice the driver and any passengers?"

"Yep. A couple of blockhead brothers who go mudding out in the forest. Jack and Seth Dawson from here in Ukiah."

I quickly jotted down the names. "Which direction were they going?"

"They turned south onto what Ukiahans call Soap Hill Road but what the damn Forest Service calls Road 52. Takes you into the Umatilla National Forest. They're probably heading somewhere up there to tear up the landscape."

I'd become pretty familiar with that part of the county, but at the moment, I had more important things to do than tackling the tangle of unpaved washboard roads and byways to find a couple of reprobate vehicle thieves. I'd radio Doug Vaughn and have him look into it instead. He'd taken off to Desolation Ridge hoping to track down that cougar while Hollis and I were putting together the murder board.

"Thank you for the information, Mr. Ulanowicz."

"Did you check the stash my next-door neighbors keep behind their propane tank?"

We'd searched the so-called stash, and without permission, but I was pretty sure this Ulanowicz fellow didn't give a damn whether or not we followed police protocol.

"Yeah, we checked it out but didn't find anything of interest."

"What *did* you find?"

"I'm not at liberty to say, Mr. Ulanowicz."

"Are you at liberty to have a drink with me sometime?"

That move surprised me. "Well, if you can wait until my baby is born next April, then sure, we can have a drink somewhere."

"Oh, you're married."

"I will be in eleven days."

"Like always, my timing is off."

Something like that.

"Thanks for the tip about the orange Scout, but I need to get back to work."

"Next time you're in Ukiah, stop by the store. Maybe we'll go have that drink."

Yeah, when hell freezes over.

14

AFTERNOON, NOVEMBER 16

I radioed Doug Vaughn and asked him to be on the lookout for Jack and Seth Dawson—the so-called blockhead brothers—possibly driving the orange Scout in the vicinity of Desolation Ridge. In the background, I heard Detective Al Bach chatting with Sherry Linn and Hollis at the front counter.

"Good to see you, Al," I said, joining the others. "How are you feeling?"

"Happy to report I didn't have a heart attack. Acid reflux, in this case a serious bout of it."

I made a face. "Doesn't sound good."

"A common condition, easily treated. But staying overnight in the hospital just about did me in."

"I have a dear friend who's in the hospital in Bend as we speak, unless she's already been released," I said.

"It's a great medical center, Maggie," Al put in. "But all the tests and visitors tired me out."

"Are you ready to get to it, then?"

Bach nodded. "Have you started your murder board?"

"Yeah, in the alcove. I decided we'd do that before wrapping up our reports on the Archer killing and the aftermath. But we'll get on those right away."

"I'm fine with that given you're down one trooper and your already limited staffing. However, don't ask me when the legislature is going to fund more positions."

"I gave up on that a while back."

"Yeah. Me too. Join me when you can," he said and carried his laptop to the alcove in back.

Hollis and I met briefly, and he agreed to take charge of putting together the report on the discovery of Archer's body, while I did the write-up on locating the man's orange International Scout out in the forest, as well as meeting up with Jenna Rhinehart. We'd move on to the assorted other encounters after that.

I drifted to the alcove, where Bach stood studying the murder board.

"You really think it's possible the DV victim killed Mr. Archer?" he asked.

"I would be surprised if that was the case, but then I've been surprised about who's capable of murdering someone before."

"I've been surprised about that a time or two myself." He pointed to Cousin Lyndon's name. "And Mr. Cummings?"

"He's Jenna Rhinehart's godfather, and they're apparently close. He had also recently fired Archer from his forest maintenance company. Thanks to me, he knew about the domestic violence the night before Archer was killed. He lives a relatively short distance from where we located Archer's body. And in our most recent interaction with him, he exhibited some nervous behavior, I guess I'd call it. But even I know all that doesn't mean he's a killer. Still, I'd like to keep him on our radar for now."

"Anyone else who you consider a person of interest?"

"Possibly Jenna Rhinehart's mother and father."

"Isn't Rhinehart the last name of the Grant County sheriff?"

"Dirk Rhinehart is the *former* sheriff and Jenna's father."

The detective was taken aback. "Since when is he the former sheriff?"

"A group of folks filed a petition to have him recalled, and he ended up resigning instead. I mean, that's not how he couched it, said something like it was time to call it a day, age and all that. Anyway, yes, I would consider him someone we'll want to question."

"Perhaps I should be the one to do that."

"Even better. The man disses me at every turn, and he's been blatantly racist in his attitude toward Hollis."

"Unfortunately, I've encountered lots of law enforcement personnel who are bigots and sexists. There is no place for that in our line of work."

"And yet..."

"Indeed. And the woman's mother?"

"It's hard to imagine her as a killer. Although she is very protective of her daughter, I don't see her picking up a gun, driving out in the middle of a dense forest, happening on the guy who'd victimized her child, and shooting him dead."

"And what is she like, the daughter?"

"Kind of indescribable at this point. I'll admit, though, she was traumatized by Archer's violence."

"Do you know how she reacted when she learned he was dead?"

"I was the person who told her, as far as I know, anyway. And there wasn't much of a reaction, although she did seem, um, surprised, I guess I'd say. Just not particularly sad."

"Well, I'd say we need to do more digging, Maggie."

"Can't disagree with that, Al. I'm hoping Harry's examination of the fifteen handguns I found in Archer's truck, as well as the one Jenna Rhinehart says she took from the guy's gun safe, gives us something to go on."

"What's the next move if Harry's examination doesn't shine a light on anything?"

"I hate to tell you this, but that's where you come in."

He sent me a mischievous smile. "It's a good thing Detective Horne got caught carrying on with a sixteen-year-old girl."

"More to the point, it's a good thing you only had a bad case of acid reflux."

"Go write your reports, Maggie. I'm going to check in to my room at Mack's Motel. Oh, and please email me Mrs. Taylor's phone number along with the audio file of your interview with Miss Rhinehart."

Just after three o'clock, Doug Vaughn called to let me know he'd pulled over the Dawson brothers and cited them for unauthorized use of a vehicle, and they were now handcuffed and sitting in the back seat of his Ram 2500.

"Good work, Doug. What kind of guff did they give you?"

"Pussycats, both of them. Didn't want to sit in a jail cell, obviously. But then I told them the Scout had belonged to a guy who was murdered last week. Said a homicide detective would need to interview them, and they clammed up tight after that."

"And Archer's old Scout?"

"Whitey Kern is on his way out here."

"Out near Desolation Ridge?"

"Nah, they were getting gas in Long Creek when I spotted them. I left the Scout in the care of the station owner—guy named Butch Robertson— until Whitey gets there."

"I'd say your visit to the Umatilla Forest turned out to be pretty fruitful."

"Except I didn't catch up with that dang cougar. Did find some inter-esting rocks along Desolation Creek, though."

"A bonus, then."

"Yeah, I guess. Well, I should get going. I'd hate for the Dawson boys to miss dinner in the Grant County jail."

"Call me after they're booked."

"Will do."

I contacted Al and relayed the information about Seth and Jack Dawson and suggested we interview them before the end of the day.

"Do you know anything about these men?"

"No. Hollis looked them up in LEDs and DMV, and they're pretty clean."

"Pretty clean, but willing to tow an old truck out of the forest and hot-wire it."

"An opportunity crime, I guess. The guy who reported seeing them in the Scout this afternoon called 'em the blockhead brothers, but he has some blockhead tendencies himself, I'd say."

"Well, let me know when it's time to head to the jail for their interview."

"All right."

"On another note, I had a nice conversation with Mrs. Taylor this afternoon. I also listened to your interview with Miss Rhinehart. And once again, I want you to consider joining my homicide squad. You're a far better interviewer than most, and certainly better than Detective Horne was."

"Oh." I hadn't expected that. "What did you think of Jenna Rhinehart?"

"I'll want to talk with her in person before I answer that. That said, you're right, she definitely experienced some distressing brutality."

Hollis and I had just wrapped up our reports when Harry Bratton arrived. I invited him to the alcove so the three of us could sit at the card table and discuss his findings, or lack thereof.

"Here's the handgun inventory," Harry said. He sat down and handed us the list of Archer's weapons, each with an accompanying photograph and its manufacturer, model, caliber, and serial number and broken down into two categories: pistols and revolvers.

"I started police academy not understanding the difference between a pistol and revolver. Just knew they both could be deadly in the wrong hands."

"Interesting that he had more pistols than revolvers," Hollis added.

Harry shrugged. "He probably just collected what he was able to purchase, trade for, or steal. Anyway, I had regional make a gun trace request in ATF's eTrace system."

"I thought a couple of them looked like ghost guns, but I guess not."

"No, but all of them are made in the US, which kind of surprised me," Harry clarified. "Guy must've been quite a patriot."

"The kind that drives a gas hog and packs a lot of heat," I snarked.

"Which means we live in a very patriotic county, right?"

"You got it, Harry."

"Some of the make and models evoke...something unfriendly, tough? I don't know," Hollis said. "AMT Hardballer. Charter Arms Bulldog. Freedom Arms 83. Smith and Wesson Bodyguard."

"Macho shit," I put in.

"Well, only two of the guns had been fired recently," Harry said. "I just don't know how recently."

"How could you tell?"

"Well, for one thing, the guy carried a utility brush, some gun cleaner, and lubricant in his ammo box, which he obviously used to clean the handguns. For another, fourteen of the weapons were spotless inside and out. Like they'd never been fired."

"So which two had recently been fired?" Hollis asked.

He pointed to the Beretta Bobcat. "This one."

"That's the pistol I found under the driver's seat in Archer's Scout," I said.

"Two sets of fingerprints were on it," Harry added. "One was Archer's. Didn't find the other in the western states fingerprint database."

"And the other gun fired recently?"

"The revolver you took from Jenna Rhinehart—the Ruger Blackhawk. Same prints as the second set on the Beretta."

I gave Hollis my *well, shit* look.

"That doesn't mean it's the gun that killed the Archer asshole. And assuming Ray Gattis turned over the slugs from both bodies to the lab in Bend, I'll get in touch with my buddies there and see what they've come up with."

"I'm sure she did," I said. "I'll be right back."

I stood and moved out front and asked Sherry Linn to contact High Desert Express, the local courier service, told her we needed to ship some evidence to the Bend lab pronto.

Hollis and Harry were discussing firearms when I returned to the alcove, but clearly the conversation was focused on elk hunting, not person-to-person gun violence.

"Sherry Linn's contacting the courier service. Hopefully we can get the two handguns to the lab today."

"The lab closes promptly at five thirty," Harry said. "But they do have an evidence drop for after hours. Or at least they did back when I worked there."

"Excuse me again, I need to get something." I walked to the evidence room, returning quickly and carrying the bagged thermos out of which Jenna had sipped milk on Friday and handed it to Harry.

"For comparison purposes. Jenna Rhinehart's prints are the only ones on this."

"Just remember, none of this nails down Archer's killer. We have to wait for the lab."

Sherry Linn stood at the entrance to the alcove. "Maggie, I talked Gus into doing an after-hours run to Bend."

"Gus is the courier?" Harry asked.

"Yeah, I had to do some sweet-talking to convince him this couldn't wait until the morning."

"That clinches it," I said. "You're getting a bump in pay."

"A whole twenty-five cents more an hour, but I'll take it," she quipped and moved back to the front counter.

"Thanks for your good work, Harry."

"And thank you for being smart enough to hire Sherry Linn."

I smiled. "That was a good hire, all right."

He looked at his watch. "Five thirty on the dot. Time for me to take your good hire home."

I still sat at the card table in the alcove, reading over the murder board. I'd tacked up the list of Archer's weaponry and added the info we'd gotten from Harry regarding the two recently fired handguns. It was looking a bit dire for Jenna Rhinehart. But there were still other questions to be answered, beginning with the info we needed from the lab.

I didn't think it was time to arrest Jenna, but Al Bach might have different ideas. Even so, I sensed I could talk him out of that, at least until we had something more definitive to go on.

I heard my desk phone ring and moved to answer it. Doug Vaughn's name flashed on caller ID.

"Are we set, Doug?"

"Yeah. The brothers are waiting in an interview room, along with a deputy sheriff."

"Thanks, Doug."

"Good night. See you tomorrow morning."

I contacted Al, and we agreed to meet at the jail, so I closed down the office, locked up, and made my way to the courthouse in Canyon City, the seat of our fair county, designated as such in the 1860s when it was a gold-mining metropolis. The building also held the county jail, which had housed some colorful characters over the years and a few too many homicidal maniacs in recent years.

Arriving before Detective Bach, I waited for him, listening to some vintage Bonnie Raitt, "Thing Called Love." Which prompted me to call Duncan and see how his day had gone, but Al pulled up next to my rig just then.

We stepped out of our police vehicles and walked to the front door, where the after-hours guard let us in. We were directed to the second floor and the larger interview room.

I knocked on the door. Chief Deputy Weldon opened it and stepped outside. He and I shook hands.

"This is Detective Al Bach," I said, making the introduction. "Chief Weldon and I got to know one another last August when Dave Shannon staged his attempted escape from jail."

Al shook the chief's hand. "Nice to meet you."

"Same here, sir."

"Please, just Al."

"And you guys are welcome to call me Jeff."

"What's the story on the Dawson brothers?" I asked.

"Not sure I've ever seen two such nervous inmates."

"From what I know, they've never been arrested before."

"Maybe that's it, Sergeant Blackthorne, but I kinda don't think so."

"Maggie, remember?"

His wizened face reddened. "I should let you get to your interrogation."

Bach and I entered the room. The first thing I noticed about the brothers was their teeth. One had had the benefit of dental care, and the other had not.

On our walk upstairs, Al had put me in charge of leading the interview, so I decided to start with the basics once introductions were made.

We sat across from the Dawsons, and I turned on the recorder.

"I'm Sergeant Margaret Blackthorne, and this is Homicide Detective Alan Bach, Oregon State Police. Please state your name, date of birth, and address."

The brother across from me—the one with all of his teeth—spoke first. "Seth Avery Dawson, August fifth, nineteen eighty-three, Soap Hill Road, Ukiah, Oregon."

"Jackson Eliot Dawson, February nineteenth, nineteen eighty-seven, Soap Hill Road, Ukiah, Oregon," the second brother said, and with difficulty.

"Those are interesting names," I said.

"Um, our ma's from back east," Seth said.

"I see. So where did you find the orange International Scout you were driving around in?"

"It just turned up."

"I don't think so, Seth. If I may call you by your first name."

"Sure, sure. I'm all about being on a first-name basis."

"That's good, Seth, because I have a delicate question for you."

"Bring it on, uh, Sergeant."

"Did either of you happen upon a Mr. Charles Archer at the Desolation Guard Station out in the Umatilla Forest?"

"I don't believe I know anyone by that name."

"Did you ever spot the 1980 International Scout you were in possession of being driven around Ukiah or out in the forest by someone else?"

"Gosh, I don't believe so."

"Is that true, Jack? May I call you Jack?"

He bobbed his head up and down but neglected to answer my question.

"Jack, is it true that you and your brother never saw the Scout being driven around by someone else?"

"Ma'am?" Jack said.

"Did either of you ever notice the Scout you moved from the woods being driven by another guy, like the man who actually owned it?"

He looked over at Seth, nervous, hanging out on a limb, and without his brother's chutzpah and confidence. "I don't think so, ma'am."

"You don't think so? Or did your brother tell you to not say anything about the vehicle belonging to someone else?"

"Don't remember him saying nothin' like that."

"Did you notice the blood on the seats and bloody handprints on the front passenger window?"

"Well, sure, but I just wiped all that off with one of my kerchiefs."

The look brother Seth passed to Jack reminded me of a character in a Coen brothers movie—a man who wished he'd committed fratricide years ago.

"Jack, did you or your brother kill Charlie Archer?"

"Don't even know who that is, ma'am."

"All right, let me put it to you another way. Have you or your brother ever killed anyone?"

"No, ma'am. But we did steal that orange truck parked out in the woods."

15

———

NIGHT, NOVEMBER 16

I answered my buzzing cell phone. "Hey, Dun. How was the opening day of Autumn Jubilee?"

"Busy. I'd say there were seventy-five to eighty customers in today."

"Wow, have you had that kind of crowd before?"

"Don't think so. I'm damned tired, though, and I wish Rain had been here to help out."

"He's probably busy with classes." Well, too busy to help out his uncle, anyway.

"Oh, I know. And I really should've hired someone after Frankie retired."

"Well, I bet if you advertised you were hiring, you'd get some decent prospects to apply."

"I have to say, this is the most romantic conversation I've had all day."

"Yeah, me too. Well, there was that short conversation I had with Al Bach..."

"Very funny. How's he doing, by the way?"

"A bad bout of acid reflux disguising itself as a heart attack."

"Sheesh. Think I'd rather have the heart attack."

"Are you hungry?"

"Starving," he said. "Let's go to the Anchor Club for dinner, celebrate the success of the sale."

"Sounds good. I'm on my way home right now."

"Me too."

"See you there."

I motored in the deep dark of our mid-November night, the moon's tiny crescent making room for the light of a thousand shining stars. I suddenly thought of Dorie. Had she been home, she would've bundled up, gone to sit out on her front porch, a cup of hot tea in hand, to take in this sky. Unexpectedly, tears formed. I inhaled sharply and willed them away.

Earlier in the evening, while driving south on Canyon Boulevard toward the courthouse for our interview with the Dawson boys, I'd passed by Dorie's place. A large *For Sale* sign had been installed at the front of the Castle Thrift Store, the business she had owned and operated for many years and where she's lived in the small apartment at the rear of the building. The lights had been out in her store and apartment, and I'd taken that as an indication she hadn't been released from the hospital today after all.

I pulled onto the shoulder of the road and idled my rig, dug my phone out of my pocket, and dialed Yolanda Young's number.

"Oh, Miss Maggie, your timing is perfect."

"Oh?"

"The hospital's in the process of releasing Dorie. We'll spend the night in my motel room and drive home in the morning."

I could feel the tears about to pop again. "That's such great news."

"Would you like to talk to her?"

"Absolutely, thank you."

Yolanda turned the phone over to Dorie.

"Hey, doll. How're you doing?" She sounded weak but still her chipper self.

"I'm great. More to the point, how are you?"

"Well, I'm coming home, thanks to everyone's prayers. I was thinking maybe you even threw one in for good measure."

"Oh, I did, but in my own special way."

"But without the cussing, I hope."

"Well, you know how I am. The cussing just reinforces my passionate nature."

"Or something," she said, giggling.

"I'm so glad you're better. I was worried."

"Well, I love you, kid, and I'll see you soon."

"Tomorrow. I'll drop by tomorrow."

"Sounds good."

"Nighty night. I love you."

"Oh, see you tomorrow, Maggie. They're here with the wheelchair to take me to the car."

She hung up, and I sighed with relief, put the Tahoe in gear, and continued driving toward home.

Raleigh Cat welcomed me in feline fashion and slipped out the front door to explore the landscape and declare his ownership.

I heard the shower running and made my way upstairs to find civilian wear for our dinner out. I chose a silk blouse that brought out the brown of my eyes, or so Duncan had proclaimed. I pulled out a pair of jeans from a dresser drawer.

"Crap." The pants no longer fit.

I wasn't a big fan of leggings, but they worked size-wise, it seemed, and the blouse was long enough to cover my growing middle. I turned to the side and looked at myself in the mirror.

"This will have to do."

I put on a pair of silver earrings and my new sneakers and headed back downstairs. I met Duncan coming up the steps as I was going down. He'd wrapped a bath towel around his waist, exposing his broad chest and muscular arms.

"Nice," he said, complimenting my outfit. "You just made me hungry for something besides dinner."

I kissed him and pressed my body into his. "How about dessert later tonight?"

"You're full of good ideas."

"I keep telling you I'm brilliant."

"And don't forget sexy."

"Well, of course."

I woke with a start. Archer's weapons. How did a man with no money afford to get his hands on all those guns? What had Harry said yesterday? Right, Archer's cache was probably made up of what he was able to purchase, trade for, or steal.

Mostly stolen weapons was my guess. I sat up. There was something else eating at me—a report or bulletin had come into the office from the FBI or the ATF a while back, or no, maybe they worked on it jointly, hell, I didn't remember. Something about a gang of gun thieves or gun traffickers —or both—on the West Coast.

All right, I was awake now. I put on my robe and slippers and tiptoed out of the room and downstairs. I retrieved my laptop and logged in to my work email. I had folders for each agency. I opened the one labeled FBI and scanned it and found the memo from both agencies with the bulletin I sought. It turned out to be the most recent I'd received from either organization back on June 11, more than five months ago.

I opened it and read through the unflowery commentary. It spelled out a hate group's rage at the state of the nation and the chaos it planned to unleash. It included artist sketches, based on witness descriptions, of seven men wanted for trafficking stolen firearms, along with a photo of the group's leader, also wanted. He was an apparently charismatic guy named Clifton Albert Massey out of Redding, California.

Known as POSSE, an acronym for Protective Order of Sovereign States Eternal, Massey's followers' names and addresses were unknown, but I was reasonably certain the illustration of the third unidentified male pictured was Charles Sean Archer, alias Archie Sean Charles and/or John Charles Archibald of Dale, Oregon, now deceased.

POSSE's eventual plan was apparently an armed insurrection of some nature. Much of their weaponry had been seized, and those confiscated firearms largely included machine guns like the PKM and FN MAG 58, along with semiautomatic rifles including a haul of AK-47s and AR-15s. Several handguns also appeared in the various photographs.

"Posse," I said. "Didn't Mario Van Peebles direct that movie back in the day?"

Before getting ready for work, I emailed the document to Hollis and Al with a note: "Is it possible guy #3 illustrated in this bulletin is Archer? I believe it might be. Might explain some or all of the guns in his possession, too."

Afterward, I took a quick shower and scarfed down a bowl of cereal before heading upstairs to get ready for work. Duncan was still asleep, so I dressed inside the closet. Then I tiptoed to his side of the bed and kissed him lightly on his forehead.

He opened his eyes and smiled.

"Time to get up, sleepy head. Day two of the big sale."

"Thanks for reminding me, Sergeant Blackthorne."

"I'm off to the office. I might've figured something out that could be important."

He sat up. "About the homicide case, I assume."

"Possibly related to it, anyway."

He pushed back the covers, got out of bed, and gave me a bear hug. "Have a good day, babe."

"You too, guy."

Hollis was already at the office and buried in his computer. He looked up as I sat at my desk across from his.

"I can't believe we made it to the office before Sherry Linn," I said.

"Most were stolen, and yes, I agree with you."

"Back up a bit, dude. Most of what was stolen, and what do you agree with me about?"

He kept tapping away on his keyboard. "Most of Archer's stash of weapons were stolen from people's residences here in Oregon, and in Washington and Idaho. Maybe they all were, and some were just unreported. And that guy definitely looks like Archer, except maybe a little younger and with longer hair."

"Ah, the joint bulletin. I guess I'm a little slow on the uptake this morning."

"I don't think so. You sent that email to the detective and me at six a.m. What made you remember it?"

"Something innocuous Harry said yesterday. Anyway, I want us to interview Jenna this morning, see if she knows anything about POSSE."

"Good idea, Maggie." Al had joined us.

"I didn't find much online," Hollis continued. "Except it seems like they operate primarily in what I'd call the US Pacific Northwest. And they're on the run."

"So not up and down the West Coast?" Bach asked. "How about Canadian influence?"

"No, just in our neck of the woods, and I can't really tell if there's any Canadian influence. But since the organization claims to be protecting state sovereignty, I'd bet Canada's provinces and territories aren't part of the deal." He picked up the bulletin he'd apparently printed out. "Although Canada may be where some of them are hiding out and/or gathering up more weapons."

"It's my understanding gun laws are much stricter in Canada," I said.

"They are, and that's probably put a damper on collecting weaponry if that's where any POSSE members took themselves."

"You two have any insights about why Mr. Archer planted himself in Grant County?"

"No, Al. That's something we should discuss with Jenna Rhinehart."

"He's from Portland originally, right?"

"And he served a couple of drunk and disorderly stays in the county jail there. Plus he took Chuck Palahniuk's *Fight Club* novel a little too seriously," Hollis said.

"Can you pull up the photograph you found last Thursday of Archer displaying his trove of guns?" I asked.

"Yeah, I downloaded it and put it in the online case file."

"Let's compare it to the list Harry brought by yesterday."

"Good thought. And by the way, Harry Bratton sent the electronic version for our records right before you arrived."

"This list," Bach said. "Do you have a hard copy for me to peruse?"

I handed him mine. "Would you like to set up at Mark Taylor's desk?" I'd noticed that someone—Sherry Linn, no doubt—had collected the family photographs from his desk.

"Sure." He placed his laptop and thermos of tea on the now-spare desk.

"So, here's the shot of Archer and those arms." Al and I stood behind Hollis. "I already compared it to Harry's list. Some appear to be on the list, and others not."

"How about the ones you mentioned yesterday evening, Maggie? The two you had couriered to the Bend lab."

"Yeah, there's the Beretta, and there in the corner is the Ruger. And before you arrived, Hollis was saying most of the guns Archer had in his possession were stolen."

"Interesting. That's Mr. Archer, correct?" Bach pointed toward the smiling guy in the photo. "Can you pull up that bulletin again, Hollis?"

"Yep."

Bach leaned toward the computer screen. "He does resemble the man you pointed out in the bulletin."

"For sure," I said and studied it again. I was unexpectedly caught by something I couldn't quite put my finger on.

"Speaking of resembling," I continued. "Does the photo of Clifton Massey remind you of anyone, Hollis?"

He gazed at the image of the large, bearded guy standing in front of a large American flag and shrugged. "Well, not to be unkind, but he looks ubiquitously eastern Oregon."

"Oh, I like that line. Maybe that's why he looks kind of familiar. At least to me."

My desk phone rang. I checked caller ID.

"I need to take this. It's Harry." I picked up the receiver. "Good morning, Harry."

"Maggie, I wanted to let you know right away. Jenna Rhinehart's prints were on the Beretta and the Ruger."

"Thanks for getting back to us so quickly on this."

"This alone doesn't prove she shot Archer."

"I know. We have to wait for the Bend lab."

"I'll call them and try to light a fire under their butts."

"Just remind them about the connection to Mark Taylor's murder."

"Exactly my thinking."

Hollis and the detective stared at me, apparently anxious to hear the news from Harry.

"Jenna Rhinehart's prints were on both guns sent to Bend."

"All right," Al said. "Let's pay her a visit."

"In the meantime, I'll continue researching the POSSE group," Hollis put in.

Sherry Linn had arrived while we were chatting and now stood at my desk. "Maggie. Sorry to interrupt, but a Mr. and Mrs. Dawson from Ukiah are here with their two sons. They would like to talk to you and Detective Bach."

Al and I moved to the front counter, where we found the Dawsons crowded into our minute lobby.

"Good morning. I'm Sergeant Blackthorne, and this is Detective Bach. How can we help you?"

"I'm Rosalie Dawson. My husband and I have bailed these two knuckleheads out of jail, although we had to think long and hard about whether to bail them out or to let them sit there for a while. Anyway, we brought them by to apologize to both of you."

I didn't remember their exact ages, but I recalled they were in their mid to late thirties.

"No apology necessary, ma'am. Your sons just need to stay out of trouble and show up at their arraignment."

"Oh, they'll do all of that, I can assure you. Now, Seth, since you're the ringleader, you go first."

"Sorry, Sergeant Blackthorne. We should've reported finding the Scout instead of just taking it. That part was my doing. Jack just happened to be along for the ride."

"Jackson," their mother said, "it's your turn."

"Uh, I was just as bad as Seth, and I'm very sorry."

I looked over at Al, and he indicated I should continue.

"Your apologies are accepted, but there is one other requirement we have in addition to you showing up for your arraignment and taking whatever punishment is ultimately meted out. And that is this, until we determine who murdered the owner of the Scout you absconded with, you are not to leave the county."

"Oh, these boys are going to be kept on a short leash from here on out, I can assure you of that, Sergeant Blackthorne."

"I appreciate that, Mrs. Dawson. Now, if you'll excuse us, we're pretty busy this morning."

"Thank you for your time." Mrs. Dawson gathered up her sons and husband, and they proceeded out the front door.

Hollis had listened to the conversation from his desk and now joined us. "What the heck was that about?"

"Oh, you missed a touching interview with those two knuckleheads at the county jail last evening, Holly."

"Those were the guys responsible for towing the orange Scout out of the forest?"

"Yeah. Goes to show, not everyone's cut out to be a member of POSSE."

16

MORNING, NOVEMBER 17

Shortly after nine o'clock, Bach and I left Hollis to continue his research of POSSE, jumped in my OSP Tahoe, and drove the short distance to Anita Rhinehart's home.

"I have a question, Maggie," Al said on the way. "What did Hollis mean when he said Clifton Massey 'looked ubiquitously eastern Oregon'?"

"Well, you may have noticed he's big on keeping his own bias in check, having been the subject of it himself all his life. So I think that was his backhanded way of saying Mr. Massey looked like a redneck."

"I see."

We arrived at Anita's place, and I knocked at the door. Twice. Wrapped in a terry bathrobe, she answered the door after several minutes, passing me a look of surprise tinged with alarm.

"Sorry to wake you, Ms. Rhinehart."

"Oh, I was just lying in bed, working on a crossword puzzle," she said from the other side of the latched screen door.

"This is Detective Bach."

Al tipped his hat.

I continued. "We need to speak with Jenna."

"I'll see if she's awake." She turned to move toward Jenna's room but faced us again and unlatched the screen door. "Please come in."

We entered her spare, spotless home.

"Have a seat wherever you'd like."

I moved to the couch, extracted the recorder and a blank waiver form from my pack. The detective seated himself next to me and exhaled.

"Everything okay?" I asked, placing the recorder and waiver form on the coffee table in front of us.

"Fit as a fiddle."

We sat in silence waiting for the mother and daughter to appear. Anita was first, now dressed and nervous.

"Can I offer you some tea or coffee?" she inquired.

We both declined.

"And is Jenna joining us?" I asked.

"Yes, I'm right here." Jenna entered the room, wearing her usual attire—the tattered black *Thundermother* shirt and black jeans. But this morning, she also wore a new, very swollen shiner.

I decided to ignore the recently battered eye for now. "Good morning, Jenna."

"Sergeant Blackthorne. I'm surprised to see you back here so soon."

I indicated Al. "This is Detective Bach."

"Nice to meet you, Detective."

"Good to make your acquaintance as well."

"Are you a homicide detective?" she asked.

He passed Jenna and her mother his card. "I am, and I'd appreciate it if both of you would take a seat."

Mother and daughter each pulled a ladder-back chair from the dining table and sat side by side across from us.

Bach continued. "Miss Rhinehart, I've read the reports regarding the investigation of Mr. Archer's death, and I've listened to the recording of your previous interview. I'm so sorry you had to go through such a harrowing ordeal, and I'm very glad Sergeant Blackthorne was in the right place at the right time and that you found her."

That was an interesting and smart place to begin.

"Thank you, Detective, um, Bach."

He nodded and looked over at me.

"We have a few more questions to ask you this morning," I said, turned on the recorder, and read Jenna her rights. She nodded and signed and dated a second waiver with all the enthusiasm of a pouting middle-schooler.

"Jenna, do you know what brought Charlie Archer to Grant County?"

"Um, well, he said he wanted to live in the mountains and where there weren't so many people. But he constantly bitched—excuse me—complained about living up in the mountains, and he didn't like most people from around here, far as I could tell."

"Did you meet him before he started working for Lyndon Cummings or after?" I already knew what Lyndon claimed, but I wanted to know if it matched Jenna's answer.

"I met Charlie when I was working at the combination gas station and grocery store in Mt. Vernon. We kind of started dating while he was living in Dale. I knew he was looking for work, so I mentioned it to Uncle Lyn last June 'cause he was hiring for the summer."

"Did he make any friends while he was working on your Uncle Lyn's forest maintenance crew?"

Jenna all but laughed. "No, not one."

"How about enemies?"

"Don't know about enemies, but he had a few run-ins."

"Anyone in particular?"

"Uh, Tess Slater's brother, for one. Brad's his name. And his cousin Calvin something. Oh yeah, James, Calvin James. And there was also Earl...somebody."

"Were all three on the forest maintenance crew?"

"I think so. And there was big problems between Charlie and Earl."

"Did you ever meet the other members of the crew?"

"Well, I already knew who Brad and Calvin were."

"Right. But did you meet anyone else?"

"No. Charlie didn't bring or invite anybody to the trailer while I was living there. Besides the smell of Tess Slater."

"Speaking of Tess Slater, does she have any relationship to that new shiner you're wearing?"

Jenna cleared her throat and sat a little straighter. "Does that matter?"

"I wouldn't ask otherwise."

"All right, yeah."

"Do you wish to press charges?" Bach asked.

"I would've done that already if I wanted to."

"Then I believe you need to explain why you're not," Al said in a voice that bordered on patronizing. Perhaps that was the intent.

"She didn't give two shits about Charlie. She was having sex with him to get back at me for turning her in last year. Her and Claire Nolan. They was smoking weed in the girls' bathroom at Grant Union."

Al passed me a quizzical look. He probably had no idea what Grant Union was.

"So all of this was a vendetta from high school?" I asked.

"Yeah. Her fucking Charlie was Tess's part of getting back at me."

Anita flinched.

"The black eye was Claire's."

"Was it worth it?"

Jenna's face reddened. "Those two bitchy snobs got in trouble for the first time in their lives. They was suspended, and best of all, embarrassed and talked about." She coughed and touched her bruised eye. "That's what made it completely worth it."

"Would you like some water?" I asked.

"No, let's get this over with. I'm sick of the whole damn thing."

"Did Charlie ever talk about POSSE? As in capital *P-O-S-S-E*. It's an acronym for the Protective Order of Sovereign States Eternal."

"An acronym?"

"Well, you know what FBI stands for, right?"

"I think so. Federal Bureau of Investigation?"

"Yeah, and FBI is the acronym used for that organization. From what I've learned, POSSE is a group with a mission to protect states' rights against the federal government. They're interested in building an arsenal of guns, uh, to resist government interference. Well, any US government interference."

She appeared stunned, or possibly attempting to remember or comprehend exactly what I had tried to explain to her.

"I heard him and Earl arguing about something like that. Thought they were talking about a TV show or something."

"But this was over the phone?"

"Yeah, like I said, I never met anyone on the crew, and I already knew who Brad and Calvin were."

"I'm sorry, I'm a little confused, I think. Charlie didn't have any friends on the crew, but he and Earl got into it over the phone?"

"All the time. Lots of back-and-forth about guns. Sometimes it was nasty loud."

"But you're sure this Earl guy was on the crew?"

She thought for a beat and shrugged. "Well, I guess I ain't sure of that."

"Okay. Are you still doing all right?"

"As all right as I can be while I'm being interviewed by two cops—one of them a homicide detective."

I nodded. "Have you ever heard of someone named Clifton Massey?"

"Cliffy? His buddy from California? I never met him, but Charlie talked about him like you might talk about a grandpa you thought was the best thing ever. Who is he, anyway?"

"He's the leader, I'd call it, of POSSE."

"Oh."

"There's one other thing, Jenna. Your fingerprints were on the gun you were carrying when you found me. Which we expected, of course. But your prints were also on the pistol Charlie had stashed under the front seat of the Scout."

"Okay."

"How did that happen?"

She thought for several beats. "Oh, that's the one Charlie tried to teach me how to shoot when he took me out target practicing. He was annoyed I'd never shot a gun before and wanted me to learn how."

Anita raised her hand.

"Yes?" I said.

"I would never allow Dirk to teach her to shoot a gun. One of the many issues between us."

"Could I pop in with a question here, Sergeant Blackthorne?" Bach asked.

"Of course, Detective."

"Why did you go along with Charlie and try and learn to shoot a gun?"

"Well, he didn't give me much choice." Her face reddened slightly.

Al continued to press. "Do people usually tell you what to do like that?"

Jenna's eyes sparked with tears. "No, sir. Not most people."

"Was it fun?"

"Not really. He was fucking pissed I couldn't hit the target he'd nailed up on a tree."

"Thank you, Miss Rhinehart. I'll turn the questioning back over to Sergeant Blackthorne."

She looked at me, seemingly weary and likely wary.

"First, Jenna, I want to tell you that we appreciate your cooperation. And we might have more questions for you as the investigation goes along," I said.

"Okay."

"Charlie's buddy from California..."

"Cliffy?"

"Yeah. Do you know where he lived in California?"

She took some time to ponder that question. "I think it had *red* in it, but I can't swear to that."

"And can you tell us anything else about Cliffy?"

"I know him and Charlie liked to talk about guns. Guns and old trucks."

"Did you ever overhear a discussion about POSSE?"

"Well, sometimes Charlie would go outside when he was talking to Cliffy. I thought of it as their friendship time. Anyway, I did wonder what they was talking about when they'd go back and forth, ranting about *the group* this and *the group* that."

"Did you ever ask?"

"I knew better than to do that, Sergeant."

"If you remember anything about those conversations, anything at all, give me a call, okay?"

"Okay." She brushed a few thick strands of hair from her eyes. "I used to really like it when Charlie would talk on the phone to Cliffy 'cause afterward he'd be less upset and mean about things."

We were quiet on the drive back to the station, until Al exhaled deeply again. "I feel intensely sorry for that young woman."

"Yep. And I'm betting she's been bullied her whole life."

"Not by her mother, I don't believe."

"Nope, just most other people she's come across."

"Including the former sheriff?"

I parked in front of the office. "In all likelihood."

"Do you think she could really have killed Mr. Archer?"

I stopped myself from answering directly. "Until we hear back from the lab in Bend, I want to pursue other possible avenues—POSSE and Clifton Massey, of course. Also the Earl guy."

"I agree. And how about those young women who sought revenge?"

I planned to wait until the detective was otherwise occupied to address that issue. "I'll have to think about that one."

"Well, my sense is, in this small town, you'll be presented with an opportunity to engage with and educate them as to the laws of our state."

I burst into laughter. "The longer I know you Al, the more I realize you're not the button-downed, strictly-by-the-book, uptight police officer I thought you were when I first met you."

"I'm pretty uptight, I'd say. Now let's go to work."

We climbed out of the Tahoe and stepped to the front door. Sherry Linn was chatting with a citizen when we moved inside.

"Sergeant Blackthorne," she said. "This is Dr. Croft. He's been waiting for you."

The name was familiar, but the context eluded me at the moment.

He stood, and we shook hands. "I'd really appreciate a brief, private conversation with you."

"I'm afraid the only place to have a private conversation here is in our storage room."

"Lead the way, please."

He followed me to the alcove where I retrieved a couple of folding chairs and continued on to the storage room where we kept most of our office supplies. Sherry Linn kept the space tidy, organized, and well stocked —to the nth degree, but it was tight quarters for a discussion.

I set up both chairs, and we sat. Dr. Croft appeared to be fairly young, well, certainly younger than me.

"I left a voicemail for you last Saturday regarding Jenna Rhinehart."

"Oh, yes. I remember now. I apologize for not getting back to you. Believe it or not, that's not like me."

"No apology needed. I realize you've been looking into a couple of homicides."

"And I remember now, you wanted to talk to me about her health, is that right?"

"Highly unusual, I know, but I've left several messages with Jenna, and she hasn't returned my calls."

"To be fair, her phone wasn't made available to her until Sunday."

"Well, I called her several times yesterday and left two messages."

"Did you consider dropping by her mother's place?"

"Yes, I stopped by, but no one answered."

"I just met with her at her mother's house."

He sighed. "I know this is unusual, but I think you need to know...this is just between us. Dr. Hilliard would... It speaks to Jenna's psychological and physical state but also to the investigation you're conducting."

"Is this something you would have to reveal under oath at a murder trial?"

"Yes. Jenna was brutally beaten and raped, and she was two months pregnant. She miscarried within a few hours of being admitted to the hospital."

"I appreciate you coming forward with this information."

"There's one other thing. Not all of the test results were available before she left the hospital. So I didn't have the opportunity to tell her, but she also has a sexually transmitted disease. One that can be cured with treatment—but the earlier the better."

"Syphilis?"

"Afraid so."

"And you want me to let Jenna know."

"Unless you know of another way since she's avoided my calls. And because I don't know how long it's been since she was infected."

"Okay, I'll figure out a way to get word to her without jeopardizing your position."

He handed me his card. "Please let me know."

I passed him my card. "If you think of anything else I should know, give me a call. And I promise I'll pick up or call you back."

We both stood and shook hands. I escorted him back to the front counter, where he thanked Sherry Linn and took his leave. On the way past the pod of officers' desks, I'd noticed Hollis was at his desk distracted by research and Al was at Mark's desk listening to the interview we'd had earlier with Jenna Rhinehart.

"I'm going to make a fairly sensitive call," I told Sherry Linn, walked back to the storage room, and dialed Ray Gattis's number. The doc answered right away.

"Good, you got my call."

"Hi, Ray. No, I was just in a meeting, and I have some information for you."

"I have big news for you, too."

"Oh, what's that?"

"The Archer guy had late-stage syphilis."

"And I just heard from Dr. Croft, the physician you met when we took Jenna to the hospital. She's been diagnosed with the disease."

"He shared that with you?"

"Reluctantly, but apparently he's left several messages asking her to get in touch with him, and she hasn't returned his calls."

"So, she doesn't know yet?"

"Well, I suppose that's why all the urgency."

"Croft must not have realized word would likely get to you from the ME's office at some point."

"And there's more. She was two months pregnant and miscarried while in the hospital."

"Did she even know she was pregnant?"

"Not sure. But I'm going to get in touch with her after I hang up. Any advice about how to present the news?"

"You read people a whole lot better than I do, Maggie."

"I don't know about that. I thought you read her pretty well the other day."

"Oh, that was just me on *kind physician autopilot*, nothing special. Anyway, tell her I called to let you know about Archer's late-stage syphilis and I recommended she get tested right away."

"That'll likely do the trick."

"Before you hang up, how's Al doing?"

"Good, I think."

"Has he met Jenna?"

"We got back from interviewing her fifteen or twenty minutes ago. Afterward, he said he really felt sorry for her."

"Does he know about the syphilis diagnosis?"

"No, and I'm not sure there's a reason to tell him. Unless, of course, it turns out Jenna already knows."

"Because that might've been a reason to kill the bastard."

"You got it."

17

———————

MIDDAY, NOVEMBER 17

On my way out of the office, I told Sherry Linn I was off to run an errand and would return shortly. I made the short drive to Anita Rhinehart's, climbed out of my Tahoe, and walked to the front door. I could hear somebody rocking out to something god-awful—possibly Thundermother? I knocked extra hard, and the ruckus was silenced.

Jenna opened the door. "Did you forget something?"

"No, I have some news to share with you. Is it possible to talk privately?"

"Sure, Mom had an appointment to get her hair trimmed at Kat McKay's salon."

Ah, my soon-to-be sister-in-law's place of business.

"Come on in."

"Let's sit down," I said.

We sat at opposite ends of the couch.

"Did something happen?"

"Well, I've had some news. You remember Dr. Gattis?"

"That nice doctor who took care of me out in the forest?"

I nodded. "She's a medical examiner with the state, and she conducted the autopsy."

"Charlie's?"

"Yes, she found that he had late-stage syphilis and asked me to tell you she recommends you get tested."

"Oh, God. Is that why Dr. Croft has called so many times?"

"Did he leave messages?"

"Yeah, but I deleted them all without listening to any," she said, tearing up. "Goddamn it, I thought Croft wanted to talk to me about something else."

"Do you have his number?"

"It's in my contacts list."

"If you'd like, I can sit here with you while you make the call."

"Please."

She scrolled through her contacts and hit the number.

"This is Jenna Rhinehart. Dr. Croft has been trying to reach me." She paused and listened. "Thank you."

She waited for him to answer.

"Hi, Dr. Croft. You been trying to reach me?" Her wan face paled even more so as he spoke, and she began to cry.

"Started dating in early July."

There was another pause.

"Okay. It's my mother's insurance, but I have my own insurance card." Tears filled her eyes again. "Will the people at the pharmacy know what the medicine's for?"

Dr. Croft was apparently explaining something to her.

"Okay. Sorry I didn't call before, I just…"

The discussion appeared to be winding down. "I will. Thank you, Dr. Croft."

She hung up, and I realized I'd been holding her hand.

"That asshole." Now angry, she made a fist and socked the couch cushion. "You said late-stage, right?"

"That's right."

"Motherfucker. He had to know, right?"

"I would think so."

"It's a good thing he's already dead. Because if he weren't, I'd get one of them guns and shoot him in his fucking balls."

I had the same thought, except I'd fire twice. Once for Mark Taylor. Once for Jenna.

I needed to clear my head, so I drove south toward Canyon Mountain, passing the turnoff to Duncan's place—well, our place. Soon enough, I pulled to the shoulder and rolled down my window, letting the autumn chill float through my heated cab. I put in *Songbird*, an Eva Cassidy CD, listened to "Fields of Gold" and watched the light of early afternoon play on the winding creek below. Sitting there, I briefly toyed with the notion that I'd lost my objectivity where Jenna Rhinehart was concerned.

My phone rang. It was Croft. Reaching out to thank me for the call he'd finally gotten from Jenna, no doubt.

"Hello again, Dr. Croft."

"Did you have a chance to talk to Jenna Rhinehart?"

"What are you talking about? I was sitting right there with her in her living room while she phoned your office and spoke with you."

"I hate to tell you this, Sergeant. Not only did I not receive a call from her, but I also didn't talk to her."

"I'll get back to you later," I said and hung up.

I smacked the steering wheel. "You've just been played, Blackthorne."

I turned around and sped toward Anita's house and called Hollis at the office.

"Maggie?"

"You know where Anita Rhinehart lives, right?"

"Yeah, you had me go to her place on Thursday to give her the news her daughter was missing."

"Right, right. Well, Jenna just served me a heaping plate of bullshit, and I fell for it. You and Al need to get over there pronto. I'll meet you there."

"The detective's at lunch. But I'll head over now."

I flipped on my siren and drove like a bat out of hell. "Shit, shit, shit! You're a sentimental fool."

Hollis was waiting out front when I arrived. After I parked, we got out of our rigs and walked to the front door. Anita opened immediately after I knocked.

"What is it, Sergeant? You look angry."

"Is she here?"

"She asked to borrow my car so she could go shopping for clothes at Martine's Department Store."

"What's your license plate number?"

"I can't remember. But my car's a silver 2014 Honda Civic."

"Trooper Jones, stay here in case Jenna returns. Anita's going to look in her files and find the plate number."

I jumped back in my Tahoe. Along the way, I contacted Al and shared a sanitized version of Dr. Croft's and Ray's interest in passing along information to Jenna Rhinehart. Told him what had happened once I'd done that, how it came to pass that the young woman had tricked me, and asked him to meet me at Martine's.

"Where's it located?" he asked.

"It's the only department store downtown on Main Street."

"See you there."

Hollis texted me the plate number as I pulled into Martine's parking lot.

I passed slowly through the small lot. Anita's car was nowhere to be seen. I idled and sent out an APB to the other local authorities with the make, model, and plate number of the car Jenna Rhinehart was driving and called for her to be detained.

Al pulled up next to me, driver's-side door to driver's-side door. I apologized for my fuck-up—or words to that effect—and told him I'd already sent out an alert.

"You let your guard down. Happens to all of us at least once. But she can't have gotten very far."

"I don't like making this kind of judgment error one bit."

"Neither did I the first time it happened."

A loud radio callout interrupted me as I was about to launch into a bout of verbal self-flagellation.

"Sergeant Blackthorne, Oregon State Police."

"Officer Bob Nolan, John Day Police. I pulled Jenna Rhinehart over. She was speeding out of town toward Mt. Vernon."

"Good work, Bob. I'd appreciate you dropping her off at the county jail."

"Can do. I'll meet you there in ten minutes or so," Bob said.

Al carried a wry smile. "All right, Maggie. I'll follow you there. Given it all turned out okay, at least so far, I'd recommend you see it as a momentary setback and a lesson. That's all the preaching I'm going to give you."

After I pulled out with the detective following right behind me, I called Hollis. "Bob Nolan stopped Jenna speeding toward Mt. Vernon, and we're meeting him at the jail. Why don't you give Anita a lift to her car and then join us?"

"I'll pick up a sandwich for you on the way."

"No need to do that."

"I'll pick up a sandwich for you on the way."

"Thanks, Holly."

"And Maggie, don't go worrying about whatever BS she fed you. For one thing, it may have given us more insight about her."

"Yeah, like she's quite capable of yarn-spinning and putting on a performance. Good to know, all right."

Arriving at the courthouse, Al and I parked side by side. On the walk to the entrance, I mentioned that Officer Bob Nolan was the father of Claire, the young woman who'd planted the shiner on Jenna.

"Is that what we call ironic?" he said.

"Nah, just small-townish."

Bob pulled up just then and idled his police cruiser. He stepped from the vehicle, opened the back door, and assisted Jenna, now cuffed and visibly contrite, in getting out.

"Thanks, Officer Nolan," I said as he removed the cuffs and handed her off to me.

"Here's her speeding ticket, too," he said.

I took that as well.

"Be gentle with her. Looks like she's already been roughed up a bit," Bob added.

Despite my heightened sense of distrust in Jenna Rhinehart, I was certain she had told the truth about Claire Nolan, something I was compelled to mention to Bob. At a later time, though.

He returned to his cruiser, and the detective and I escorted Jenna into the courthouse. Instead of requesting a holding cell, I asked for the keys to one of their second-floor interview rooms.

We mounted the stairs, Jenna between Al and me. I unlocked the door and told her to have a seat.

"I need to have a word with Detective Bach."

She seated herself, and I shut the door.

"What's up, Maggie?"

"I explained to you earlier that Dr. Croft had some important information—a dangerous diagnosis, actually—to discuss with Jenna."

"Yes, and she pretended to talk to him over the phone about it."

"For whatever reason. Anyway, as I also said, she fooled me completely. So my concern is that she's told us nothing but lies this whole time."

"I got that."

"And I wanted you to be aware of one other thing. I'd find it unethical to be the one to reveal her diagnosis while we're interviewing her."

"So don't. Allow her to do that if she's so inclined."

"All right, let's get this over with."

"Is there room in there for me?" Hollis stood behind us holding a small cooler. "I brought your sandwich and also one for Jenna, assuming she missed lunch too."

"We're having a picnic now?" I said.

"Well, I've made it my business to make sure you eat your lunch."

"So I've noticed."

"Have you been ill?" Bach asked.

"Oh, crap. I thought you knew, Detective. Maggie, I..."

This was all it took to embarrass Hollis Jones?

I felt my face redden too. "I'm pregnant, Al. I'm also getting married to Duncan McKay on Thanksgiving."

He beamed. "Congratulations. There's nothing like having children. Am I right, Hollis?"

"I've mentioned that to her myself."

"All right, you two. Let's get this over with." I opened the door. "Trooper Jones brought us sandwiches, Jenna."

"I'm not hungry. Thanks anyway."

Al, Hollis, and I took a seat at the table.

"Okay, let's get to it," I said. "But first, I want you to know I haven't shared the recommendation Dr. Gattis passed along to you with anyone else. I also want you to know that Dr. Croft reached out to me right after I dropped by your mother's house this morning. He let me know he hadn't heard from you, and he was quite worried about you. That's how I knew you'd put on a little act in front of me and hadn't actually contacted him."

"Sorry I did that, but I was so scared, I couldn't think."

"Just have to say, you're dang good at acting. You must've been in a lot of theater performances in high school."

"No, I never done that kinda thing."

"So, you're just a natural actress, then?"

She shrugged.

"You see, Jenna, it just makes me wonder if you've been pretending this whole time. But before you say anything, are you willing to submit to another interview?"

"Yeah, I guess."

"Are you willing, or aren't you?"

She sighed. "I said I am."

I Mirandized her for the third time and got her signature on a waiver form.

"Were you at Desolation Guard Station on the morning of Friday, November thirteenth of this year, and if so, did you shoot and kill Charles Sean Archer?"

"No, I don't know what or where any guard station is, and I've never been to it far as I know. And no, I did not shoot and kill Charlie."

"What was that charade you put on for me this morning all about?"

She bowed her head slightly. "I already thought there was something wrong. Was already afraid it mighta been what the lady doctor said. It's disgusting. Just wanna die, knowing it's true. Didn't even really like, you know, the sex. He slapped me around 'cause uh that, too."

"Where were you headed this afternoon in your mother's car?" Hollis asked.

She gazed down at her hands. "I don't know. Away from all of this shit, I guess. I mean, I done a bad thing by faking the call to Dr. Croft. But I couldn't take no more. Everything else, and now an STD...it was too fucking much."

"You may not believe me, Jenna, but Dr. Croft can help you get well."

"All right, I really will call him and make an appointment right away."

"Sounds good."

"I do have one question for you, Sergeant," she said. "No offense to anyone here, but are most men assholes and bullies?"

"Many are," Holly answered.

"I've known several myself," Al put in.

"Jenna, you and I know a lot of unkind people—to put it another way—who live right here in good ol' John Day, are female, and also fit into that category."

"True. And one of 'em has a kind dad who I met for the first time today."

"Yes, Officer Nolan's a pretty nice guy, all right," I said. "Anyway, we're done for now, but you know the drill."

"Until you wrap up the case, I gotta stay in the county."

I clicked off the recorder. "You got it."

"Don't have any place else to go, anyway."

There was a light knock at the door. Chief Deputy Weldon opened it and peeked inside. "Sorry to bother you, but Mrs. Rhinehart is here with an attorney."

Jenna rolled her eyes.

"Thanks, Deputy. You can show them in," I said.

I didn't recognize the woman with Anita, but she was dressed like a recent Willamette University Law School graduate. Might've been University of Idaho College of Law, though.

"Everyone," Anita began. "This is Ms. Flannery. She's agreed to represent Jenna."

"That means this conversation is over," Ms. Flannery said and gave each of us one of her cards.

I noticed the first name, Eve-Lyn. Her practice was in Burns, ninety miles or so south of John Day. Which probably meant Anita had called her earlier in the day, certainly before Jenna had been escorted to the courthouse.

Al stood and passed his card to Ms. Flannery. "The interview wrapped up just before you arrived."

"And like I told you before, Ma. I don't need a damn lawyer."

"Your mother and I think you definitely need legal advice," the Flannery gal shot back.

"Am I free to go, Detective Bach?"

"I think Sergeant Blackthorne made it clear you were."

"Thank you. Let's go, Ma."

Jenna, Anita, and Eve-Lyn filed out of the tiny interview room.

"All right," I said and stood. "We have lots of work to do. First on the list is to track down the Earl guy Jenna mentioned this morning."

"That's interesting," Hollis said. "The name Earl Ziegler popped up during my research today. He might be one of the men pictured in the joint bulletin from the FBI and ATF."

18

___

AFTERNOON, NOVEMBER 17

On the drive back to our cop station, I was pumped about the possibility of a relevant lead in our investigation and also famished and low on energy, and I all but inhaled the sandwich Hollis had bought for me.

Speaking of Holly, he'd managed to track down the Earl Ziegler dude in Idaho, or at least that's where he'd been spotted around eighteen months ago in the mountain town of Golden Pine. Unfortunately, that tip came to authorities too late. The man had moved on, and his trail had since gone cold.

A photo of Golden Pine was displayed on the screen of Hollis's computer when I arrived at our pod of desks. Unincorporated like Dale, but with about forty residents or so, in contrast to Hi Appleby and his so-called daddy tucked in the living quarters at the rear of Blue Mountain Gas & Groceries and the few folks residing in the Dale trailer park. The countryside near each small burg was mountainous and densely forested, places where a person might easily get lost or just as easily hide out.

"It's really thick with trees, isn't it," Hollis said. He stood behind me now.

"Very. Just like the Umatilla Forest outside of Dale and Ukiah."

"And both places are near wilderness areas."

He moved the mouse and brought up a second website with a map of eastern Oregon and western Idaho. "Do you know anyone who might know all of the back roads between Dale, Oregon, and Golden Pine, Idaho?"

"My father. And as you know, he's long dead. But that was his thing when I was a girl. Drive a Jeep, the kind from back in the day, cross-country on old logging roads or the routes between former mining towns. Sometimes there was nothing but a broad patch of land to cross over, so he'd use his instincts, memory, whatever and keep going until he met up with another unpaved byway. One that linked to some Forest Service road or maintenance easement until he found a passageway that took him to a highway."

"Did he ever drive from somewhere in eastern Oregon to western Idaho?"

"I have no idea, but I do know there's a large river, major highways, and freeways that might block the way."

"Maybe, but I have a theory." He paused.

"Are you going to tell me your theory, or do I have to do some trick in order to get it out of you?"

"I think it might be doable. That a person could travel between eastern Oregon and western Idaho and pretty much avoid major highways and freeways, probably not the Snake River, but some of the crossings over it are in the middle of nowhere."

"And so what?"

"For now, just hang in there with me."

"I'm all ears, sir."

"Well, I got called away by my boss before I could work on figuring it all out, so you'll need to give me some time. And I just have to say, such a route would largely be impractical."

"Yeah, well, these are impractical people we're talking about," I said.

"Impractical, but successful on some level."

"On to Earl Ziegler. You said he might be one of the men pictured in the joint bulletin from the FBI and ATF."

"Well, here's a decade-old photo of the guy." He scrolled to another tab and opened Ziegler's black-and-white photograph.

"Something about that guy is familiar," I said. "What is it?"

"Don't see how you'd recognize anybody under the beard and all that hair. But he does look like *this* guy." Hollis opened the bulletin and scrolled until he found the illustrated version of what appeared to be Earl Ziegler. "Don't you think?"

"Yeah, you're right."

"So do we call the FBI or ATF and tell them we think we've identified two of the guys featured in the bulletin?"

"Well, one of them is probably our second homicide victim, and the other might be someone who argued over the phone with our second homicide victim."

"Since you put it that way, I guess the answer is no, we're not calling either federal office."

"I say we focus on finding the killer of Mark's killer and then consult with the feds."

He indicated his agreement. "And my theory? Should I set that aside for now?"

Like I could stop him from going down that road, so to speak. "Nah, I value your instincts and certainly your ability to pull things out of the ether that ninety-nine percent of the time end up being useful."

"I'd say it's more like ninety-nine-point-nine percent of the time."

"Come on, have some humility."

"I'll try. But let me begin with a confession. I was having trouble tracking what was going on with Jenna Rhinehart today. Except Archer's treatment of her and the condition he left her in. What was your 'heaping plate of bullshit' comment about?"

"She faked an entire phone call to her doctor. I sat there and listened to her side of the supposed conversation. She even shed tears. Worse, I held her hand."

"Ouch. No one punks Maggie Blackthorne and gets away with it."

"That's right. Now get to work before you end up getting punked yourself."

"Yes, ma'am. By the way, I know you have a report or two to put together, but you can find that photo of Earl Ziegler in the online case folder."

"Yeah, maybe I'll print it out and frame it."

"Whatever tickles your fancy, boss."

By four o'clock I was exhausted, and I couldn't tell if it was my pregnant body rebelling or the stress a murder investigation was putting on my pregnant body. I'd put in ten to twelve hours a day most days since last Thursday, the exception being my promise to Duncan to take most of Sunday off. And even then, I worked the case some or thought about it constantly.

I reminded myself that earlier, I'd felt hopeful we were getting somewhere. I sighed and opened the file titled "Ziegler Photo" and stared at it. There was something there, but what was it? After five minutes, I closed the file.

Our office was exceptionally quiet except for Holly's tapping, sighing, tapping, sighing. Sherry Linn had departed earlier for a dental appointment or something. Doug Vaughn had driven out to the Murderers Creek Wildlife Area to check out a couple of reports of nearby gunfire, and after that he planned to drive to Dead Point to make sure any chukar hunters were in possession of a valid license. And with the budget always tight for the Oregon State Police, Al was stuck in his motel room providing long-distance oversight of a couple of homicide cases that had once been assigned to Detective Bryce Horne, who now was the subject of an internal affairs investigation himself.

I read back through my reports on the two interviews we'd had with Jenna Rhinehart and signed off electronically on both. Next, I opened Earl Ziegler's photo again.

Staring at the mountain man's face, I suddenly remembered I had a question for Cousin Lyndon, looked up his contact info, and dialed his number. When he didn't answer, I left a message asking him to call back at his convenience and listed off the numbers for both of my phones.

I wandered into the alcove and began filling in information on our murder board. Afterward, I stood back and stared at what was missing. Everything? Nothing? A clear motive? I suspected there might be several people in addition to Jenna Rhinehart who could answer that last question.

"Maggie?"

I jumped but fortunately didn't scream.

Hollis was standing in the entrance to the alcove.

"Your phone was ringing, so I answered it. Lyndon Cummings is on the line."

"Thanks, Holly."

I followed him back to our desk corral and picked up the receiver.

"Thanks for getting back to me, Lyndon."

"Sure. How's it going?"

"I'm assuming you mean the investigation."

"Well, yeah. The whole thing has been hard on Anita. And Jenna, of course."

"Speaking of Jenna, she mentioned that Archer used to speak with a guy named Earl on the phone. She never met the man but thought he was on the maintenance crew with Archer."

"There's nobody named Earl on the crew. Seems like an older man's name to me, but all my crewmembers are generally younger."

I was pretty sure someone, somewhere, under forty was named Earl, but whatever.

"Thanks, Lyndon," I said as cheerily as I could muster. "Do you happen to know anybody living in the county, let's say, named Earl?"

"Well, you probably remember our great uncle Earl, but he passed away a long time ago."

"Right, right."

"He's the only Earl I know about, I guess."

"Appreciate you getting back to me."

"You're welcome, Maggie."

"Good night."

Hollis had closed down for the day and looked like he was ready to scram.

"I just listened to the interview of Jenna Rhinehart from early this morning. She put up with incredible abuse, didn't she?"

"Might your other question be, *or did she*?"

"No. She sounded believable."

"Well, she sounded believable while making the fake call to her doctor too. But I agree with you, she lived through some bad shit and survived. At least physically."

"Good night, Maggie."

"Night, Holly."

I sat in the total quiet for a few minutes, finally reaching to shut off my computer. Instead, I opened the Earl Ziegler photo again and stared at it again. "Shit."

I leaned into the screen. "My God, is that him?"

I pulled out my cell phone and called Hollis's number. It rang three times.

"Mags?"

"Come back to the office. Please. I think I know who Earl Ziegler is."

"See you in five."

Hollis moved his desk chair next to mine, and we both stared at the photograph.

"Anything?" I asked.

"Just tell me who you think this is?"

"He might live in the Dale trailer court."

Hollis studied the photo. "You think it's the guy who works at the hardware store in Ukiah?"

"I think it could be. Name's Max Ulanowicz."

"Hmm. Wasn't his hair blondish-brownish, not dark brown or brunette?"

"Well, it's a black-and-white photo, so it's hard to tell the hair color for certain, and/or maybe he's dyed his hair. Anyway, this is where your magic comes in."

"I want to remind you I'm not a forensics expert. Also, I read an article recently that questioned some supposedly proven methods of photographic analysis by law enforcement."

"You misunderstand. The only thing I had in mind is for you to do whatever it is you do online to chase down information on Ulanowicz."

"One question, though. What makes you certain Mr. Ulanowicz is actually Earl Ziegler?"

"I'm *not* certain. But there's something about the facial features that resembles Ulanowicz, I think. And you've got to admit he seemed to sic us on Brad Slater and Calvin James. Might've had that in mind when he reported the Dawson brothers joyriding in Archer's orange Scout, too."

"He seems more like the nosy neighbor type to me."

"Can't disagree with that assessment. Anyway, I probably shouldn't have asked you to come back to the office," I said.

"Well, I'm here now, so I'll see what I can find out about Mr. Ulanowicz."

"Don't spend any more than fifteen minutes, Holly."

"Uh-huh." He moved his chair back to his own desk and turned on his computer.

I sat looking at the photo but broke away when a text came in.

"Hey, babe. It's quittin' time," Duncan wrote.

"Soon..."

"See you at home."

"Mags?" Hollis said. "Come look at this."

I rose and stood behind him and read the headline from an article published eighteen months ago in the Redding, California, *Times Review*: "Local Man Dies of Gunshot Wounds." The subheading clarified further, "Shooter unknown."

"Not much popped up when I searched for Max Ulanowicz, except for something about the guy's accounting firm in Redding and a few other people with the same surname who live in the Midwest or on the East Coast. However, there was this article. He's the local man identified as having been killed."

"What the hell?"

"Yeah, and as far as I can tell, the murder has yet to be solved."

"If I remember correctly, the feds' bulletin noted that Redding is where Clifton Massey's from."

"Yep. And Earl Ziegler is originally from Weed, California, about seventy miles north of Redding."

He opened another page and pulled up a map of Oregon, Idaho, and northern California. "About my theory. A person could take a number of paths from Redding and/or Weed—or elsewhere—and discreetly keep in contact with their fellow compadres, revolutionaries, gun thieves, gang members, whatever you want to call them—who have also taken up residence in various small towns or villages scattered throughout the West, and without anyone giving it much more thought than the initial suspicious once-over."

Hollis switched on his cursor highlighter and pointed out several routes using back roads and lesser-known state highways that could take someone from northern California to Dale, Oregon, and Golden Pine, Idaho. And other places too, obviously.

"Okay, I get what you're saying."

"And all you'd have to do is buy your groceries, gas, and what-have-you from locals and start to blend in, even if you're crotchety or aloof. Maybe take a job at the local hardware store. Pretty soon nobody would really pay much attention to your comings and goings. Then you sit and wait for the right time or a signal from your grand pooh-bah to pick up where you left off and go back to building an arsenal and planning the revolution."

"Wow, how long has this theory been percolating in that head of yours?"

"Since earlier today when I started researching the POSSE people."

"So at this point, here's what we know about the POSSE people. Archer was one of them if the bulletin is correct and if we're correct that he's one of the illustrated members of the group."

"Yes, and Earl Ziegler's photo matches one of the other men in the bulletin. And there may be reason to believe that Ziegler took the name of Max Ulanowicz of Redding after Mr. Ulanowicz was murdered by some unknown party, and Ziegler-turned-Ulanowicz now lives in Dale."

"Seems...I don't know, operatic?" I said.

"Well, however operatic it seems, we need more to go on."

"Exactly. I'm going to pay a visit to my buddy Max tomorrow after Mark's funeral."

"Your buddy?"

"He flirted with me, even asked me out for a drink."

"When did that happen?"

"When he turned in the Dawson brothers for taking Archer's Scout."

"Ah..."

"I even told him I was pregnant and getting married, but he still thought we could go out for a drink sometime."

"Well, since you're pretty certain he's Earl Ziegler, I don't think it's a good idea to confront him on your own."

"Oh? I was planning on taking you or Al with me."

"I still don't like the idea."

"Does he have a criminal history?"

"Not that I saw, but if he is Earl Ziegler, he's part of a band of gun thieves who want to overthrow the federal government."

"I didn't just fall off the turnip truck, Hollis. Besides which, I'm a police officer investigating a murder. And I know how to take care of myself. And I pack heat. And you or Al—or both of you—will be with me."

"Can we talk about this in the morning? And with the detective present?"

I knew he was worried about my health and safety, but it was getting out of hand from my perspective. Still, I didn't plan to argue with Hollis or with Al Bach.

"Sure," I said. "And let's call it a day."

He nodded, closed out the several documents and websites he'd opened, and shut down his computer. I walked back to my desk and did the same.

"Good night, Maggie."

"See you in the morning, Holly."

19

—————

MORNING, NOVEMBER 18

Duncan lay with his back to me, his body rising and falling as he slept. I'd been awake for nearly half an hour thinking back over my last conversation with Hollis. I didn't remember ever feeling anger toward him before, but I woke pissed as hell.

Finally, I pulled back the covers, stood, and tucked myself into my robe. Raleigh Cat stretched his long body on the carpeted floor and followed me downstairs. I attended to his food and water before climbing into a hot shower. Afterward, I opened the glass garden door, stepped onto the back deck, and sat at our little table. More snow had fallen on Strawberry Mountain over the last few days, and its peak was stark and magnificent in the scarlet light of daybreak. A beacon, at once primeval and new, in high desert country.

I heard the door open behind me. "Hey," Duncan said in his morning voice. "When did you get up?"

"Not that long ago."

He sat in the chair next to mine. "What's bothering you, babe?"

"Oh, I got a little bent out of shape about something Hollis said yesterday, but I'll get over it. And today is Mark's funeral."

"I know. I'm closing the store to attend."

"What about the Autumn Jubilee sale?"

"Some things are more important." He put his arm around me and looked to the east of us. "The mountains are beautiful this morning."

The entire Strawberry range was now bathed in vermilion. We sat quietly and watched the sun ply the land with shine and shadow, until the morning chill drove us back inside.

———

By the time I arrived in the office, I had decided there was some truth in what Hollis had been getting at last evening. Mr. Ulanowicz could actually be Earl Ziegler, a member of an ominous organization according to the feds, and not someone to toy with or give the impression of toying with. I needed to bear that in mind no matter how harmless or fatuous he came across as being.

"Morning, Maggie." Sherry Linn sat at the front counter opening the mail she'd picked up at the post office on her way into work. She wore a dark wool suit and a subtle scarf.

"How's it going?"

"Well, I shouldn't say this, but I'll be glad when Mark's funeral service is over."

"I know what you mean. I find them..."

"Depressing, right?"

"I completely agree."

"I do have some happier news to share with you, though. Harry and I are getting married in Reno next month."

"Congratulations. He's a great guy."

"But it does mean I'll be asking for time off."

"And you deserve it. Just fill out the leave form, and I'll sign it."

"Um, Hollis was here before I arrived this morning. I should probably mind my own business, but he seems kind of upset about something."

"Maybe it's the funeral."

"Maybe."

I sauntered back to our desks, at this point completely over the internal tiff I had awakened to this morning.

"Good morning, Holly."

He looked at me sheepishly. "Maggie, I apologize for being overly protective last night. I was out of line," he said, his deep voice set at an octave somewhere between Johnny Cash and Barry White.

"Yeah, I wasn't happy about that, but the more I thought about it, the more I think you're right. If Ulanowicz is actually Ziegler, he could be more dangerous than we think."

"That's why I came in early. I unearthed some more information about Ziegler. He's wanted for questioning by authorities in Texas and has been for about five years."

"What do they want to question him about?"

"Gun theft and assault with a deadly weapon."

"Did you find a photo of him from Texas authorities?"

"Yeah." He moved to another webpage and pointed to the photograph. "Earl Ziegler appears to be the spitting image of Mr. Max Ulanowicz of Dale, Oregon."

"I tried to tell you."

"I know, and I should have listened to you."

"Where's a witness when I need one?"

"What's all this?" Al had arrived at our pod of desks with his laptop and thermos of hot tea.

"Well, it all began with Hollis figuring out that one of the other unidentified men pictured in the feds' bulletin was Earl Ziegler."

"Let's hear the rest."

As I had expected, Mark Taylor's funeral was well attended, primarily by members of his family and church, but the bigwigs from the Oregon State Police in Salem had also sent an honor guard, so the whole affair took on a kind of military air unlike most of these local commemorations.

After the honor guard silenced attendees, Reverend Bill led everyone in prayer. Next, Alice and Dave Hanover sang "You'll Never Walk Alone," which, under the best of circumstances, has a difficult range of high notes and low notes to keep under control. Mark's brother, Jim, read the eulogy, which was a little long, but it was followed by Ellie and Mark's children reading their father's favorite poem, "The Toucan," by Shel Silverstein, a very sweet touch in my view.

Duncan and I sat next to Dorie, who normally would've been the pianist for the event, but she had returned from her stint in the hospital in Bend only the day before, so Ellie had asked Reverend Bill's wife, Vera, to play a few hymns.

Afterward, Al prayed briefly with Ellie, holding her hands and remarking on her kind husband and lovely children. Duncan and I gave her a hug, and then Dun returned to McKay's Feed and Tack, and I walked Dorie to her car.

"That was a lovely service," she said as I opened the driver's-side door.

"Yes, it was." I wasn't going to tell her my favorite part had been the reading of "The Toucan," but it turned out I didn't need to.

"Like you, I really liked the kiddies reading that poem." She got into the car. "Are you going to solve your case before Thanksgiving—you know, your wedding day, a week from tomorrow?"

"We're working really hard on that. Which reminds me, I apologize for not coming to see you yesterday like I'd promised." I reached in and gave her a long hug. "Love you."

"I love you too, Maggie. Very much. And I like your new look."

"My new look?"

"You know, preggers."

"Preggers? I haven't heard that since high school."

Prior to Mark's funeral, Sherry Linn had put together a warrant for Judge Campbell to sign off on his approval of the search of Earl Ziegler's mobile home, along with a warrant for his arrest. That last was attributed to his suspected participation in POSSE and based on information in the bulletin from the FBI and ATF. I delivered it to the judge myself, interrupting Wednesday traffic court in dramatic fashion, and we took off for Dale just before eleven thirty.

In the event Detective Bach was called away on one of the other homicide investigations he was supervising, he followed me in his vehicle. We had yet to contact Texas authorities, but our plan was to question Ulanowicz/Ziegler, preferably at his residence but at the hardware store where he worked in Ukiah, if necessary.

Driving north on Highway 395 along Beech Creek, the last of this year's autumn leaves on the quaking aspen, cottonwood, and poplars were carried away by a whirling bash of wind and deposited on the highway, the gray earth, and the canyon's basalt scarp. Suddenly, it began to rain, shifting rapidly into a violent downpour and turning the sky to a dark bruise.

Before departing the office, Al had gotten word from the lab in Bend that Charlie Archer had likely been killed by a larger weapon—specifically, a big-bore handgun—than he appeared to have in his collection, which seemingly meant that Jenna Rhinehart was off the hook for the murder of her abuser.

"Holly, what is it about Americans and their guns?" I asked.

"That's interesting. I was just wondering that myself."

"I guess I see the purpose of having a hunting rifle or two, possibly even something for protection."

"Protection against what?"

"Well, it's not like we haven't had seven murders in this county in the last couple of years."

"Just to remind you, three reprobates hung Guy Trudeau in his kitchen, and Janine Harbaugh was pushed off the Aldrich Mountain Fire Lookout. And both of those victims were gun owners."

"All right, I get what you're saying. But what's the point of having a big-bore handgun?"

"Overkill?"

"Oh, very clever."

As we drove on, the sky cleared, and we pulled into Dale and passed by Blue Mountain Gas & Groceries on our way to the trailer court. I noticed the Airstream that Brad Slater and Calvin James had been living in was no longer parked there, but the next-door neighbor's mobile home was still in its place. I pulled up to it, and Al did the same. I got out, put on a pair of latex gloves, and knocked on the metal front door.

"Try opening it," the detective said.

I moved the handle, but it was locked. I tried the back door, but it was also locked. "Guess we're paying a visit to Jacoby's Hardware Store in Ukiah."

"How far away is that?" Bach asked.

"About fifteen miles up the road, give or take a mile or two."

"All right, let's go."

We jumped back in the rigs, and Al followed mine to the highway. We turned north, drove past the edge of the Umatilla Forest and further up, a separate wildlife area, and continued to motor along the winding road until we arrived at Route 244. There we turned east and into Ukiah. I parked in front of the hardware store across from Cousin Lyndon's place, and Detective Bach pulled up next to my Tahoe in his Interceptor.

Hollis and Al followed me into the store. The man smiled when he saw me enter, but he took on a look of surprise when he caught sight of the men following me. I hadn't noticed before, but his eyes were hazel in coloring, leaning more to green than brown. He wore reading glasses that sat low on his aquiline nose, and his Jacoby's Hardware shirt had been laundered too many times.

"How can I help you, Sergeant Blackthorne?" he said.

"Are you the only clerk working in the store today?" I asked.

"I'm the only clerk every day."

I gazed around the store. "No customers?"

"Do you see any?"

I was momentarily thrown off by his sarcasm, but then I'd spoken to him only twice before, and both conversations were brief.

"What's this all about, anyway? And why do you have two other officers with you?"

"You've met Trooper Jones before. And this is Homicide Detective Bach. We need you to place your hands on top of your head and move slowly from behind the counter."

"What the hell is going on?"

"Hands on your head," I said darkly.

"I don't think I can do that until you tell me what this is about."

"We have reason to believe your name is not Max Ulanowicz. Instead, we have a recent bulletin telling us you're Earl Ziegler, originally from Weed, California. Further, we believe you took the name of a man named Ulanowicz who was murdered in Redding, California."

"How'd you come to that damned conclusion?"

"We're cops. We investigate people. For instance, we also know you're wanted as a member of a gun-trafficking organization known as the Protective Order of Sovereign States Eternal. POSSE, as the organization's referred to, and the long-term goal of POSSE is to overthrow the federal government, or at least undermine it."

"You know squat about POSSE, woman."

"Hands in the air, Mr. Ziegler," Al said behind me.

The front door opened. "Hey, Maggie, I thought I saw you go into the hardware store."

I turned ever so slightly. Cousin Lyndon had just entered the premises.

"What's happening here?" he asked me.

"You need to leave, Mr. Cummings," Hollis told him.

"No, he needs to stay." Ziegler had pulled a short-barreled rifle from somewhere. "Or rather, he needs to come with me. Now, if you officers would just put your holstered weapons on the floor and step out of the way, Lyndon and I are going for a ride."

"You don't want to do this, son," the detective said.

"I'm not your son, mister. Put the damned holsters on the floor before I decide to take Sergeant Blackthorne with me instead of old Lyn here."

We did as we were told.

Ziegler drew out a large shopping bag from the stack by the checkout counter and tossed it to Lyndon. "Put the guns in there."

Lyndon placed the guns in the bag as Ziegler walked to the front door and peered out the window.

"I assume the fancy Interceptor belongs to the detective, but who drives the Tahoe?" he asked.

"I do," Hollis answered.

"Get the man's keys, Lyn. And the older guy's too."

Lyndon took a set of keys each from Hollis and Al and moved to hand them to Ziegler.

"Dump the keys in with the guns, Lyn, and then go open the front door.

Slowly. And remember, I'm right behind you."

Ziegler backed up, his rifle remained pointed at us, and followed Lyndon outside and locked us in the store. Afterward, we paced to the window and watched him pull away from the curb in a newer, dark blue Jeep four-by-four with Lyndon and our weapons inside.

"That was smart to tell him the Tahoe was yours, Hollis," I said.

"Well, I took a chance he wasn't going to try and drive away in it."

"He likely would've taken the detective's Interceptor, anyway. Still, that was a wise move on your part."

"I agree," Bach said.

I looked around the store again and noticed a hallway behind us. "I'm going to see if there's a back door."

Hollis and Al followed me to the rear of the building. A set of heavy boxes had been stacked in front of the back door.

"Detective Bach and I will get those, Maggie."

The man was not going to cease patronizing me while I was pregnant, but this was not the time to go into all of that. Besides, I was sure Al fully agreed with him.

They had shifted the boxes away from the back entrance. Fortunately, it was locked from the inside. After opening the door, we reset the lock, stepped outdoors, and moved to the sidewalk at the front of the hardware store.

The detective hustled to the driver's side of the Interceptor and unlocked it. I'd forgotten his rig had a keypad entry system.

"I've got a spare key for the ignition in the glove compartment, along with a second revolver," Al said.

"And I've got two extra Glocks in the safe at the back of my Tahoe," I added.

"Mr. Ziegler's only five or six minutes ahead of us, so let's head back to his trailer house. I'm betting he'll stop there on the way to wherever he plans to head next."

I wasn't sure about that, but I didn't have a better suggestion at the moment.

"I'll contact dispatch on the way," Hollis put in. "I memorized his license plate number."

20

AFTERNOON, NOVEMBER 18

I waited until Hollis had gotten word to regional dispatch regarding Earl Ziegler before I brought up the matter that had been bugging me since we left Ukiah.

"Why didn't he just kill us?"

"Ziegler?"

"Yeah."

Holly considered my question for about thirty seconds. "Here's my guess. It's one thing to blow away some citizens as you flee town, it's a whole other something else to gun down three cops—in terms of the level of law enforcement response, anyway. Plus, if he'd started shooting, he might've attracted the attention of a resident or two. Especially since Jacoby's Hardware Store sits in the center of town, right across from the one grocery store."

"I suppose, but I have to say you're giving him a lot more credit than I would."

"Is that Lyndon Cummings?"

It was, and he was walking toward us on the shoulder of the road. I slowed, pulled over, and idled my vehicle. Al Bach parked behind me.

I rolled down my window as Lyndon met up with us. "Are you okay?"

"Guess so. The guy drove about five miles south on Highway 395 before pulling over. Scared the crap out of me 'cause I thought he was going to kill me. But he just told me to get out of his Jeep. I did, and he took off."

"Don't suppose he told you where he was going."

"No, and I didn't ask."

"Afraid we can't give you a ride back to town. Can we call someone to pick you up?"

He shrugged. "It's not that far to go, but thanks for offering."

"We need to get going," I said.

He tipped his hat and continued walking toward Ukiah.

We drove on, arriving in Dale about ten minutes later, and I motored slowly to the trailer park. Patti Hutchens was outside feeding her pet goat. She waved when she saw us, and I decided to stop by to see what she knew about the man calling himself Max Ulanowicz. I parked next to her place, and Al did as well.

The three of us stepped out of the two rigs, and Patti greeted Hollis and me.

"This is Detective Bach," I said, indicating Al. "Ms. Hutchens took care of Mark Taylor after he was shot last Thursday."

He removed his cap. "Nice to meet you, Ms. Hutchens."

She nodded and tucked her wool scarf closer to her neck. "I noticed all of you this morning at Mark's funeral, but there wasn't an opportunity to say hello."

"It was a very nice service," Bach said.

"It was beautiful, all right," she answered. "And the children were so charming."

"Patti," I began. "Do you know Mr. Ulanowicz, the man who lives in the small mobile home at the end?"

"Not very well. He's pretty standoffish."

"Do you know if he owns his trailer house?"

"Oh, no. Like mine, it's one of the mobile homes Hi rents out. Folks don't usually stay in that little one for very long. It used to be rented mostly in the summer, until Max moved in, gosh, more than a year ago. Maybe a year and a half, even."

"Thanks, Patti."

"Just curious, why are you asking about Max?"

"We have a warrant to search his place."

She took in that information, then hugged herself. "It's cold out here this afternoon. Think I'll go back inside."

"Nice to see you," I told her.

We watched her enter her double-wide.

"I'm walking over to Blue Mountain Gas and Groceries to find out if Hiram Appleby's got a spare key to Ziegler's trailer," I said. "You're welcome to stay here."

"You've got the search warrant, right?" Al asked.

"Yep. I'll be right back."

"I'm coming with," Hollis said.

Al put his cap back on. "As am I."

"How do you feel about the taxidermy of wild animals?" I asked him.

"Don't believe I have a philosophical opinion about that."

"How do you feel about several of them packed into a small space?"

"Claustrophobic?"

"Just wanted to prepare you for the experience."

Zeke Ponder was at the counter inside the gas station and grocery store he and his stepson, Hi, ran. He heard the door open and peeked around the large, glass-eyed bear that blocked his line of vision.

"Oh. It's you again. Hiram!" he called out fraily. "Them cops is back!"

"Coming, Daddy!" Hi emerged from the back of the store. "Sergeant Blackthorne and Trooper Jones, how can we help you this afternoon?"

"Good to see both of you again," I said. "This is Detective Bach. He's been helping us with our investigation."

"Hiram Appleby, sir." He held out his hand.

"Pleased to meet you, Mr. Appleby."

"This here's my daddy, Mr. Zeke Ponder."

Daddy barely acknowledged Al before taking his leave.

"How can I help you this afternoon?" Hi asked again.

I placed the search warrant on the counter. "Judge Campbell has given permission to search the home of Max Ulanowicz. However, he fled before we could conduct the search."

"Oh, I get it. His trailer house is locked."

"Yes."

"Is he Charlie's killer?"

"We haven't determined who the murderer is yet, but Mr. Ulanowicz is wanted for questioning regarding other matters."

"Gotcha." Hi opened a drawer and drew out a small box of keys. He picked out the one marked with a spot of green paint. "It'd be good to get it back from you when you're done."

"Of course, Mr. Appleby," I said.

"Just Hi, remember?" He handed me the key.

The search of Ziegler's home came up empty. No bills, photos, correspondence, personal items, extra clothes, or weapons, unless we counted the kitchen knives. The place was spotless, almost as if he hadn't been living there at all.

"I don't think anyone lives here," Al said.

"Maggie and I have seen him open the door and go inside before."

"Oh, I believe he rents it, Hollis, but I don't think he actually lives here."

"Let's have another conversation with Patti Hutchens, and then let's stop back in and chat a bit with Hiram Appleby," I suggested.

I locked up the trailer, and we wandered back to Patti's place. She opened the door as I was about to knock.

"Saw you coming up the walk. Come on in. I'll make us all some hot tea."

Even I thought a cup of hot tea sounded good. The sun was already waning, and a biting cold had moved in from the mountains.

Her warm living room, the charming dachshund décor, and comfortable couch had me yearning for a short nap while waiting for her to serve us. I could've almost gotten away with it. Detective Bach was in the kitchen helping her put together the cups and saucers, and Holly was thumbing through her latest *National Geographic Magazine*.

Al followed Patti from the kitchen carrying a tray holding the teapot, dishes, utensils, sugar, and cream. He placed it on the coffee table and served us all.

"I don't usually like tea, but this is delicious," I said.

"Good old oolong," she answered.

"So, I noticed the Airstream where Brad Slater and Calvin James were staying is no longer parked in the trailer court."

"No, the Forest Service ended maintenance work for the season, and they moved back to John Day, I think. They were such nice young guys."

"We have what's probably a strange question for you."

"What's that, Sergeant Blackthorne?"

"You're welcome to call me Maggie. How often do you see Mr. Ulanowicz at his mobile home?"

"I don't think he spends a lot of time there. I've always assumed he's got a girlfriend in Ukiah or something. His lights are usually off, and there's rarely a car parked out front. And a few times, I saw another guy hanging around his place."

"Could you describe this other guy?"

"Big guy. A lot of white hair."

"Caucasian?" Hollis asked.

"Yes."

"Can I borrow your keys, Maggie? I want to get the laptop out of my pack."

"I have a computer you can use," Patti offered.

"That would be great."

"It's in my office." She stood. "Follow me, everybody."

We squeezed into her office, and Hollis sat at her desk. He logged in to our case file remotely and opened the feds' bulletin stored in the folder. He scrolled to the photo of Clifton Massey, the supposed leader of POSSE.

"Is the man pictured here the other guy you saw at Mr. Ulanowicz's place?"

She stared at it for a full minute and sipped her tea. "Can you enlarge it, please?"

Holly enlarged the photograph.

"I believe that's him, all right. He has less hair in the picture here. But I'm pretty sure it's him. And he drove a red sports car."

A red sports car didn't sound like something a person wanted by the FBI and ATF would drive, but perhaps it was the perfect automobile for someone wanted by the FBI and ATF to tool around in. Sure beat a gargantuan orange International Scout.

"Patti," I said. "Do you remember the last time you saw him there?"

"It's been since Mark Taylor passed. Over the weekend, I think. Yeah, the day I came back from staying with my sister in Mt. Vernon. Sunday."

"And I don't suppose you know what kind of sports car he drove?" Hollis asked.

"Heavens, no. I'm not even completely sure it was a sports car, but it looked like one to me. And I know absolutely nothing about cars, other than when to put gas in the little Volkswagen I own."

"You've been very helpful, Ms. Hutchens. And I really appreciate the tea," the detective said. A hint that it was time for us to go.

"You're welcome. But I suppose you can't tell me who the man is."

"We can only say that he's a person of interest."

"So if I see him out here again, I should give you a call?"

"Yes," I answered and handed her another one of my cards.

"Do I have reason to be afraid of the man?"

"If he's who we think he is, I believe the last thing he wants to do is call attention to himself."

"Then he probably shouldn't be driving around in a red sports car, then, should he?" Patti said mischievously.

"I did wonder about that myself."

Hollis and I stopped in at Blue Mountain Gas & Groceries on the way out of Dale to ask about the guy we presumed to be Clifton Massey. Meanwhile, Al took the opportunity to check in on the other cases he was supervising.

Hi was in the process of dusting his dead animals and whistling the tune to *Jeopardy!* when we entered the store. Daddy must have been in the back office because it took a bit for Hi to notice he wasn't alone in the store.

"You're back already," he said and climbed down the ladder he was standing on.

"We have another question for you. We just met with Patti Hutchens, and she may have recognized a photo of a person wanted by federal authorities and who's possibly connected to our investigation."

"Patti's a smart lady, all right."

Hollis set his laptop on the counter and opened it to the photo in the FBI/ATF bulletin. "We're curious to see if you or your dad recognize the guy."

Hiram stepped to the counter and took a look at the photo displayed on the screen. "Cliff is wanted by the feds? That's hard to believe."

"How do you know him?" I asked.

"Well, he lives around here somewhere. Drops by for gas and groceries every once and a while."

"Did you ever see him hanging out with Max Ulanowicz or Charlie Archer?"

"No, but I don't usually make it my business to know who hangs out with who."

Just the opposite, was what I was thinking.

"Do you happen to know Cliff's last name?"

He thought about that and raised his shoulders up and down, indicating he didn't. "The guy always pays in cash, and I guess I've never asked what his last name is."

"How about his vehicle?"

"An older Honda, don't know the model. Some kind of sporty thing, I think."

"Color?"

"Well, I'd call it tomato myself."

"Do you remember the last time he stopped in and got gas?"

Hi appeared to put on his thinking cap. Literally. "Let's see. Sometime in the last week, I think."

Patti had said she'd seen him this past Sunday, so I took the question in that direction. "Last Sunday, maybe?"

"Nah, it was sometime before that. Oh, I know, it was the day Charlie killed that officer. Late in the afternoon."

"Did you mention it to him? Charlie murdering Trooper Taylor?"

"I mighta. There's never been such a thing happen in Dale, far as I know."

I put the key to the mobile home and another one of my cards on the counter. "We'd appreciate you letting us know if he drops by again."

"Sure thing."

Al was waiting in his rig when we emerged from the store. He appeared to be exhausted and damn sick of murders.

"Everything under control?" I asked through his now open driver's-side window.

"Well, things here in Grant County are pretty much under control, but down in Lakeview and over in Prineville, not so much. I'm heading to Prineville right away, but I wanted to hear what you learned from the shopkeeper."

"Hiram Appleby recognized Massey, but he only knew him by the name Cliff. Said he lives somewhere nearby and drops by occasionally for gas and groceries. Drives an older, sporty Honda. Called the color tomato."

"Well, we need to send out an APB for that, too. And I'll contact my FBI source in Portland while I'm on the road. I'll be in touch tomorrow, hopefully early."

After Al took off for Prineville, Hollis and I headed back toward John Day. We rode quietly for several miles, each of us deep in thought. It had been a strange day, and there was some possibility we were on the verge of solving a mystery even more significant than a backcountry murder case.

"Everyone in the trailer park had to know Charlie Archer killed a State Police officer," I said. "They learned about it from Patti Hutchens or more likely Hiram Appleby, and then the news spread to the towns and outposts nearby. By the next morning, everyone living in this county and the county next door knew."

"Sounds like Clifton Massey might've known before the next morning."

"Jenna Rhinehart said Archer had heated arguments with Earl over the phone. And she mentioned there was a lot of back-and-forth about guns."

"Was it over the phone because they couldn't be seen together? And they were all supposed to be hiding out?"

"That's the theory I'm operating on, Holly. Earl became Max Ulanowicz and worked at the hardware store in Ukiah."

"And faked living in Dale. But why?"

"I don't understand that either."

"Well. I hate social media," he said. "But that might be the rabbit hole I should go down next."

"God, I hate that shit, too."

"Doesn't seem to have made the world any better or people any smarter."

We drove on for several miles in silence, but my brain was on fire, or it was shorting out, I couldn't tell which. Until I finally pulled some pieces of history out of nowhere.

"Remember Ruby Ridge or the Waco siege back in the nineties?" I said.

"Of course. The Montana Freemen, too."

"Maybe POSSE has put together a compound of sorts. Up in the mountains? Or buried in the forest? Or both?"

"There are eight men in total, including Clifton Massey. That we know about, anyway. Would they all be hiding out in the vicinity of one another?"

"That's possibly even a better way to hide out. Archer lived in Dale, and Ziegler pretended to live there."

"I don't know, Mags. My rabbit hole analogy is starting to seem like the conversation we're having."

"Come on, Holly. Humor me."

"Well, I could be enticed by a raise in pay."

"So granted. Now hear me out. Let's say some of them are holed up in one of those abandoned mining towns we talked about."

"If you're right, I hope and pray it's Cracker City."

"We couldn't be that lucky."

21

EVENING, NOVEMBER 18

I reminded Hollis about the armed standoff between law enforcement and protesters who had converged at a spot in the Elkhorn Mountains last August. "That small range of mountains is only a hop, skip, and a jump from the Umatilla Forest and all those old mining towns."

"And so…?"

"Those demonstrators last summer were arguing with the government over a mere twenty-five acres of grassland where antiquities had been discovered. Ranchers believed their grazing rights trumped the history of indigenous peoples and the place's archeological relevance. For them it was the principle of the thing, I guess, and they had the support of like-minded folks from around the country, especially here in the West."

"Ah, another iteration of the culture wars."

"Not sure about that, but as far as I know, those protesters weren't aiming for a full-blown insurrection."

"All right, I can see you're serious about all this. And it does seem like more and more people get hotter under the collar about all kinds of things these days," he said.

"I'm mostly trying to say it's at least possible the POSSE members identified in the FBI bulletin—not just the three we know about or suspect—

are hanging out somewhere nearby. And where they might encounter like-minded individuals."

"You're saying 'somewhere nearby' means one of those old mining towns. And what got you thinking along those lines?"

"Kind of started with your suggestion about being able to drive on secondary highways and forest roads through backcountry between eastern Oregon and Idaho."

"Lots of places, really." He drew out his phone and began thumbing.

While he searched, I put on Tedeschi Trucks Band's *Revelator* and waited for him to report out. It was fully dark outside and the time of year when migrating mule deer often crossed the highway, foraging for bunch-grass and any remaining mountain mahogany leaves. That damn cougar was likely out too, hunting the deer.

"Well," Holly finally said. "The most populated of those old towns is Granite, with gas, groceries, gravel roads and everything."

I turned the music off.

He continued, "The place closest to Granite is Greenhorn. It has some leftover structures, but it's hard to tell if they're habitable. Interestingly, Greenhorn has a city council, but they all actually live elsewhere in Oregon, as far as I can tell."

"Strange. I wonder what that's about."

"Don't know, but people apparently liked their towns to have G-names back in the day because there's also a place called Galena. Again, I'm not sure if anything's habitable in Galena."

"Isn't there a Susanville somewhere around, too?"

"Yeah. Bunch of run-down buildings and one that appears to be locked tight."

"The towns you mentioned. Are any close to Desolation Guard Station?"

Hollis dove back into his search. "Granite sits at the junction to Forest Road 10," he said after a few minutes. "Which, if you remember, goes right by the guard station. It would be a bit more of a trip from the rest of those old towns, but it could still be done."

"How about Cracker City?"

"I know Cracker City is a town on that atlas of yours, but the worldwide web tells me the name was changed to Bourne."

"Born? As in being born?"

"No, as in someone's last name."

"Well, shit. That's no fun," I countered.

"Bourne is located pretty far up in the mountains. In the Elkhorns, actually. So I suppose it's possible that a POSSE member or two are hiding out up there. Guess it's also possible they were a party to that brouhaha last August."

"I think we need to take a trip to Granite tomorrow. Make some inquiries about the POSSE crew."

"And maybe go take a peek at Greenhorn?"

I yawned. "Sure, unless we get some kind of lead in Granite."

"Would you like me to drive tomorrow?"

"Not especially."

"What was that music you had on earlier?"

"Tedeschi Trucks Band. Susan Tedeschi and Derek Trucks."

"Nice mix of blues and rock. And she's got a voice."

"It's something my dad would've liked back in the day."

"That surprises me, I guess," Holly said. "I figured him to have been a country-western kind of guy. And possibly a conservative Republican."

"Hardly that last. He was a working-class Democrat. And a lonely, confused alcoholic who wanted things to be like they'd been when he was younger."

"Like what?"

"Not so much unfriendly back-and-forth about politics. And not so hard to make a decent living."

"Huh."

"How about your dad?"

"As one of the few Black men in Medford, Oregon, he mostly wanted to lay low and bring home a paycheck every month," Hollis said and paused. "Don't want you to freak out, Mags. But when I looked over at the outside rearview mirror just now, I saw a cougar dart across the highway behind us."

"I wondered about that fucking cougar earlier."

"It was weird. His eyes looked red in the light."

"I'm begging you, shut the hell up."

He laughed. "Sorry."

The house was cold when I arrived, and Raleigh Cat was in need of his evening constitution. I let him outside and stood in the darkened entryway of our small home. It wasn't late, but it was after six.

I wondered about dinner, knowing I'd counted on Duncan to take care of that, even though I hadn't spoken with him since Mark Taylor's funeral. A wave of guilt rolled over me. What kind of a life partner was I? A bad one, it seemed. Hell, I probably made a lot better patrol partner for Hollis when it came down to it.

The door opened and Duncan stood behind me holding a warm pizza from the Cave Inn. "Hi, babe."

We kissed and removed our coats. I hung them in the closet by the front door, and Duncan carried the pizza into the kitchen.

I pulled salad fixings from the fridge and began chopping veggies while he set us up at the so-called breakfast nook. I dressed and tossed the salad as he put out paper plates and napkins, served us each a piece of pizza, and poured himself a glass of wine, along with a glass of flavored fizzy water for me.

"We're the epitome of domesticity, I'd say." He clinked his glass to mine.

"And I was just thinking what a shitty partner I am."

"What?"

"I came in the door, the lights and heat were off, and I thought to myself, 'It's cold in here, and where the fuck is my dinner?' And then I felt guilty about that and wondered, 'What kind of a partner am I?'"

"Well I knew you were probably home safe and likely hungry, and I was feeling too lazy to make one of my sophisticated-cowboy, showoff meals."

"How'd you know I'd be here?" I asked.

"I saw the lights on at the station and stopped to find out what was up. Hollis was there and said you were on your way home."

Hollis had intended to make his way home to Lil and Hank, too, or at least that's what he'd said. But something must have sparked his curiosity and sent him on a goose chase. I willed myself not to wonder what that might have been about until tomorrow.

"And as far as feeling guilty, you've got the whole night to make it up to me."

"Well, it doesn't really sound like I need to make anything up to you," I teased.

He pulled my stool closer to his and wrapped his arm around me. "I love you, and you'll never need to make anything up to me. Who you are is all I ever want, do you understand?"

"Damn it, Dun. Now look what you did. I'm about to start crying."

"There's an entire night ahead for me to make it up to you, babe."

I placed a hand on one side of his face, "It's a date."

———

Later, in the warmth of the covers and our bodies, we lay whispering about our future, our child. As we fell into sleep, I felt strangely recharged, ready for what was to come in the investigation.

Tomorrow was the one-week anniversary of Mark Taylor's murder, and I was convinced there was reason to continue following the path we'd stumbled onto. Hollis and I were smart cops with good instincts and common sense, and we knew when to let the facts show us the way. But we also understood we had to be open to any turning point in our investigation.

A question, one I'd had earlier in the day, came back to me. Why *hadn't* Earl Ziegler, alias Max Ulanowicz, blown us away with his short-barreled rifle?

Tucking myself next to Dun's muscular back, I was very happy Ziegler had chosen to lock us in the hardware store as opposed to making that deadlier choice.

I woke believing Hollis might've been on to something during our rambling conversation about Earl Ziegler. I quietly climbed out of bed, put on my robe, and crept downstairs.

How was it that Ziegler had sped from Ukiah without killing the three cops whose weapons he'd absconded with? As Hollis had suggested, maybe we were all alive now because we're police officers. Killing us would've risked greater law enforcement interest in finding Ziegler and rooting out the rest of the gang.

Was cop-killing verboten inside the POSSE organization, at least until the grand revolution was called? Or were they simply FOPs—friends of police? I was pretty sure that last was not the case unless some of the members had been officers themselves. Always a possibility.

In addition, Clifton Massey had no doubt learned Charlie Archer murdered a police officer last Thursday, the day before Archer himself was shot to death with a big-bore handgun. Had Massey sent someone to track the man down and cancel his POSSE membership forever? Had he done the deed himself?

Massey had to be the Cliffy that Jenna Rhinehart had mentioned, and what was it she had said about the relationship Archer had with Cliffy? Something about the way Charlie talked about Cliffy—like somebody who goes on about their grandfather being the best person ever.

Made me wonder if Archer had been referring to the man's ability to sway his followers. I wasn't a political scientist or a psychologist—perish the thought—but I knew there was such a thing as charisma. Some people had it, and other people were drawn to them by virtue of that affect. And it often didn't matter if the charismatic person was a psychopath or a saint, some could be convinced of that person's moral significance.

"All right, Blackthorne. Don't go on the road with that *moral significance* BS."

"Maggie, are you okay?"

Duncan had slipped downstairs and found me eating the last of my raisin bran at the dining table while I stared out the garden door windows at an intensely ice-blue sky and talked to myself.

I turned to look at him. His sweet face, his shock of graying red hair, and those green eyes of his made my heart skip a beat. And then there was that voice—deep and kind. It felt right to fall in love all over again every morning.

I smiled. "Nah, I was just philosophizing to myself."

"That can be dangerous."

"If not stupid." I stood, cereal bowl in hand. "Would you like some coffee?"

He took the bowl from me, placed it back on the table, and coaxed me to again take in the view from the garden door. "Sunshine. How'd we get so lucky?"

"Don't know, but I'll take it as a good omen."

"Are you getting close?"

"I think so, Dun."

"Be careful out there, babe. Promise me that."

"You have my word."

———

Driving toward town, the morning sky brightened, thin layers of Oregon jade shimmered in the light now striking the basalt cliff rising above Highway 395. The veiny gray trunks of the gnarled and leafless cottonwoods stood along the banks of Canyon Creek as though awaiting the return of snow melt. Cold as it was, I cracked open the window and allowed the scent of damp sagebrush to fill the cab of my police Tahoe.

Arriving at the office, I cornered Hollis first thing with my notions. But he was already with me or ahead of me on all counts.

"Duncan might have told you, but I stayed here for a while last night, went through our case file, peeked at the murder board, and did some more research."

"Yeah, he said he stopped by the station and chatted with you."

"So, I decided to contact an FBI buddy of mine, a researcher of sorts."

"You and Bach and your FBI buddies. Since when did you have one?"

"Went to college together. He's an intelligence analyst in the Salt Lake City field office, and he owes me a favor. Even though he wouldn't plug me into the non-public information gathered by him or other analysts, he suggested a few sources to access. Those were work, though, but I was able to dig up a few nuggets."

"Can't remember where I heard this, but doesn't the Salt Lake City field office cover activities in Idaho and Montana, as well as Utah?"

"Yep. Anyway, the first thing I figured out was Clifton Massey had been a police officer in a few jurisdictions in Idaho."

"I actually did wonder if any members of POSSE had been in law enforcement. Was he ever an officer in Golden Pine, by any chance?"

"No, but speaking of Golden Pine, there's something called the Flag Tenders Rendezvous near there every other May. The most recent one was held last year."

"Eighteen months ago. That's when Earl Ziegler was spotted in Golden Pine."

"That's right."

"Flag Tenders?"

"Don't ask, but I bet you can guess."

"Jesus Christ."

"They're big fans of that fellow too."

"Remind me. Golden Pine is up in the mountains?"

"That's right."

"It's still kind of cold in the mountains for a rendezvous in May."

"I would think so. Maybe only the truly dedicated would attend."

"And what exactly are the Flag Tenders tending to?"

"The values they say the American flag represents, as I understand it."

"Let me guess, there aren't a lot of people of color among the Flag Tenders."

"Doesn't seem like it." Hollis kneaded his temples. "In terms of what values they claim the flag represents, well, that isn't really defined, as far as I can tell. But it appears to have a lot to do with gun rights. And the call to *Hold Firm!* seems to be code for something I haven't figured out yet."

"Catchy slogan."

"The other bit of news I wanted to give you was about the Max Ulanowicz from Redding, California."

"I'm all ears."

"He was an undercover FBI agent who had been detailing Clifton Massey's activities."

"What? You were able to figure that out by perusing unclassified files?"

"Um, no."

"Okay, Fox Mulder. You're sure he was an undercover FBI agent?"

"Yes. He had even pretended to show an interest in joining POSSE."

"What tipped off Massey that he was the subject of FBI surveillance, which no doubt led to the murder of Ulanowicz?"

"I don't know."

"Anything else?"

Hollis shook his head. "Sorry, but I needed to spend some time with my family last night."

"All right, but that may delay the raise I promised you yesterday."

"Well, that and the Oregon state legislature. Anyway, I have a few more things to sort through, see if anything else interesting pops up."

"I also continue to wonder why Ziegler released Cousin Lyndon? It would've been so easy to kill him—and as a lark, use one of our police weapons to do it—and then push his body into a ravine somewhere."

"Zero-sum game, I'd say. Offing Mr. Cummings would only buy Ziegler more trouble and make him more of a target."

"I guess. Although I'm not sure we would've necessarily found the body right away."

"No matter what, I think we're getting close, Mags. Really close. But I have a couple more things I want to dig into."

"I think we're close, too. Even mentioned that to Duncan not more than a half an hour ago. But this is when I always start getting anxious."

"It's also when things start clicking into place."

"Speaking of that, I think I want to pick Jenna Rhinehart's brain a bit more about Clifton Massey. But when I get back, we're heading to Granite."

22

MORNING, NOVEMBER 19

Jenna Rhinehart had washed her hair and was dressed in clean jeans, a white oxford shirt, and a sweater. She had yet to put on shoes, and I suspected the footwear would likely be black combat boots. It wouldn't have mattered, though, because she had utterly transformed her appearance and came off looking like a typical college freshman.

The young woman wasn't a student, but perhaps someone should encourage her to think about becoming one. Someone besides me.

"How are you, Jenna?"

"Well, I got a job interview this morning."

"That's great. Do you have a minute for a couple of questions?"

"Um, what time is it?"

I peeked at my watch. "Nine fifteen."

"Yeah, my interview's not 'til ten. Just let me put my shoes on first."

"Sure, I'll wait for you in the living room, if that's okay."

"I'll be right back."

I took a seat and listened to the three versions of miniature grandfather clocks placed in various locations around the room tick away time. When the girl returned, she was indeed wearing a pair of black combat boots, but the whole ensemble was just right in some way. Certainly in comparison to her usual holey *Thundermother* shirt. But really, who was I to pass judgment about either outfit?

"Where's your recorder?" she asked, taking a seat on the couch.

"Oh, I'll just take notes today. No Miranda, either."

Jenna smiled, realizing she wouldn't be recorded or under oath this time. Which, in the scheme of things, didn't really mean as much as she might have thought. But in truth, she had moved down on the list of suspects in Archer's murder. For a variety of reasons, but primarily because the man had been shot to death by someone with a big-bore handgun, and no such a weapon had been in his collection as far as we could tell.

I drew a small notebook from my back pocket. "I want to start with a question about the conversations Charlie had with his friend Cliffy."

She shrugged. "Okay."

"As far as you know, did Cliffy ever drop by the trailer house in Dale or meet up with Charlie somewhere nearby?"

"I was never, um, I was supposed to stay at the trailer and not answer the door and definitely never let anybody come inside."

"So when anybody knocked on the door, you had to what, hide?"

"Well, nobody ever knocked." She looked at her lap. "Except that police officer."

"So, let's back up some. I think what you're telling me is that Cliffy never dropped by Charlie's mobile home."

"No, he didn't."

"How about Mr. Ulanowicz?"

"Mr. Who?"

"Mr. Ulanowicz. He lived in the trailer court, too. And he worked at Jacoby's Hardware in Ukiah."

"I don't know who that is."

"Tall guy. Really tall in comparison to either of us."

"I saw a tall guy around from time to time."

"At the trailer court?"

"Yeah. He lived next door to Brad and Calvin."

"Did you ever see him talking to, or arguing with, Charlie?"

"Don't know if they was just talking or arguing, but they was outside together a few times, having some kind of conflab."

"Was Charlie ever upset afterward?"

She gave that some thought. "I'm sorry, Sergeant, but Charlie was upset most of the time, so I don't remember if he was especially upset with that guy."

"Did you ever see a man with white hair at the trailer court?"

"I don't think so. Can you tell me why you're asking about the tall guy and the white-haired man?"

I mulled over my answer. "They're both people of interest."

"In Charlie's death?"

"In matters possibly connected to it."

"Um, are we going to be done soon? I have to walk to my interview, and I don't want to be late."

"Just one more question. Do you have any thoughts about why Charlie had a couple of fake IDs?"

"Charlie was anxious about something, but I knew not to ask about it. Guess it doesn't surprise me much he had a couple of fake IDs."

Which I found to be an astute answer. "Well, good luck on your interview, Jenna."

"I'm kinda nervous. I sure hope Mr. McKay is nice."

"You mean the owner of the feed and tack store?"

"You know him?"

"He's a really nice guy. But can I give you some advice?"

"Sure."

"The second syllable of *McKay* rhymes with *sky*, not *hay*."

"Really?"

"Yeah, it's the Scottish pronunciation. And it's how the family has always said their last name."

"Thank you, Sergeant Blackthorne. That's helpful."

"You're welcome. If you think of anything we should know about, you can call me anytime." I wrote my cell phone number on the back of one of my business cards and handed it to her.

"Do you have any more advice for me? About the interview, I mean."

"Well, I know you've been through a lot lately, but you've proven you're tough. Which means you really are self-confident. Turning in Tess Slater and Claire Nolan last year took guts, no matter your motivation. It shows that you can be bold, maybe even assertive if you have to be."

"Oh, I can be assertive, but it's got me in trouble before."

"I assume you're talking about Charlie Archer."

She nodded.

"He was the troubled one, Jenna. You're young and you made a mistake, but there's probably not a person alive who hasn't made a mistake when they were younger."

"Even you?"

"Oh, yeah. For starters, I've been divorced twice, and that's not even the half of all the messes I got myself into along the way."

"Thanks for the advice, Sergeant."

"I should go and let you get to your interview. Or would you like me to drop you off?"

"I don't want to insult you or nothing, but I don't think it would look too good showing up for my interview in a cop car."

Duncan would've wondered about that, too. "You're probably right."

As I gathered my notepad and moved from the room, Jenna practiced saying Duncan's last name.

Sherry Linn was on the phone when I returned to our cop station. It seemed she was taking a missing person report and having a difficult time grasping what the caller was telling her.

She crossed her eyes as I passed by the counter on my way to the corral of officer desks. Hollis was staring at his computer and taking notes while Doug Vaughn scrolled through memos from the Oregon Department of Fish and Wildlife. Shortly after I sat at my desk and began entering the notes from my latest discussion with Jenna Rhinehart in the case file, Sherry Linn handed me the report she'd taken.

I invited her to take the empty chair beside my desk, and she sat down.

"That was an elderly gentleman on the phone just now. A Mr. Karl Jacoby. He owns the hardware store in Ukiah and called to report the guy he'd hired to staff the place had gone missing. Apparently, Mr.

Jacoby doesn't know how long the clerk's been gone, and the only reason he learned the fellow wasn't there is because someone needed to pick up something at the hardware store earlier today but found it locked tight."

"The missing clerk, Max Ulanowicz, right?"

"Yeah, isn't that the man whose property you got a search warrant for just yesterday, along with a warrant for his arrest?"

"That's right. Long story short, he got away."

"But I shouldn't let Mr. Jacoby know that, right?"

"Definitely not."

She ran her fingers through her hair. "Mr. Jacoby has an accent. German, I think. We were having a hard time communicating."

"Thanks for hanging in there."

"I felt bad for the old guy. Well, I know I'm not supposed to call him old. Ageism and all that. But he was really struggling to tell me what he called to say. Mostly because of the language barrier, I think."

"Excuse me, you two," Hollis said. "Maggie. I think you need to see this."

"See you later, guys," Sherry Linn said, stood, and sashayed to the front counter.

I moved to Holly's desk. "What's up?"

"Found a twenty-five-year-old jail shot of Earl Ziegler, back when he was in his early thirties. He'd been picked up in Northern California. Humboldt County, to be more specific, on suspicion of car theft. The charge didn't hold up, or he got off for some reason. But while he was there, they took his mug shot standing next to a height chart."

"I see that. And he was almost six feet tall then."

"I'm six two."

"Okay, I'll say it. You're taller than Earl Ziegler."

"But not as tall as the guy calling himself Max Ulanowicz."

"Are you sure?"

"I'm positive. Or if he's not taller than me, he's for damn sure taller than six feet."

"Wait. You're saying Max Ulanowicz is Max Ulanowicz? And did you just say a cussword?"

"Yes, to both of those questions. Well, I'm pretty sure Max Ulanowicz is Max Ulanowicz and not Earl Ziegler."

"Christ on a crutch, my brain's about to explode. That means Ulanowicz is undercover FBI. And that's why he didn't blow us to smithereens and kill Cousin Lyndon."

"Yeah, I'm pretty sure. But don't let your head explode just yet, because I also think you're on to something about those old mining towns. First of all, there are also a bunch of abandoned logging towns out there too. In Grant County and neighboring Baker County combined, there are twenty of these kinds of ghost towns or almost ghost towns."

"Twenty?"

"Yep. Six in Grant County and thirteen in Baker County. And one more, Greenhorn, supposedly rides the border between the two counties. Now, a fair number are not anywhere near Desolation Ridge, but all appear to be accessible. Although I haven't researched the condition of every road and byway."

"You slacker, you."

"But I did check the sheriff report logs in both Grant County and Baker County going back some. Reported crimes have climbed to unprecedented levels in those largely unpopulated areas, even before that dust-up in the Elkhorn Mountains last August."

"What's an example?"

"Several weapons charges, including trafficking and theft. Poaching of deer and elk, hunting on private property posted with *No Hunting* signs. Reports of camping or building shelter on private or public forest land. Most of it in parts of the Umatilla and Wallowa-Whitman National Forests."

"Why haven't we heard anything about all of this?"

"Probably because it's random and not all in one place."

Doug's desk was maybe eighteen inches from where Hollis and I were talking, so he was obviously privy to our conversation.

"Fish and Wildlife—both the OSP division and the state department—have been trying to get to the bottom of that for a while," he chimed in. "At least the illegal taking-of-game issue. The camping thing is more of a nuisance than anything else."

"Unless someone sets fire to the place," I said.

"You're right. That would be a tough thing to deal with. As you probably noticed when you were out in the Desolation Ridge area, the deeper you go into the woods, it becomes more thickly forested and much steeper."

"Ripe for an inferno," Hollis added.

"Not this time of year, I would hope."

Doug sighed. "I don't know, our county ranged between abnormally dry to extreme drought this year, depending on the location."

"On the heels of that happy news, I think we should get out to Granite while the getting's good, Hollis. What's the rest of your day like, Doug?"

"Now that both deer and elk hunting season are over, I'm taking a trip out to the Murderers Creek Wildlife Area to check for any scofflaws."

"Be careful out there."

"I will be, Maggie."

We each gave the other a serious glance. I was pretty sure he was thinking about Mark Taylor. How bad things can happen unexpectedly. How some people were assholes, and in the case of scofflaw hunters, some were assholes with guns.

From our State Police shop in John Day, we took the fastest route to Granite, the old mining town of about forty souls. This time traveling east on Highway 26, we rode past Prairie City and then headed north on Route 7 until we met up with a connecter road that took us west to our destination.

Entering the village, we passed under an impressive metalwork sign depicting a horseback rider leading a troop of pack mules. The weather had held, and Granite, built on several small hills and surrounded by Ponderosa and lodgepole pine, juniper, and the occasional blue spruce, was charming in the midday sun. Even the dilapidated, 150-year-old buildings held a certain appeal. I could imagine happening on the place and being enchanted by its historic, ethereal vibe.

I had forgotten about the trips here as a girl. My father, Tate, would pan for gold, and I could remember on one such occasion, Zoey, my mother, brought oil paints and an easel and sat one afternoon immersed in capturing the image of the surrounding mountains on canvas. That was a lifetime ago and long before the Earth's center of gravity slipped and tore our family apart.

We drove through the town and parked in front of the country store, assuming it was the main attraction in Granite. The relatively large wooden building stood out, in part for its size, if not for the sparse collection of antlers adorning the front of the broad portico.

Inside the store, more antlers graced the interior walls, but unlike Blue Mountain Gas & Groceries in Dale, the taxidermy specimens were limited to one elk head. A small kitchen and dining area was placed near the front but off to the side. It offered fresh breakfast, coffee, and sandwiches for sale, according to the menu posted on a blackboard, but it appeared to be devoid of a cook or waitstaff.

Center-front of the business's large open space, a man dressed in a red-and-black-checked flannel shirt sat in a rocking chair behind the checkout counter. An elderly cash register was parked in front of him, and he was reading through a hunting magazine. The guy didn't bother saying howdy or looking up as we entered and sauntered to the counter.

"Excuse me," I said.

"Somethin' I can do for you?" he answered in an unfamiliar drawl.

"I'm Oregon State Police Sergeant Blackthorne, and this is Trooper Jones."

He glanced at Hollis. "She your boss, is she?"

"She is," Hollis answered.

He looked directly at me. "What you want?"

The man needed to wash his hair in the worst way.

I pressed my hands into the countertop. "Are you the owner of the store?"

"Yup."

"May I have your name, please?"

"What you need that for?"

I took out the notebook I'd used earlier when chatting with Jenna Rhinehart, along with the photographs of Ziegler, Massey, and Archer. "Is there some reason you don't want to give me your name?"

"What you need it for?"

"So I can write down the name of the person who gives an answer to my questions."

"I don't know."

"Well, you do own the store, right?"

"For fifteen years."

"It's pretty easy to look up a business owner's name online. Trooper Jones could pull out his phone and do it in about three minutes."

The flannel dude relented. "Name's Gregory."

"First name or last?"

"Both." He placed his hands on top of the counter.

"Both?"

"That's right. Gregory R. Gregory. My pops thunk that up. Thought it'd be funny. Most people just call me G.R."

I wrote down his name. "Okay, Mr. Gregory. Are you familiar with someone named Earl Ziegler? Sixty-ish, close to six feet tall." I placed the photo on the counter.

"Never met no Earls around here."

"Check out the photograph, please."

He stared at the black-and-white image. "Don't know 'im."

"How about a man named Clifton Massey?" I laid Massey's picture on top of Ziegler's.

"He go by Cliff?"

"I'm not sure." I glanced over at Hollis. "Did your research indicate if he used that name?"

"No, but we do have a witness who referred to him as Cliff."

"That's right. Does he look familiar, Mr. Gregory?"

"Maybe. Lot of white-haired old folks come out here. History nuts, mostly."

"Take a good look, please."

He stared at the photo briefly. "Don't know if I seen him afore."

I placed Charlie Archer's photograph on top of the other two. "How about this man. Ever see him around?"

"I know Charlie, all right. Heard he's dead, though. Somebody shot him." He moved out of his rocking chair. "That why you be here? You lookin' for his killer?"

"Yes, that's why we're here."

"He used to come in most every Saturday morning for breakfast. Before he got that girlfriend uh his."

"Was he alone?"

"He'd meet up with a...with a white-haired guy..."

I put Massey's black-and-white photo beside Archer's.

"Uh-huh, now I see the two pitchers together. That white-haired guy's who Charlie met with, all right. They'd talk about guns a lot and other things I didn't care nothin' about."

"Like politics? How the country was being run?"

He grimaced dramatically. "Shit like that."

"What kind of vehicle did Charlie drive?"

"An ugly, old orange Scout."

"How about the white-haired guy?"

"He never bought gas from my pump out back uh my store, so I didn't notice no vehicle."

"Have you ever noticed a sporty red automobile around town?"

"Not unless whoever drove it stopped for gas."

I placed my card on the counter. "Trooper Jones and I are leaving our contact information with you."

Hollis pulled out his card and put it on the counter as well. "Thank you for your time, Mr. Gregory. I was wondering if we could trouble you for a couple of sandwiches?"

"Why, sure. I just picked up some fresh lunch meat in John Day. Got roast beef or got roast chicken, and a lady up the road sells me her home-made bread once a week."

"I'll take the roast beef, thanks," Holly said.

"Want some good hot mustard on that?"

"Most definitely."

23

____

AFTERNOON, NOVEMBER 19

Detective Bach hadn't checked in this morning as he'd indicated he would. I took that as a sign things weren't going very well with the homicide case in Prineville and/or he'd also been required to head down to Lakeview. I tried his police radio, but he didn't pick up, and we were currently out of cell tower range and had been for a while. I decided to give him a call once we wandered back into service.

In the meantime, we sat in my Tahoe on a hill overlooking Granite chowing down the sandwiches G.R. had prepared for us. The windows were shut tight due to the wind having picked up again. Typical November weather in eastern Oregon. Sunshine one minute, blizzard the next.

"You're a genius, Holly. Having G.R. put together a lunch for us. My chicken sandwich is delicious," I said.

"My roast beef is too."

"Who'd uh thunk?"

"Are you making fun of the chef?"

"Right, he did say 'thunk,' didn't he? As in, his daddy thunk up his name."

"I got the feeling G.R.'s daddy wasn't a very nice person."

"G.R. sure softened over the course of that conversation, didn't he?"

"I'd say so. Seemed almost sad about Charlie Archer's death."

"You buying the shirt for Hank with the country store logo on the front was a nice touch."

"You noticed I didn't buy one for myself, though."

"Christmas is just around the corner, dude. And I finally know what I'm getting you."

"You get wittier with each passing day."

We ate and watched the few comings and goings in Granite. Nearly every vehicle was a four-wheel-drive pickup or SUV, which made sense, certainly for fall and winter driving, anyway.

When I had devoured half the sandwich, I wrapped the other half back in the wax paper G.R. had bound it in and placed it inside my small cooler. I retrieved my binoculars from my pack and checked out the Blue Mountains, the range that ran to the northeast and the southeast of us.

Further out and not visible from this vantage point were the Elkhorns, a stark cluster of formidable volcanic peaks that rose up from the high desert floor. Those mountains were a comparatively isolated range which, when a traveler happened upon them, stood out by virtue of their isolation.

I turned the binoculars toward Granite proper and scanned the town.

"Hollis, is that a red, older sports car parked next to that little cabin, the furthest one back up the hill from the country store?"

He fetched his own set of binoculars and checked out the little village. "Maybe."

"Buckle up. We're going to go take a closer look."

"Are you sure we want to do that? A police vehicle driving around this place stands out like a sore thumb."

"We already drove around this place."

"We went to the store, bought sandwiches, and left."

"What's your suggestion, then?"

He thought about that. "Wasn't there a small lodge not far from the store?"

"Yeah."

"Let's park near it and walk up to the cabin from there."

"Oh, I get it. You need some exercise."

He gave me a look.

"I don't mind parking at the lodge and walking," I said. "I'm not sure we're any less conspicuous trudging around Granite than we would be driving through in a cop rig. Either way, it'll take us no more than three or four minutes to go check out the red car."

"Well, it's up to you, Sarge."

"Gee, thanks, Holly."

I drove to the lodge and parked. We got out and walked toward the cabin. We must have been quite a sight—short female cop and tall male cop—traipsing through town, because all the village looky-loos drew back their curtains and stared.

"Okay, I see what you mean," Hollis said.

We quickly reached the cabin, walking past it a couple of yards, then turning to check out the vehicle parked in the back.

"It's a Honda, all right," I said.

"Yep. California plate, 4-R-A-L-7-1-8. S2000 is the model, a lot sportier than their other sedans. And the tags are about a year out of date."

"We can't confirm ownership until we can connect to the net."

"So true."

"Hey, officers." A man had appeared out of nowhere and was now blocking our path back to my Tahoe. He was bundled in winter gear and packed a holstered sidearm on one thigh.

"Fuck," I whispered under my breath.

He moved toward us.

"What can I do for you, sir?" I said.

"What's going on?"

"Who's asking?"

"Name's Clyde. Clyde Dalton."

Clyde had a giant wad of chew tucked between his bottom lip and gums.

"Are you concerned about something, Mr. Dalton?"

"Well, I saw you parked outside G.R.'s store, then I saw you parked on the hill across the way. After that, you parked in town, and now you're checking out my automobile."

"Not that it's your business, really," I said. "But we stopped at the store and got a couple of sandwiches. After that, we parked across the way to enjoy the view and eat our lunch. My partner here's a car buff, and while we were having lunch, he noticed your Honda. An S2000, right? He's always wanted to own one."

"It ain't for sale."

"Well, he wasn't thinking about buying it. Just admiring it is all."

"Okay, um, officer?"

"Sergeant Blackthorne."

"Oh, a lady sergeant, huh?"

"Yeah, and did you know your tags on the Honda are expired?"

"Gosh, I keep forgetting about that."

"How long have you lived in Oregon, Mr. Dalton?"

"About a year 'n a half."

"You need to get you some Oregon plates on your vehicle, too."

"Been meaning to do that, too."

"Uh-huh. Well, consider that a warning."

"Okay, Sergeant. I just wanted to find out if there was something going on around Granite. We've had a few incidents of late—a couple of break-ins and some odd strangers hanging around."

"This was all reported to the authorities, right?"

"I guess so."

"I have another question for you, Mr. Dalton. Do you happen to know a man named Clifton Massey?"

He spat a brown spray of tobacco juice onto the ground between us. "Can't say as I do."

"White-haired guy."

The man yanked the floppy-eared tuque from his head. "Hell, *I* got white hair."

Hollis broke in. "I have a question for you, Mr. Dalton."

Dalton smiled. "And here I thought the sergeant didn't want you to do any talking."

"I notice you keep your Honda unlocked with the keys in the ignition."

"That ain't illegal, is it?"

"No, but what with the break-ins you mentioned, I'd think you'd want to lock up your car."

"Well, I...I get tired of hunting around the house for my keys, so I just leave 'em in the car."

"Mr. Dalton," I said. "I think we'll be on our way now."

He stepped back to allow us to pass by. "Nice meeting you both, ma'am."

After we had moved out of the man's earshot, Hollis asked me what I thought about that encounter.

"I think these backwoods hollers attract some interesting individuals."

"I'd say you're right. But what do you think about his answer when you asked him if he knew Clifton Massey?"

"A fifty-fifty chance he was lying."

"At least. Either way, it would be easy for someone to make off with his Honda."

"Someone like Massey, you mean."

We got in the Tahoe, and I drove slowly back through Granite and under the metal entrance sign.

"I think we need to try to get some information on Mr. Dalton, don't you?" I asked Hollis.

"Agreed. And he looked sort of familiar, too. When we pick up cell service, I'm going to pull up our case file and look at the joint bulletin from the FBI and ATF."

"And the Honda's plate number."

"Yeah, that too."

We had moved down the road in silence for a beat or two when a radio call came in from Officer Bob Nolan of the John Day Police.

"How are things this afternoon, Bob?" I asked after acknowledging the call.

"Picked up that guy from yesterday's APB."

"Max Ulanowicz?"

"That's him. He's sitting here in our holding tank. Would you like me to transport him to the county jail?"

"Nah. Hollis Jones and I are on our way back to town. We were out in Granite."

"That old mining town?"

"Yep."

"Business or pleasure?"

"That murder case of ours, I'm afraid. We'll be back in John Day in a little over an hour."

"Maybe I'll still be here at the office. If not, it was good talking to you again."

Bob was a nice guy, but I still wanted to let him know his daughter Claire had gone too far in meting out her revenge on Jenna Rhinehart.

"All right, Bob. Thanks for the heads-up."

I signed off and glanced over at Hollis. We must have come into cell range because he was thumbing away on his phone. While I waited for him to report out on what he did or didn't find on his internet search, I concentrated on the road and considered all the loose ends we had to pull or let go of.

Max Ulanowicz was likely one loose end we could soon let fall away. More importantly, he might be able to supply us with something tangible enough to break our murder case wide open. And then I felt vaguely apprehensive, having not dealt with the FBI much. His having skin in the game after all this time might prompt Mr. Ulanowicz to undermine our work or usurp our authority in the investigation of Archer's murder.

"Just calm down, Blackthorne," I said to myself.

"What's that?" Hollis asked.

"Never mind. I was overreacting to something that hasn't happened and won't happen."

Besides, the FBI was in a period of having to walk on eggshells lately. In addition, undermining or usurping our authority would prompt Detective Al Bach and the OSP superintendent, maybe even the governor, to call on our two US senators—lawmakers who weren't always big fans of that particular federal bureau's actions.

"All right, it took some digging, but I was able to figure out that Clyde Dalton once lived in Smith River, California. Near the Pacific coast and just over the Oregon border. The Honda belongs to him, and there's not much on him anywhere except a few traffic infractions, including two for his failure to renew his vehicle registration. And I thought he might've been one of the men in that bulletin, but I decided I was wrong about that."

"That's okay. It turns out you were mistaken about that once before."

"Uh, remember? Technically, I wasn't," Hollis countered.

"Speaking of that, let's hope Ulanowicz will be helpful as opposed to turning out to be an undercover FBI dickwad."

"Ease up there. Remember he had the chance to kill us, and he didn't."

"I think he might've gotten in trouble for that, don't you?"

"I'm just glad that's nothing more than a rhetorical question, Mags."

I decided we'd transport Mr. Ulanowicz to the courthouse after picking him up at the John Day Police Station. Their cop shop was but a block from our cop shop and about the same square footage, although they had room for a holding cell at least. But it was a small holding cell, and Max Ulanowicz barely had room to sit down in the barred-in space, let alone stand up.

"Afternoon, Bob," I said as we entered his police station. He appeared to be the only officer on duty.

"Hey, Maggie."

"You know Hollis Jones, right?"

"Of course. Good to see you again. Did the city ever fix that set of potholes near your house?"

"They did," Hollis said. "But we waited two years for it to happen."

"I'm surprised they got to it that soon. Did the mayor drive up there and fall into one or something?"

"I didn't ask, but that's a pretty good guess."

"How's Mr. Ulanowicz been behaving?" I asked.

"I don't think he appreciates the size of our holding cell."

"Well, we're going to escort him to the courthouse and avail ourselves of one of their interview rooms." I turned to Hollis. "Would you mind cuffing Mr. Ulanowicz and taking him out to my vehicle? I need to talk to Bob about another matter."

"No problem."

I handed my Tahoe key fob to him, and he unclipped his handcuffs as Bob unlocked the cell.

Once Hollis and Max Ulanowicz had moved outside, Bob asked me what I needed to talk to him about.

"Sorry to be so mysterious. It's about Claire."

His face reddened. "My daughter?"

"Yeah."

"What is it, Maggie?"

"I'm assuming you know Jenna Rhinehart and Claire had a little set-to last year at school."

"No, I didn't know that."

"Jenna turned Claire and another girl in for smoking in the bathroom."

"I knew someone turned her and Tess Slater in for smoking pot, but I didn't know who."

"Here's the thing, Bob. Claire paid Jenna back recently. That's where that black eye of Jenna's came from."

"That's terrible. The Rhinehart girl has been through more than her fair share of hurt lately."

"Jenna didn't want to press charges, but I thought you should know."

"Well, thanks, I guess." He sighed. "Claire's starting college in LaGrande in January. Had to offer to buy her a car to get her out of this place, to go get an education and grow up. But she's damn well going to enroll in that school, I'll make sure of that. And she can forget about the car."

I nodded. "Do me a favor. Tell Claire I'm the one who let you know. You can also tell her I pressed Jenna to file a complaint, but she wouldn't."

"Will do."

"Thanks for your help today, Bob."

"Sure. And before I forget," he said, picking up two large evidence bags, the first containing Ulanowicz's wallet and items from his pockets. The second held the man's short-barreled rifle and the keys and sidearms he had collected from us inside Jacoby's Hardware Store. "The rifle wasn't loaded, if that means anything."

The three of us were quiet on the mile-and-a-half drive to Canyon City and the courthouse. We were directed to one of the interview rooms upstairs. A deputy led us there and unlocked the door. The place was cold and bare, except for a table and four chairs.

Hollis unlocked the handcuffs. "Have a seat on the other side of the table, Mr. Ulanowicz."

He did as he was told and sat staring through the small window at the dark clouds.

"When can I make a phone call?" he asked, turning to face us.

On the drive back from Granite, I had finally connected with Detective Bach. He was now in southern Oregon just outside Lakeview, so nowhere near John Day. Over speakerphone, we all agreed our strategy was to be straightforward with Ulanowicz.

"After our conversation is over," I said.

"Conversation?"

"Yeah. We know you're an undercover FBI officer collecting intelligence on Clifton Massey and his gang of seditionists."

The man smiled. "What makes you think that?"

"My partner here, Trooper Hollis Jones, is a miracle man when it comes to tracking down such details."

"Is that so?"

"That is so. Your supposed death down in Redding, California, was staged, and we're relatively certain the FBI has Earl Ziegler on ice so you can act as his replacement in the POSSE gang."

"You're saying I faked my death so that I could pretend to be this Earl Ziegler person?"

"That's right," I said.

"For what purpose?"

"To draw out Clifton Massey and capture him."

"What's a Clifton Massey?"

I turned to Hollis. "Tell him, Trooper Jones."

"He's a former police officer. Worked for a number of local jurisdictions in Idaho. Somehow, he wound up being influenced by someone, or some orthodoxy, or simply developed his own radical views of government, particularly the feds."

"There are thousands of nutcases like that in this country."

Hollis continued, "Eventually, he formed the Protective Order of Sovereign States Eternal—or POSSE—ostensibly to protect states' rights."

There was a pause.

"Does that sound about right, Mr. Ulanowicz?" I asked.

"I need to make that phone call."

"To whom?"

"My supervisor in the FBI resident agency in Redding."

I pulled out my Tahoe's key fob again. "Trooper Jones, would you mind retrieving the two evidence bags Officer Nolan turned over to us?"

After Hollis closed the door, Ulanowicz directed his blue-eyed gaze at me. "You're correct, Sergeant Blackthorne. Jones is a wonder at digging up information."

"He's one of OSP's secret weapons."

"OSP?"

"Oregon State Police."

"Of course. It's a world of acronyms."

"FBI. ATF. CIA. WTF."

"SOS. I definitely wish I'd met you before your fiancé came along."

"Yeah, well, I doubt it would've come to much."

"Oh?"

"I prefer people who are straightforward."

"So, I should've told you I was an agent with the Federal Bureau of Investigation the first time I met you?"

"I'm done with stupid questions today. Tell me how you learned Ziegler was planning to kill you?"

"You know I'm not at liberty to say."

"Let me guess, then. One of the POSSE gang members is an informant working for the FBI."

He maintained his well-practiced poker face, put his hands at the back of his neck, and stretched his folded arms taut as a pair of wings.

It was my turn to smile. "I have a better theory. One of the POSSE gang members is another undercover FBI agent."

I knew in my gut I was right.

Hollis returned with the evidence bags before I could take the line of questioning any further, placed them in front of me, and sat down.

I put on gloves and removed Ulanowicz's iPhone from one of the evidence bags.

"Open it and send it back to me," I said and slid it across the table.

He tapped the phone with his thumb, and it lit up. He passed it back to me.

"What's your supervisor's name, Mr. Ulanowicz?"

"Lewis Ingram."

"And what's his code name in your contacts list?"

"Beth Heppner."

"We're going to listen to both sides of the conversation." I found the name, put his iPhone on speaker, and dialed the number.

"Good afternoon," the professional voice said on the other end. It was a woman.

"Beth, this is Agent Smart."

"I'll patch you through, sir," she said.

"Thank you."

After a pause, a man came on the line. "Where the hell have you been, Max?"

"Well, right now I'm being interviewed by a couple of Oregon State Police officers."

"Oh, for Christ's sake. Tell me what the fuck is going on up there? I got a similar call from Agent Dalton earlier today."

24

LATE AFTERNOON, NOVEMBER 19

"Well, sir. I'm also on speakerphone, and the two officers are sitting here with me in an interview room at the county courthouse, where they had it in mind to stick me in jail."

"This is Sergeant Margaret Blackthorne, Oregon State Police. Here with my patrol partner, Trooper Hollis Jones."

"Blackburn, did you say?"

"Blackthorne, sir."

"Are you part of the homicide crew?"

"No, we're local officers. Detective Alan Bach of the Homicide Division is our lead in the investigation."

"Why am I not talking to Detective Bach?"

"At the moment, he's the lead in other homicide investigations elsewhere in the state."

"You're able to, uh, how shall I say, conduct a murder investigation?"

"Let's just say my patrol partner Trooper Jones and I are getting used to conducting murder investigations."

"I see. Well, it's not the most fun job in the world, I'd say."

"I guess if we'd wanted to have fun for a living, we would've chosen a different profession."

"You and me both, Sergeant. I assume you were the officers who visited with Agent Clyde Dalton today."

I glanced at Hollis. "Not that we knew he was FBI at the time, but yes."

"And as I understand it, this began with the murder of an Oregon State Police officer by one of the POSSE members, who was subsequently murdered himself?"

"Yes, sir," I said.

"Maxwell?"

"Here, sir."

"We shall be cooperating fully with Sergeant Blackthorne and Trooper Jones."

"Happy to, Special Agent Ingram. I think together, we can make considerable progress."

"And I think we have different aims," Ingram replied. "You're to keep your eye on the agency ball but pass on whatever information your Oregon State Police partners need to bring in a killer. If it happens to also serve our purpose, all the better."

"Got it, sir."

"Keep me apprised."

After hanging up, Ulanowicz looked squarely at us. "So you also wouldn't be surprised to learn a large part of Massey's and POSSE's platform is primarily to protect what they view as the rights of white citizens."

"I don't find it surprising." I turned to Holly. "How about you?"

"Hardly," he replied. "For one thing, I didn't see one person of color pictured on the bulletin sent out jointly by the FBI and the ATF."

"The bulletin. Is that what sent you two down this track, Trooper Jones?"

"The murder of our colleague initially sent us down this track."

"Right."

"And then Sergeant Blackthorne remembered that bulletin from last June."

"I have another question for you," I said. "Why keep using your own name?"

"Speaking of names, since we'll be working together, do we need to be so formal?"

"Most people call me Maggie."

"Yes, I remember. And your partner's name is Hollis. Anyway, you were right, Maggie. Clifton Massey had gotten wind of the fact that I worked out of the FBI's Redding office and called on Earl Ziegler to decommission me. Fortunately, we were able to neutralize Ziegler, put him on ice, as you said."

He paused.

"Is that it, Mr. Ulanowicz?"

"Maggie, call me Max, okay?"

"Sure. Max."

"You've already figured out there's a strong resemblance between Ziegler and me. The thing is, Massey had only met Ziegler once before, so even though I'm taller, I ended up being able to pass for the guy."

"Okay, but that doesn't answer my question."

"I was supposedly dead, right?"

"Yeah, Hollis found an article from the *Times Review* in Redding that told us, and probably told Massey at the time, that an accountant named Max Ulanowicz had been shot to death."

"So why not follow Massey to the eastern Oregon outback, pretend I was Earl Ziegler using my own name as an alias, get a job somewhere nearby, and wait for Massey to send me word when the time for our glorious uprising was nigh."

"You said Massey got wind you were in Redding and called on Earl Ziegler—who lived not far from there in the town of Weed, California—to assassinate you?"

"That's right."

"Why did he want you dead?"

"I was leading the FBI's surveillance team charged with keeping track of him in Redding. And I'm still in charge of gathering intelligence on him and the remainder of the POSSE crew, as well as hopefully preventing a large-scale armed insurrection."

"You guys don't have a great track record where armed insurrections are concerned," I said.

"I'd be the first to admit the bureau has a lousy track record when it comes to that."

"So there are other agents out there besides you and Dalton?"

"Yes."

"How did Massey learn you were surveilling him in Redding?" Hollis asked.

"I hope to be able to ask Massey that exact question one day."

"Speaking of being able to ask Massey questions," I began. "How does he set up a meeting with you, and how would he let you know the glorious uprising was nigh?"

"He doesn't send out messages on the dark web or communicate with me directly about when and where to meet. Doesn't own a phone or any computer as far as I know."

"Really?"

"Harder for someone to keep tabs on him that way. He mails me notes telling me when and where to meet. Dale residents' mail is sent to Ukiah, and since I work there, I can easily walk over to the post office and pick up whatever's in my personal mailbox."

"He'd send notes to you from where?"

"All over. Cryptic messages about when to meet him at the trailer."

"Why didn't you arrest him at one of these meetings?" Hollis asked.

Ulanowicz paused. "Our mission was to capture Massey *and* his men."

"And as long as he believes you to be Ziegler, you're assuming you're not vulnerable?"

"I always assume I'm vulnerable, Hollis. This is a dangerous job. Just like yours."

Holly shrugged. "Most of the time my work involves driving around the county on patrol and citing any scofflaws I meet up with."

"Well, I know you know this, but that doesn't mean your job can't be dangerous."

Ulanowicz punctuated that last statement with a yawn, after which he furiously rubbed his eyes with the palms of his hands.

"Sorry, I barely slept last night, and I've had nothing to eat today."

"Just one more question for you."

"Fire away, Maggie."

"Do you actually live in that trailer house in Dale, or is that also a ruse?"

He laughed. "I stay elsewhere most of the time, but I used it to keep an eye on Charlie Archer, as well as occasionally meet with Massey."

"Didn't you keep tabs on Archer by arguing with him over the phone?"

"Yeah, I'd call him on occasion from the old farmhouse I rent outside of Long Creek, hoping to track down where exactly Massey and most of his entourage are holed up in backcountry. But the guy had a hair-trigger temper, and about the only thing I learned from him was some new and unusual profanity."

"You heard Massey was in backcountry from informants, other agents, or both?"

"I wish we had informants."

"And Agent Dalton, who Hollis and I talked to earlier today out in Granite, does he lend Massey his red Honda on occasion?"

Ulanowicz appeared to be surprised. "How do you know about that?"

"I didn't know about that until you told me just now."

That puzzled the man.

"Believe it or not, we've interviewed several people. A couple of Dale residents recognized the photo of Massey and had seen him driving a small red car. One person was even able to ID it as a Honda." Talking to possible witnesses is something cops do when a homicide occurs, I was tempted to add.

"And Agent Dalton loans Massey his Honda to what, build trust?" Hollis asked.

"The chewing tobacco is a nice touch of authenticity," I said.

"How many agents are out there on watch?" Hollis continued.

"I'd have to get the okay from Special Agent Ingram before answering that question."

"Is there any intel suggesting Massey is recruiting new members?" I said.

"Not that I know of, or I should say not that we've uncovered."

"We spoke to the owner of the country store in Granite this morning. He contends Massey met up with Charlie Archer in his little diner on occasion."

"Yes, I know."

I locked eyes with the man. He clearly wasn't going to elaborate further.

"On another matter, Karl Jacoby filed a missing person report about you with my office yesterday."

"Poor old guy." Ulanowicz actually seemed concerned.

"Are you going to try and patch things up with him so you can continue working in his hardware store?"

"Does that mean I'm free to go?"

"Not unless you give me your phone number."

He listed it off, I dialed the number, and his phone rang.

Ulanowicz smiled again. "I'd like to have your numbers as well."

We each handed him a business card.

"I should tell you, if we determine that Massey *is* or is *possibly* Charlie Archer's killer, we're going to do everything we can to find him and bring him in for questioning."

"Would you let me know before you do that?"

"Well, Detective Bach will need to have the last word on that subject."

"That'll have to do, I guess. One other thing. From what I know about Mr. Massey, it would be verboten for anyone in his circle to kill a police officer."

"Hollis and I had wondered about that."

"Was it verboten because Clifton Massey had been a police officer himself?" Hollis asked.

"Maybe, but I think his primary concern would be to keep from drawing attention to POSSE and their possible location."

"That pretty much captures my thoughts exactly," I said. "Where's your Jeep parked?"

"In the lot at Chester's Market. I'd stopped to pick up something to eat when Officer Nolan spotted me."

"We'll give you a lift to Chester's."

"Thanks. But before we leave, I'd like to go wash up."

"Restrooms are down the hall and to your left."

He stood, moved from the interview room, and shut the door.

"God," I said after a beat, "this whole thing is beginning to seem like a bad movie."

We handed over Ulanowicz's belongings tucked in the evidence bags and dropped him off at the parking lot outside Chester's Market. I drove back to the station and scarfed down the other half of my sandwich before reaching out to Detective Bach. This time, I connected with him. Turned out he was pulling into Bend after his trek back from Lakeview in southern Oregon.

"How many miles did you add to your Interceptor this week, Al?"

"It's gotta be about five hundred fifty miles or so. And that's on top of what I put in traveling to John Day and then up to Dale."

"Ack."

"I'm taking tomorrow off, unless you need me over there." He sounded out of sorts, but I knew it was fatigue.

"Well, let me give you an update, and then you decide what makes sense."

It had only been a little over twenty-four hours since Al had taken off from Dale and driven the 160 miles to Prineville to help another murder investigation get back on the right track. He'd then left early this morning and driven the two hundred and twenty miles from Prineville to Lakeview for the same purpose. From there, he had driven the one hundred seventy-five miles back to Bend, where he was stationed.

In the interim, we'd learned quite a bit, including that Clifton Massey and likely most of the POSSE gang were holed up somewhere nearby. I gave him the lowdown about Hollis being able to figure out that Earl Ziegler was actually shorter than the Ulanowicz guy.

"So you're telling me Mr. Ulanowicz is not Earl Ziegler?"

"No, he's not. To Massey—and I assume the other POSSE members—he is, but in actuality, he leads a team of FBI agents actively pursuing the whole lot of them."

"Seriously?"

"He was also stopped this morning by the John Day Police on the basis of the APB we put out yesterday. Hollis and I interviewed him a short time ago."

"Okay."

"During that interview, Ulanowicz put in a call to the FBI's office in Redding, California, and spoke to his supervisor about the situation. Special Agent Lewis Ingram instructed Ulanowicz to cooperate with our investigation."

"And you're sure he was actually speaking with a special agent of the FBI?"

"I was the one who dialed the number, and we listened to their conversation over speakerphone and were ultimately a party to the discussion. Not only am I certain Ulanowicz works for the FBI, but we inadvertently spoke with someone this morning who turns out to also be on the same team of agents seeking out Massey and his gang."

"Well, Sergeant, I have to confirm all of this through the proper channels and get back to you. The names and titles are Special Agent Lewis Ingram and Agent Ulanowicz, whose first name is Max?"

"Special Agent Ingram referred to him as Maxwell."

"And the other agent?"

"Clyde Dalton."

"And Sergeant..." He was angry. "You're not to make another move on the case until I've confirmed all of this."

"Detective, I really did try to connect with you before now."

"I'm sure you did, but you should've spoken with me before interviewing Mr. Ulanowicz." Al paused. "I'm about a mile from my office, and I'll try to get everything confirmed tonight."

Bewildered, I sat at my desk. Had I fucked up the case and my career? That last, maybe, but I knew we'd done what we would've done had Bach been with us.

Hollis had listened to my side of the conversation. "We didn't do anything we shouldn't have, Maggie. Well, I might've. I went down a path I don't really have clearance to go down for some of that information."

"You do that all the time. The detective even knows it, I believe."

"It's probably because this involves the FBI, don't you think?"

"I guess."

"Which report should I work on, our trip to Granite or the discussion with Mr. Ulanowicz?"

"I'll write up the discussion," I said.

"Sounds good."

"I could use a stiff drink."

Holly smiled. "I hear you."

I had finished writing up the discussion with Ulanowicz and sat waiting for the next shoe to drop. Hollis had also completed his report on our visit to Granite and was going back over some of the research he'd come up with earlier in the day.

My gut was roiling, the effect of rapidly chowing down the rest of my sandwich, no doubt. I sipped some water to see if that would help, but no. I stood to take a walk in an effort to be distracted from my distractions and ease the stomachache.

My cell phone buzzed. It was Ulanowicz.

"Blackthorne," I answered.

"Got a call from one of my people. Something's up out in the hinterlands. Appears to be a gathering of the POSSE members. I'm waiting for my invitation."

"That was fast."

"A call's coming in. This might be it."

"Let me know."

His news didn't lessen my body's complaints or general anxiety. "Hollis?"

He looked up from his computer. "What's up?"

"That was Ulanowicz. Sounds like some possible POSSE action, but he got another call and had to go."

"He's calling back, though, right?"

"I believe so."

My desk phone rang. "Sergeant Maggie Blackthorne here."

"Sergeant, this is Sam Damon. Mr. Archer's sister has called and would like to claim her brother's body. I told her I needed to touch base with the local Oregon State Police."

"Let me check with the homicide detective. I'll get back in touch as soon as I can."

"Thank you, Sergeant Blackthorne."

I hung up as Ulanowicz rang in on my cell phone. "What's up?"

"Reunion time's tomorrow morning in an old ghost town out there.

You'll need a warrant from a local judge before we can turn him and any of his people over to you for questioning in Archer's murder."

"Which ghost town?"

"Susanville. You know where that is?"

"Yeah. What time's the party?"

"Eight in the morning. We're taking advantage of better weather and setting up out there tonight. My plan, if all goes well, is to bring him to you at the courthouse. But I'll let you know if plans change or the arrest goes south."

"Sounds good."

"Don't forget the warrant."

"Right."

I hung up as my cell phone rang again. Detective Bach.

"What's the word, Al?"

"Well, first is an apology. I'm run ragged, and I took it out on you. Second, I've spoken to Special Agent Ingram, and he confirmed that Agent Ulanowicz is in charge of the FBI unit keeping track of Massey and his people. He also said he spoke to you earlier today and let you know the FBI and the task force would cooperate with our investigation."

"And I was on the phone with Agent Ulanowicz just now. They plan to confront and capture Massey and other members of POSSE tomorrow morning at an old ghost town called Susanville out in some nearby mountains. They'll deliver Mr. Massey to us for questioning in Archer's killing."

"What time in the morning?"

"POSSE plans to meet up at eight o'clock."

"All right. I'm going home to get a hot meal and a good night's sleep. I'll do my best to be at your office early in the morning. I'd like to be there when Massey's questioned."

"One other thing, Al. Charlie Archer's sister would like to claim his body."

"I'm pleased the sister was located, but I'll have to pass that by my boss and the lab folks first."

"I'll let Sam Damon know."

"You and Hollis did good work today. I'll see you tomorrow, bright and early."

25

PRE-DAWN, NOVEMBER 20

My cell phone rang a little after four thirty a.m. Duncan bolted upright in bed, and I popped out from under the covers, grabbed my robe, and stumbled to the desk in the corner where I'd left the phone to charge. The name Ulanowicz shone brightly from the screen.

"Blackthorne here. Give me a second," I croaked and moved from our bedroom, down the stairs, and into the kitchen dining area. I turned on a light. "Did something happen?"

"Massey and his followers already decamped."

"And he didn't mail a note letting you know ahead of time?"

"Well, I haven't picked up my mail in a couple of days. I plan to make a trip to Ukiah and do that in about ten minutes. Anyway, a note from him aside, Massey may have heard I'd skipped town on Wednesday and that three Oregon State Police officers had paid a visit to the hardware store right before that."

"You think that prompted him to get out while the getting was good."

"Maybe."

"Where do you think he might be headed?"

"I have no idea, but my team and I are meeting at seven this morning to strategize and plan next steps. You and Hollis are welcome to join us."

"Where's the meeting?"

"My place in Long Creek," he said and gave me the directions. "Drive a non-police vehicle, if possible, and park inside the old barn. Wear street clothes just in case."

"In case of what?"

"In case we're tipped off as to their whereabouts and go confront them. If they see anyone looking remotely like law enforcement or driving a police vehicle, there'll be an all-out battle."

I wondered who might tip them off, but I let that go for the time being.

"I need to check in with the homicide detective leading our investigation. I'll call you back as soon as I can."

I hung up and dialed Bach's number. He picked up on the second ring and groggily barked his last name.

"Sorry to wake you, Al. I'm afraid there's been a change in plans."

"What's up?"

I told him what I knew and that Hollis and I had been invited to the FBI's seven o'clock strategy session.

"I won't be able to make it over there by then, but you and Hollis should go. Just keep me in the loop while I'm on the road."

"Will do. And if you want to reach out to us while we're on the way, I'll be in my personal rig, but I can connect with you on Bluetooth, of course."

"Why your personal vehicle?"

"To avoid attracting more attention than is wise under the circumstances, according to the FBI."

"I see. Can I give you some advice, Maggie?"

Like I could stop him from giving me advice? "Sure, Al."

"If you and the FBI team decide to go after Massey and his people with the assumption there will be a firefight, it almost guarantees one will happen."

"I don't know about Ulanowicz and his team, but I'm unlikely to ever assume that, Al. Which might be a different kind of problem given the number of weapons the group is reported to have collected. And there's the real possibility the whole crew might be long gone."

"Let's hope that's not the case."

I almost made a comment about the FBI pulling out all the stops but thought better of it. That might've made for a complicated discussion I didn't want to have.

"We'll keep you apprised, Al."

After hanging up, I stared at my reflection in the garden door windows. The blue-black darkness outside seemed relentless, the morning sun a long way off. I moved back upstairs momentarily overcome with despair. I wanted all of this to be over.

———

"Hey, babe," Duncan said as I crawled back under the covers and wrapped myself around him.

"Gotta go to work."

"You mean me?"

"I wish."

He pulled me closer. "Be careful out there."

"Have a good day."

I got back out of bed and again went downstairs, dialing Hollis's number on the way.

"Morning?" he said in a voice an octave lower than usual.

"Meet me at the office in an hour. We're heading to Long Creek."

"You keep taking me to all the hotspots."

"Yeah, we're meeting with Max Ulanowicz and his team at seven to strategize. Apparently, Massey and his gang flew the coop."

"See you in an hour."

"I'll explain when I see you, but dress in civilian gear."

We both clicked off, and I dialed Ulanowicz.

"Are you in?" he said.

"Yep, see you at seven."

———

By the time I got out of the shower, Duncan had decided to get up and fix us breakfast. He was in the kitchen frying potatoes and making a couple of omelets. I raced upstairs, put on a pair of warm leggings, a bulky sweater, and my old Jack Purcell high-tops. I grabbed the oversized varsity jacket I'd saved my allowance to buy when I played on the high school volleyball team. I was too short to be much of a spiker, but I'd had a dead-on serve. *Blackthorne* was embroidered in gold cursive on the front upper-left side.

I checked out my outfit in the mirror. I looked like a plump, jolly kid, not a cop.

Back downstairs, Duncan took a gander at my attire and laughed. "You're trying for the teenager look today?"

"No, but I'm going incognito and taking my Subaru Crosstrek."

"Is Hollis going with you?"

"He is. Want me to text you a photo of him in his civilian gear?"

"Only if he's wearing a varsity jacket too. Are you ready for breakfast?"

"I'm starving."

He handed me a glass of milk. "I'll be right back with our plates."

Glancing at my reflection in the garden door windows again, I decided I was an idiot. It was possible Massey or someone in his bunch of clowns knew there was an Oregon State Police trooper named Blackthorne stationed in John Day. I moved to the closet next to the front door and pulled out my wool peacoat.

"You decided the teenager look wouldn't work?" Dun asked.

I took a chair at the dining table. "Yeah. Plus I don't think I want to advertise my last name."

"Ah."

"Breakfast looks delicious."

"You might need a bit more salt."

I forked a mouthful from my plate. God, the man could cook. "Will you marry me?"

"Oh, sure. Will next Thursday work for you?"

"Sounds good."

"Are you certain you're going to have this case wrapped up by then?"

I sighed. "I'm hoping I'll have it wrapped up by end of day."

"End of what day?"

"This day."

He reached across the table and took my right hand as I forked another mouthful with my left hand.

"I love you more than anything. Please tell me you're going to be safe."

I finished chewing and swallowed. "As safe as I am on any given day, Dun. And I love you more than anything. I feel damn lucky to have you in my life."

"Same here, babe."

Hollis pulled up outside of our office and parked next to me. We both got out of our vehicles and walked to the front door.

"Where's your cruiser?" he asked as we stepped inside.

"No police rigs today."

"Got it. And I take it I'm riding with you."

"Yeah, I didn't think you'd want Lil to be without the Vanagon."

"Well, the Vanagon is about twenty years old and needs to be near a mechanic at all times, so that was a good call."

"On life support, huh?"

"Practically."

I peeked at the schoolhouse clock hanging on the wall. Five forty-five. "Let's take fifteen minutes to check email and pack up anything we think we might need today."

"Sounds good."

"You're wearing a shoulder holster, right?"

"Yep."

"I wish I knew what the game plan was for the day."

"Isn't that why we're heading to Long Creek? To talk about the game plan?"

"It is."

"Were you able to get Judge Campbell's signature on the warrant?"

I nodded. "And he didn't balk when he saw I'd had Sherry Linn make it out for the arrest of Clifton Massey and associates."

"So, he didn't care you couldn't name any of Massey's associates?"

"Nope. Especially after I told him they were all also wanted by both the FBI and the ATF."

"Makes sense," Holly said and sat down at his desk. "He'd want us to have the first crack at questioning Mr. Massey and his followers."

I moved to my desk and fired up the computer. "Speaking of Sherry Linn, I need to leave her a message about the two of us being out of the office this morning."

"Did you also mention POSSE and their sentiments to Judge Campbell?"

"Of course. But that was like pouring sugar on ice cream."

"Now that's some expression you came up with there, Mags."

"Oh yeah, the old noggin's on fire this morning."

"If you say so."

By six thirty, we were again winding our way north on Highway 395, this time headed to Long Creek and Max Ulanowicz's rented farmhouse. Sunrise was close to an hour away, so I was on the watch for mule deer breaking through the tall pines in an attempt to cross the road in front of us. It wouldn't do to total my little Subaru, not to mention kill an unsuspecting animal.

As we traveled, Venus—the morning star—lit up the sky and silhouetted the rugged mountains, mesas, and steep canyon walls. The sight was a wonder and gave me hope this day would bring good closure to events of the past eight.

That reverie of optimism was counter to my earlier despondency but certainly not the first time bearing witness to the beauty of this stark land moved me. Also not the first time my pregnancy sent me bobbing back and forth in a sea of dissonant emotions.

My phone rang. Detective Bach checking in. "Good morning again, Al."

"Have you arrived at the meeting spot?"

"We're still on the way but should be there soon."

"I'm on the road, too. But I had a thought."

"Let's hear it."

"Hollis is with you, right?"

"Good morning, Detective," he answered.

"Good morning, Hollis. So I was thinking the two of you could suggest to the FBI team a joint reconnaissance force with other relatively nearby Oregon State Police troopers as a possible tactic. That is, if it makes sense in this case."

"I guess my only concern would be what you mentioned earlier this morning."

"You mean my 'if you go expecting a firefight' comment?"

"Yeah."

"Well, I could enlist some troopers from Baker City who have good instincts in this kind of situation. I worked with a few during last summer's siege over federal lands in the Elkhorn Mountains."

"We'll offer up your suggestion, Al."

"All right, and in the meantime, I'll make a few calls and figure out who might be available."

Once we'd signed off, Hollis asked me what I thought of Bach's idea.

"I'm not sure what I think about it. But I'm beginning to realize that if we're heading back to the Desolation Ridge area and all those old mining and logging towns—not to mention the dense, steep forest—it could get tricky."

"Meaning?"

"You can easily get lost out there, or you can easily lose someone out there."

"So you're saying we're among those who can get lost out there?"

"And we could lose Massey and his men out there."

"Are you suggesting more OSP officers might not be a big help?"

"Hell, the two of us might not be of much help."

Long Creek was a lovely little burg and enough higher in elevation than John Day to get slightly more snow in winter. It sat in an upland valley surrounded by rolling hills and mountains in the distance.

Shortly before seven o'clock, I turned right onto Keeney Forks Road in the center of town and drove the four miles to the farmhouse Ulanowicz rented. As instructed, I parked inside the old barn.

Hollis and I took the steps up to the front porch, and I knocked on the door. Ulanowicz opened it immediately, and we moved inside.

"Glad you could make it. But I meant to tell you to come to the back door."

"I probably should've thought of that," I said.

"It is what it is. Anyway, let's go into the parlor so you can meet everyone."

Parlor? People still called it that?

We traipsed behind Ulanowicz and found four individuals sitting in comfortable-appearing furnishings and sipping coffee or black tea. I recognized Clyde Dalton and nodded. He smiled and offered to pour each of us a cuppa.

"I'd take a coffee, thanks," Hollis answered.

"I'd love some herbal tea if you have it."

There was a bit of a back-and-forth between Clyde and Max about whether or not herbal tea was available, but they managed to find some.

Hollis and I took a seat on a frilly settee and sipped our beverages.

"This is Sergeant Maggie Blackthorne and Trooper Hollis Jones, Oregon State Police and stationed in John Day," Max said, introducing Hollis and me to his team.

"You've already met Clyde," he continued. "And over there is Sue Rassmussen, and next to her is Oliver Wayne. And across the way is Ben Kennedy."

They didn't seem very friendly, but we didn't drive out here to make new friends.

Ulanowicz opened up the discussion. "We don't know very much so far, but here's what we do know. Someone took off with Clyde's Honda yesterday—probably in late afternoon—and didn't return it. It could've been a local, but Clyde doesn't think so."

"So you were right, Trooper Jones. I shouldn't leave my keys in the ignition," Clyde said. "Although, in my defense, that's what most folks in Granite do."

Max went on, "Whoever took it—and it might've been Clifton Massey himself—left it parked behind the Desolation Guard Station, where we all know Charlie Archer met his demise."

"Who discovered it there?" I asked.

He gestured toward the young woman on his team, who I'd noticed frequently attended to her oversized, dark-framed spectacles. "Sue here. She was posted near there last night."

"What did you find in your mailbox this morning, Agent Ulanowicz?"

"A crude photocopied flyer from Jacoby's Hardware Store naming Lyndon Cummings as the temporary clerk and announcing ten percent off of all merchandise purchased between Thanksgiving and Christmas."

"No note from Massey, then?"

"Nope."

"So you weren't invited to the glorious uprising after all."

Max's team laughed at that.

"Apparently not. Anyway, what's interesting about finding Clyde's Honda at Desolation Guard Station is that whoever drove it there *was able* to drive it there."

"Meaning?" Hollis asked.

"Meaning they likely didn't travel out there by any unpaved roads or rudimentary logging tracks."

"But someone could've hauled it there, right?"

"Why? And how, other than by hiring a tow truck and calling attention to where it was being taken."

I could see his point, and he was right. Whitey Kern owned the only towing service in the area, and he was aware someone had recently been murdered at Desolation Guard Station. He would've immediately alerted me about a request to move any vehicle to that location.

"Earlier this week, we arrested a couple of men who used a heavy-duty tow chain and a wench to move Archer's International Scout out of the forest. Couldn't someone have used similar tools to move the Honda over unpaved or rudimentary roadways?"

It appeared Hollis was still not satisfied with Agent Ulanowicz's reasoning.

"Again, why, Hollis? The keys were in the car."

"All right, I'll let it go."

Then one of the men we'd been introduced to earlier piped up. "On the other hand, Trooper Jones has a point."

"In that such a method of towing a vehicle is possible, I'll give you that."

I thought of something I intended to ask earlier. "An all-points bulletin has been issued, correct?"

"Special Agent Ingram was reluctant, but yes, an APB was issued."

"Why was he reluctant?"

"It means the end of this operation. There are...matters we haven't been able to resolve. That's all I can say about it, Maggie."

I indicated I understood, but I wasn't sure I did. "When you called me last night, you said Massey and his mob were planning to meet in Susanville at eight a.m. today. And then when you called me at four thirty this morning, you said they had already taken off. How were you sure about either?"

"Well, first of all, I'm never sure about the intel we get."

"I don't understand. You said you and your team don't have informants."

"I'm talking about the intelligence arm of our field office outside of Sacramento. They gather rumblings and follow what they assess as communication between parties, that kind of thing. They were very sure POSSE's departure from the area was imminent. Then Ben sent word a few hours ago they had gathered in Susanville around two this morning and moved out en masse."

I glanced over at the men we'd just met. "Were you present in Susanville?"

"I was posted close by," the young red-headed guy responded. "And like Max said, Sue was stationed near Desolation Guard Station while Oliver was at a spot called Galena."

"Special Agent Ingram needed to send more of you on this mission."

"He looked at the population size of Grant County and decided a team of five would be plenty," Max pointed out. "None of us understood the number of square miles of backcountry or the terrain, at least at the time. And then came the FBI staffing cuts."

"Speaking of the backcountry and terrain, Maggie was saying earlier this morning how someone could get lost out there or you could lose someone out there," Hollis put in. "Words to that effect, anyway."

Team Ulanowicz expressed their agreement.

"All the effort and time it seems you've put in on your operation only to see it shut down—Hollis and I would call that a deal."

"A deal?" Sue asked.

"You folks don't use that expression?"

"I guess not," she answered. "What does it mean?"

"Well, it's cop code for, um, a fucked-up situation."

There was an extended pause, and finally Ulanowicz took a breath. "I think we might agree with you. This is a deal, all right."

26

MORNING, NOVEMBER 20

We spent some time talking over a possible game plan, but without more to go on, we hadn't gotten remotely close to any kind of strategy for moving forward. We needed more information, beginning with the direction Clifton Massey and his entourage had headed. Determining that might take local intel as opposed to relying on the intelligence arm of the FBI's field office in Sacramento.

"I have a question for you, Max," Hollis said. "I just remembered I was able to dig up some information about Earl Ziegler. Specifically, he was spotted in Golden Pine, Idaho, around eighteen months ago, about the time Massey sent him to Redding to assassinate you. Was that you posing as Ziegler, or was that the man himself?"

"It was Ziegler. Why?"

"I have an idea," Holly answered. "Maggie, I don't suppose you brought your atlas?"

"I did, just in case we needed it to navigate through backcountry." I stood and put my peacoat back on. "I'll go get it."

"Through the kitchen and out the back door, remember?" Max reminded me.

I did so, slipped outside, and hurried to the barn. My phone buzzed as I stepped inside the Crosstrek.

"Sherry Linn?"

"Maggie, Harry said he needed to talk to you ASAP, but I wasn't sure if he should call you since you're meeting with the FBI."

"I stepped away for a minute, but I'll call Harry right now."

"Okay, he's right here."

"Thanks. You made the right decision to get in touch with me, Sherry Linn."

"Good. Be careful out there."

"You sound like Duncan."

"That's because we both love you," she said and handed the phone over to Harry.

"Maggie, I think we finally caught a break in Archer's murder."

I'd never known Harry to get excited about anything. But he definitely was.

"We could damn well use a break," I said.

"The lab rats in Bend ended up with a set of prints they couldn't identify. They weren't in Oregon LEDS, the western states fingerprint databank, or the FBI's fingerprint ID system. But one of the up-and-coming techs—a woman named Christine something—dug a little deeper, including checking out the state's Public Safety Standards and Training's records on cop candidates."

"Are you saying a set of prints from Desolation Guard Station were from an Oregon law enforcement officer or trainee?"

"A former cop, and an interested party."

"Holy shit, are you talking about Dirk Rhinehart?"

"I am."

"Mother of God. Christine needs to be promoted."

"She's thorough, all right. She also contacted the Forest Service to find out the last time Desolation Guard Station was thoroughly cleaned. Monday, November ninth."

"Four days before Archer was murdered. Man, Christine is damn meticulous."

"Thoroughly clean means walls, floors, all of it. The best thing is, she called me before going through channels. Otherwise, it might've been days before I got the news."

"Thanks, Harry. I've got to wrap up another matter, but I'll get on this ASAP."

"Keep me posted."

After clicking off, I grabbed the atlas and stepped out of my Crosstrek. A message had come in from Al Bach while Harry and I were on the phone. I listened to it while hurrying back to Ulanowicz's farmhouse.

The detective had gotten in touch with the Baker City OSP officers he'd worked with during the Elkhorn Mountains siege. Apparently, Clifton Massey and POSSE were already on their radar, so they planned to send a sergeant and two troopers to patrol the interstate and a couple of tributary routes.

I dashed through the back door and to the parlor, where everyone was waiting. "Sorry that took so long, but I had a call from the forensics guy we're working with on the Archer killing."

I could see Hollis was curious about what that conversation was about, but he took the atlas and quickly turned to the two pages he had in mind. He spread it out on a large coffee table. "Sue, what time did you station yourself near Desolation Guard Station yesterday?"

"Around eight o'clock last night. I didn't discover Clyde's Honda until early this morning."

"And Ben, how did you know Massey and company had gathered in Susanville and moved out around two this morning?"

"Well, I saw them. Recognized Massey and assumed he was traveling with his people."

"My guess is protocol doesn't allow you to go after them on your own."

"That's right, Hollis," Ulanowicz answered for the young agent.

"Which direction did they head?"

Ben peered at the atlas. "South on Road 45 toward Middle Fork Road."

"If they had cut to the north after meeting up with Middle Fork Road"—Hollis indicated the spot on the atlas page—"Oliver would have seen them moving through Galena, right?"

"That's right," Oliver said, passing his hand over his bald pate. "I'd camped out there and couldn't have missed them."

Hollis continued. "So here's a possible scenario, although there could be others. Massey takes Clyde's Honda late afternoon yesterday and drives to Desolation Guard Station. He leaves it parked behind the building so it's less noticeable, and he's picked up by the rest of the other POSSE members at some point, and they all drive south on Middle Fork Road."

"And then what, according to your hypothesis?" Max asked.

"Based on learning Earl Ziegler was reportedly in northern Idaho some time ago and knowing that the rural areas of that state tend to attract the kind of folks who might agree with POSSE's ideals, I did some research."

"Like I told you, research is one of Hollis's gifts," I put in.

"Please, keep going," Max said.

"I studied the backcountry roads and lesser-traveled highways out of here," he said, circling the swath of atlas territory he was referring to. "There's a decent route that could take a person from Granite or any of those old towns and hideouts all the way to northern Idaho without having to spend much time, if any, on an interstate freeway or major highway."

The parlor was quiet, so Hollis continued. "I speculate they took Route 7 from Austin rather than meeting up with Highway 26—less traffic, fewer police. They then headed toward Idaho, taking mostly back roads, forest tracks, and rural thoroughfares."

"If you're right, Hollis," I said, "that would take them largely through Baker County next door to Grant County and eventually across the Oregon-Idaho border."

"Yes, it would."

Ulanowicz raised one pointer finger. "They would have to cross the Snake River, right?"

"The best spot, if my research is correct, would be the Baker-Adams Bridge." Hollis turned to a different page of the atlas and put his finger on the spot. "Near the village of Homestead, just south of Hells Canyon."

"Remind me, what's the name of that mountain town in Idaho where Earl Ziegler was seen a year and a half ago?" I asked.

"Golden Pine."

"Maybe they're headed there, just not for the Flag Tenders Rendezvous."

"Flag Tenders?" Sue asked.

"I know about that...philosophy, I guess I'd call it," Oliver said. "Even researched the group, well, the individuals who subscribe to its amorphous ideals, if I can call it that."

"Hollis, remind me, what was their rallying cry?" I asked.

He traded looks with Oliver. "Go ahead, you've done more research about the group than I have."

Oliver raised his fist slightly and said, "Hold firm!"

"Do we know what's intended by that?" Max asked.

Oliver reddened. "Don't tread on me?"

"The saying on the Gadsden flag from the Revolutionary War?" I asked.

"Yes, Sergeant. Of late, in some quarters, anyway, it's come to be associated with far-right sentiments as opposed to freedom from the rule of the British monarchy," Max noted. "Which is fine as long as no laws are broken and the Constitutional rights of others are upheld. But some individuals have their own ideas about following laws and the Constitution."

Professor Ulanowicz would get on my nerves if I had to spend much time around him.

"So I've noticed," I said. "But I wasn't aware that historic saying had been appropriated. Anyway, do we have a game plan where POSSE is concerned?"

The agents sitting or standing in the parlor appeared to need a long nap. I could relate, but I was anxious to follow up on Harry's news.

"I think Hollis's theory that they traveled through backcountry and minor roadways—at least largely—is an interesting possibility," Max began. "And they would likely know or be able to connect with sympathetic individuals living in parts of northern Idaho, if that was their plan. What does the rest of the team think?"

Clyde stepped forward. "It's worth putting feelers out to our people closest to either side of the Oregon-Idaho border."

"I agree," Sue chimed in. "I also know an agent out of Coeur d'Alene who has a keen interest in all of these groups. You're all probably aware, but Coeur d'Alene's in northern Idaho, and there has been plenty of far-right activity in the area."

"Ben? Oliver?"

"I'd say make the call to our people closest to the Oregon-Idaho border," Oliver said.

Ben coughed, then put in his two cents. "I'm with you all on that. But, Max, I think we want to see what kind of intelligence we get from them before we pack up and head over there."

Ulanowicz nodded. "I'm not even sure Special Agent Ingram would approve of us heading anywhere. But I'll contact him right away and let him know our thinking."

"There is one other thing," I said. "Don't know if this will be helpful, but Detective Bach contacted the Baker City unit of the Oregon State Police. He'd worked with a few officers during last summer's confrontation over a parcel of grazing land in the Elkhorn Mountains."

"Yeah, we remember that. A tense few days," Max remarked.

"It was indeed. Anyway, two troopers and a sergeant from Baker City OSP are out on patrol in the area." That reminded me of a question I'd yet to ask. "Ben, how many vehicles were Massey and his entourage traveling in?"

"Just two old crew cab pickups. He was in the second truck, sitting in the front seat on the passenger side."

"And you weren't able to get plate numbers?"

"No. I was parked in my truck and camouflaged by trees and such. I heard this hideous racket, the two crew cabs—black or dark blue in color—plowing through the muddy roadway."

"But you were able to recognize Clifton Massey?"

"The light was on in the front cab, plus he was holding a flashlight and looking at something. I would've recognized him anywhere. That shock of white hair and the scar."

"Scar?"

"Down the right side of his face."

"I didn't notice a scar in his photo in the bulletin."

Ben looked over at Max, who nodded for him to continue.

"He got the scar at some point after that photograph was taken. We only knew it existed because of witness testimony."

"What happened to him? The scar, I mean."

"Supposedly, he did it to himself. In an effort to avoid being recognized. Me, I think he'd have been better off dyeing his hair."

As we pulled away from Ulanowicz's farmhouse, Hollis contacted our State Police colleagues in Baker City to report the probable color and make of vehicles in which Massey and his cadre of disciples had likely made their way out of the Umatilla Forest.

"All right, tell me what info you got from Harry earlier," Hollis said after signing off with Baker City.

"Guess whose fingerprints turned up in the batch he collected from Desolation Guard Station?"

"Crap, not Jenna Rhinehart's."

"Nope, but you're close."

"I'm assuming not the mother's. Maybe Lyndon Cummings?"

"No. They ended up with a set of prints they couldn't ID in the usual systems. So one of the more tenacious techs at the Bend lab checked out the state's Public Safety Standards and Training records."

I could hear Holly's brain ticking.

"You remember. All police trainees have to submit to a background check."

"Which includes fingerprints. And this lab tech found a match to Dirk Rhinehart's prints?" He was a hair shy of incredulous.

"That's right."

He placed another call. "Hey, Sherry Linn. We need you to fill out another search warrant. This time for Dirk Rhinehart's property, including his home, outbuildings, and equipment."

Hollis paused. "Yeah, that's right, the former Grant County sheriff. He lives near Mt. Vernon. Maybe try the phone book for his exact property address. If that doesn't work, try County Elections. He would've had to enter his address on the filing form he filled out when he ran for sheriff during the last election."

He paused a second time, listening intently.

"You should be able to find all of that online. If not Grant County's website, I know the Secretary of State's Office has all of that on theirs." He glanced at his watch. "We'll see you in about forty minutes or so." He hung up. "Now we're getting somewhere."

"Haven't we said that already in this case?"

"I'll admit, we've been flailing around some."

"And helping out the FBI."

"Speaking of people flailing around."

"Not nice, Holly. Not nice at all."

The sky had maintained its splendor into the full light of morning, now cloudless and ultramarine against the snow-covered Blue Mountains. It would've been a perfect day to drive to the John Day Fossil Beds, a nearby national monument showcasing the ancient leavenings of the Eocene Epoch's uplift and erosion. All of it riven and carved by its namesake river. Instead, we were driving back to our modular cop station in hopes of solving a murder.

Just north of Mt. Vernon, we passed Dirk Rhinehart's place. He was in the field next to his house standing atop a wagon, pitching alfalfa hay to his small flock of Suffolk ewes. With luck, he wouldn't head out somewhere before we had an opportunity to get Judge Campbell's signature on our search warrant and make it back out here.

Detective Bach had arrived by the time we got to the office. I parked beside his Interceptor, and Hollis and I both became aware of the unseasonably warm temperature as we stepped out of the Crosstrek.

"Man, it must be close to sixty out," Hollis speculated.

"Feels fantastic, all right." I opened the door to our cop shop. Unfortunately, the sunshine hadn't improved our dark, cramped quarters any.

"Hi, you two," Sherry Linn called out from her seat at the front counter.

Dark, cramped quarters aside, I didn't know what the hell we'd do without our office manager. Hiring her was the best thing I'd done since convincing Hollis to leave his Oregon State Police post in Burns and come work for me.

This morning Sherry Linn was decked out in the frilliest flower-print dress I'd ever seen and wearing a necklace made of large turquoise glass beads. But in case anyone, say, a member of the public, were to mistake her outfit and generally positive disposition as signs of her being an airhead, she had the chops and the vocabulary to make one regret making such an assumption.

"Your search warrant is set to go," she said. "I would've taken it to the judge myself, but I assume it's a sensitive matter. And he'll no doubt want an explanation for why you're asking to search the former sheriff's personal property."

"Thanks. We can always count on your good judgment."

"Are you getting close?" she asked.

I sighed deeply. "I sure as hell hope so."

"Are you feeling okay, Maggie?"

"Just tired."

Hollis was already sitting at his desk and chatting with Al Bach and Doug Vaughn by the time I made it back to our circle of desks.

"How's everyone this morning?" I asked.

"The trip was long," Al put in, "but I'm enjoying the weather."

"I hear you about that."

"Maggie, I was about to drive out to Seneca and over to Izee. Haven't been out that way for a while."

"Sounds good, Doug," I said. "I'm going to head home and change clothes, and Hollis, you'll want to do the same thing. Then we should go see Judge Campbell after that."

"What's up with Judge Campbell?" Al asked.

"Sorry, Al." I sat down at my desk. "Somehow I thought I'd called you and given you the news from Harry Bratton."

The detective looked concerned. "You seem like you're running on empty?"

"Not quite. But I would like to get this investigation over with."

"Yeah, me too. So what's the news from Harry?"

"The lab in Bend was finally able to track down the owner of the final unidentified set of prints found at Desolation Guard Station."

"Oh?"

"Former Grant County sheriff Dirk Rhinehart."

He was taken aback. "Well, that's strange."

"Not if you think about it. Remember, his daughter had been beaten by Archer and left to fend for herself out in the Umatilla Forest."

"Of course. Why didn't we consider him a suspect before?"

"Well, as problematic as he was as our sheriff, none of us would want to believe a former law enforcement officer would murder anyone. And there still could be a legitimate reason why he had gone out there."

"Like what?" Hollis chimed in.

"I don't know, but I do know I need to keep an open mind since I already dislike the guy quite a bit."

Holly shrugged. "Copy that."

"All right," Bach began. "Do what you need to do. Then let's go talk to that judge as soon as we can."

A wave of nausea caught me by surprise. "I'll be right back," I said, moving from my desk chair and pacing to the lavatory in back.

I locked the door and peeked at my reflection in the mirror above the sink. "Fuck, you look like shit, Blackthorne."

27

MID-MORNING, NOVEMBER 20

On my return from the lavatory, I found my three male compadres and Sherry Linn waiting for me, seemingly worried. No longer nauseous, I'd consumed a Dixie cup of water and attempted to pull myself together before I rejoined the crew.

I raised my hands, not in surrender but simply as a gesture to encourage everyone to calm down. "I'm fine. Just pregnant. Plus, I've been up since four thirty this morning. And right now, I'm going home and changing into my uniform, and I'll be back as soon as I can."

I checked my posture, walked through the office, and opened the front door. I hadn't noticed Hollis shuffling behind me until I stepped outside.

"Are you following me?"

"No, Sarge. I'm going home to change into my uniform."

"Wasn't very bright of me to not suggest we bring our uniforms to the office when I called you this morning."

"Most people aren't very bright that early in the morning."

"I love you, Holly."

"I know. See you in half an hour or so."

Motoring along Canyon Creek to the bridge that took me home, I lowered the driver's-side window to let the scent of late autumn fill my Subaru while the cool breeze fussed with my hair. Today could be the last day of full sun we might see until early spring, and I wanted, and needed, to take advantage of it.

Raleigh Cat was happy to see me, and I spent a few minutes entertaining him with a belly scratch before going upstairs and changing into my uniform. On the way back through the great room, I ducked into the kitchen and snared the sack lunch I'd thrown together earlier—and promptly forgotten to take with me—out of the refrigerator. I locked the house and hopped into my cop Tahoe feeling considerably more energetic.

I snacked on the carrot sticks I'd fetched from my lunch bag and put in a call to Sherry Linn asking her to have Al and Hollis meet me at the courthouse with the search warrant. Soon thereafter, I pulled into the asphalt parking lot and waited for them to arrive.

Bach drew up next to my rig several minutes later, but I could see he was engaged in a conversation over his police radio. Hollis got out on the passenger side of Al's vehicle and joined me.

"Looks like the team from Baker City stopped one of the crew cabs POSSE was traveling in," Hollis said. "Fortunately, it was the one Massey was riding in."

"That's terrific. If our discussion with Rhinehart comes to nothing, we'll take a drive to Baker City, assuming the detective is on board with that."

"I'd think he would be."

After Al signed off on his radio conversation, the three of us stood in the parking lot for a few minutes and discussed the capture of Clifton Massey and three of his followers.

"The FBI agents you met with this morning were on their way to Baker City. Apparently, they're planning to extradite Mr. Massey and the other men to California in the next few days. So, if we decide to question any of them about Mr. Archer's homicide, we'll need to do so right away."

"Depends on how our conversation with Rhinehart turns out, don't you think?"

"I don't disagree with you, Maggie. So let's go talk to the judge and get on with it."

The three of us crossed the parking lot and headed inside the courthouse. We were lucky Judge Campbell wasn't presiding over cases when we arrived. However, he was shut up in his office with the door closed. His receptionist had apparently gone on her lunch break, but even knowing he generally insisted on privacy, I knocked. Twice.

He finally opened the door, napkin in hand and a spot of mayo on his chin. The good judge was not much older than me, and I vaguely remembered him from my high school days. He had been a shy, gangly teenager who was one of the few to go to college from our town, let alone end up in law school. He moved back to John Day years before I did and had aged into a tall, frail-looking bachelor.

"Maggie?" he said and wiped his narrow lips and chin.

He never referred to me as Sergeant Blackthorne unless I was testifying in his courtroom or was present in case my testimony was needed.

"I apologize, Judge Campbell." I indicated the others standing behind me. "I'm here with Trooper Jones and Homicide Detective Al Bach."

"And this can't wait?"

"We're hoping to get your signature on another search warrant."

"Another one so soon?"

"Yes, sir. Another one having to do with our murder investigation."

He opened the door wider. "Let's all take a seat at my conference table."

His conference table appeared to be where he had been eating his lunch, I now saw. He moved to the opposite end of the table away from what remained of his lunch, and the three of us took a seat near him.

"Let me see the warrant, please."

I passed it to him. And as soon as he unfolded it and began reading the text, he sent me a blank look. "You'll definitely need to explain this to me."

"Mr. Rhinehart's fingerprints were found in that old Forest Service building where Mr. Archer was murdered."

"Well, there could be any number of explanations for that."

"You're right, sir. But there is a link between former sheriff Rhinehart and Mr. Archer."

The judge shook his head. "Help me understand. I know Mr. Archer shot and killed your colleague, Trooper Mark Taylor. And I know Mr.

Archer was subsequently found shot to death in a building in the Umatilla Forest, but that's all I really know."

"Archer had driven out to the forest after killing Mark Taylor, but he'd taken his live-in girlfriend with him. The reason Trooper Taylor had gone to Archer's home in the first place was because a neighbor had called in a case of domestic violence in progress."

"I still don't understand what this has to do with Dirk Rhinehart."

"The woman Archer was abusing, had abused severely, is Rhinehart's daughter."

The judge's eyes widened. "Dear lord." He pointed at the container of pens in the center of the table. "Please pass me a pen, Hollis."

Judge Campbell took the pen and signed the warrant, and the three of us stood.

"Thank you, sir," Al said. "I'd also like to apologize for interrupting your lunch."

"Appears it was necessary, Detective."

The detective sent him a respectful nod, and we moved from the room.

Bach following close behind me, the three of us arrived at Dirk Rhinehart's small ranch five miles northeast of Mt. Vernon. His acreage sat between Beech Creek and Highway 395, and he obviously took great care of his property—house and barn freshly painted, no rusted-out farm equipment, and his classic 1969 Ford pickup truck was shiny as new.

I'd never been invited to his home, but I'd heard from Dorie that he was a meticulous housekeeper, something that was apparently common knowledge in church-lady circles. I'd never been tempted to ask how any of the church ladies had become aware of this detail, but I suspected its discovery subsequently required a long prayer session or two.

As we pulled onto the dirt road leading to Rhinehart's house, I noticed him driving his all-terrain vehicle and towing a cart across the field where he'd earlier been feeding his sheep. He sped up when he noticed two Oregon State Police rigs pulling up to his house.

A few days ago, I had encouraged Al to take the lead in our discussion with Rhinehart, and I let him know the man had very little respect for Hollis and me. The detective had acknowledged bigotry and racism were problematic among the rank and file in law enforcement.

I almost asked why something wasn't done about that, but I'd worked in a paramilitary organization long enough to understand that *baby steps* was a euphemism for *not in our lifetimes*.

Hollis and I flanked the detective, who stood slightly ahead of us as we waited for Rhinehart to pull up in his driveway. As he did, he made sure he maneuvered the cart so that it ended up being parked squarely in front of us. He apparently didn't want us to miss out on his gruesome cargo—one of his ewes and my cougar nemesis. Both had been slaughtered; the sheep clearly by its predator, and the wild cat by Rhinehart and his gun.

The man hopped off of his ATV and stood on the other side of the cart from us, smiling.

I cringed at the sight of the cougar's long yellow teeth. "Guess you taught that guy a lesson."

"Son of a bitch killed one of my best breeders."

Al put out an arm. "Detective Alan Bach."

Rhinehart shook his hand. "Nice to meet you. You from the Patrol Division?"

"Homicide."

"Oh?"

"Your fingerprints were found inside Desolation Guard Station, where your daughter's live-in boyfriend, a Mr. Charles Archer, was slain. We're here to question you about that, and we have a warrant to search your property." Bach handed over the document.

"That chicken-shit Campbell signed it?"

"Judge Campbell signed it." Al put on gloves, and Hollis and I followed suit.

"So search away, since I don't seem to have a choice," the man said.

"In the meantime, we'll take temporary possession of your weapon." Al was as cool as a cucumber. "Remove the gun and holster. Slowly."

Rhinehart did as he was told.

"Hand it carefully to Sergeant Blackthorne."

As he passed me the leather sheath and fat handgun, his bloodshot eyes burned through me.

"You'll regret this," he told Al. "I'm a personal friend of Superintendent Bronson's."

"Give him my regards next time you speak to him," Bach replied wryly.

God, I so wished someone had been recording this.

"Trooper Jones," the detective said. "Pat down Mr. Rhinehart."

"Yes, sir." Hollis began the body search.

"Oh, for shit's sake," the man whined.

When he'd completed the pat-down, Hollis turned to me. "Sergeant, shall I lock the weapon in your vehicle?"

I passed him the holstered weapon and the keys to my Tahoe. "I'd appreciate you retrieving my pack as well."

Once Hollis returned, the detective asked Rhinehart to lead the way. We followed him inside, and as I expected, the church ladies had pegged it correctly. The place was spotless. Sterile was probably the more apt description.

The front room contained two couches, side tables, lamps, a bookshelf, a dining table, a locked gun cabinet, and a few antiques. But most notably, a gargantuan photograph of Sheriff Rhinehart on horseback hung on the wall. In it, he carried an American flag while riding in a parade during a previous '62 Days gathering. An event held annually in Canyon City in celebration of the 1862 discovery of gold and the mining boom that followed. A giant three-day drunk fest was more like it.

"Have a seat, Mr. Rhinehart," Al said.

He sat on one of the couches, and the detective sat across from him. Hollis and I took the stairs to the second floor. Once there, my partner signaled for me to join him in one of the two bedrooms. He all but closed the door.

"The gun he used to kill the cougar?"

"Yeah?" I said.

"A Glock 29 ten-millimeter semiautomatic. Sub-compact."

"Okay?"

"A big-bore handgun, like the weapon used to kill Archer."

"That alone proves nothing."

"Well, of course not."

"But we could call Harry and tell him we need his ballistics expertise out here."

"My thought exactly."

"I'll make the call. Meanwhile, you check out the other bedroom." I brought up my cell phone while Hollis moved into the hallway.

"Maggie?" Harry answered.

"Hey, do you have the ability to test a weapon remotely?"

"Remotely? You mean bring equipment to a different location?"

"Yeah, as in run a test on a specific weapon to see if it matches what the lab in Bend came up with regarding the big-bore handgun used in Archer's murder?"

"I can. Ballistics are my true specialty, but it would take some packing up of equipment. Where would I need to go?"

"Dirk Rhinehart's place outside of Mt. Vernon."

"The dude who used to be the county sheriff?"

"One and the same."

"Email me the address, and I'll try to be there in an hour."

"Thanks, Harry. And text me when you get here so I can give you the all clear." I hung up, emailed the address, and turned my attention to the room. It was empty except for the bare hangers in the closet.

I stepped inside the bedroom Hollis was searching. It held a twin bed, a dresser, and some of the frilliest, pinkest accoutrements I'd ever seen. I would've killed to have had a room like this as a kid. This one had all of the early 2000s toys targeted at little girls, including a set of Troop Groovy Girls, all of it preserved and well cared for. Waiting for six-year-old Jenna to come home to daddy.

"The man should be embarrassed," I said.

"It does reinforce what you've inferred about the guy. The outraged father going after the man who beat his daughter."

"Oh yeah, he had plenty of motive for killing Archer. But it doesn't explain all of this." I signaled the over-the-top froufrou.

"Well, sometimes there's no satisfying you, Maggie."

"I know. But people should try harder."

The second-floor memorial to Jenna Rhinehart's childhood contained nothing of interest homicide-wise, so Holly and I made our way back to the first floor to scope out the remaining rooms.

"Everything copacetic, Detective Bach?" I asked.

"You could bring us some water."

"Sure. Coming right up."

I found the kitchen and filled two glasses with cold water. Looking out the window over the sink, I watched a few dark clouds sweep across the mass of blue sky above a thicket of lodgepole pine. The days preceding winter solstice had grown shorter and shorter, as was the natural state of things, but every year I seemed to forget the inevitability of that fact, at least until the Earth and sun sent a joint signal to remind me.

Passing back through the kitchen, I noticed a stack of assorted papers affixed to the refrigerator with a large magnet. That was the closest thing to messy I'd noticed in the entire house, and still it was damned neat. I decided I'd begin my downstairs search perusing through those after I delivered the water.

I placed the glasses of water on the table between Al and Rhinehart. Hollis was not to be seen, so I assumed he'd begun searching one of the other first-floor rooms.

Returning to the kitchen, I closed the door and began going through the paperwork hanging from the outside of the refrigerator. Near the top of the documents clipped together by an Oregon Sheriffs Association magnet was a Forest Service map of Desolation Ridge and the surrounding expanse of land, including Road 10 and the area where Desolation Guard Station was located.

The next item in the stack was even more interesting, and more familiar. He'd attached a copy of the joint FBI and ATF bulletin alerting law enforcement to be on the lookout for Clifton Massey and POSSE.

"Were you thinking of joining them?" I said under my breath.

I reminded myself that the bulletin was issued last June, a couple of months before a group of Grant County voters launched an effort to recall our ignoble sheriff. But the man took the hint he was no longer wanted by the electorate and resigned. The Sheriff's Office no doubt had also received the bulletin, and Rhinehart likely recognized the illustration of Archer and secured a copy of it for his own purposes.

I moved to the kitchen table and began going through the rest of the documents, but other than a graphic article about neutering male lambs, nothing popped out at me.

I looked at the two bills clipped atop the map. One was from the local water district, and the other was from a dentist in John Day. Rhinehart had opened them and overlaid them, along with their return envelopes, on the map. Both were dated for last Friday. Which meant they had arrived in his mailbox after Archer was killed.

"Sarge?" Hollis whispered behind me.

I was deep in thought and hadn't heard the door being opened, so I jumped, of course.

"Are you finding anything interesting, because I'm not," he said.

"Yeah, look at this." I removed the bills and revealed the bulletin and the map.

"Now that's interesting."

"I haven't checked drawers and cupboards yet. Let's do that before we have a chat with Rhinehart."

Hollis looked through the broom closet and cupboards while I went through the drawers and open shelves. The room appeared to be set up by an old bachelor who didn't seem to do much eating in or entertaining, given the dearth of cookware, utensils, or dishes.

That said, Hollis found something interesting on the top-most shelf of the last cupboard at the end of the row of cupboards. There appeared to be a false door at the back of the empty cupboard. It was fronted with small shelves similar to a spice rack but without spices or anything else stored there. He'd inadvertently given the door a little push and heard a latch give way, and the false door opened a crack.

"Now why would he have a false door?" Hollis said.

"Is there a safe or something built into the wall?"

He pulled up his Maglite and directed the beam inside. "Nope. Just a cardboard box."

"So pull it out and check the contents already."

He opened the door fully and brought out the box. "Here, you take the first peek."

I peered inside and examined some of the contents. "Good God."

Hollis took his turn scoping out the items Rhinehart kept stored behind a false door at the back of his kitchen cupboard. "Oh, my."

"Who knew?"

"That Sheriff Rhinehart was a collector of kiddie porn? No one, is my guess."

"My question was rhetorical, but I'm betting someone knew about his fetish. In fact, I'm almost sure of it."

Harry Bratton had arrived slightly earlier than expected, and his text letting me know interrupted my conversation with Hollis.

"Ah, Harry's here," I said and sent a message letting him know I was on my way.

"Before you retrieve the Glock semiautomatic for Harry, tell me what you meant when you said you were almost sure someone knew about Rhinehart's, um, proclivities?"

"Well, for one thing," I said, indicating the box full of smut. "These all appear to be old VCR cassette tapes, so he's been at this for some time, assuming he's still a connoisseur. His ex-wife, Anita, might've known. And Jenna, too. And if Jenna knew, then maybe Charlie Archer knew about it. Here's a theory. Somebody out there discovered his cache of child pornography or was possibly supplying him with this crap. But someone, probably more than one someone, knows or did know."

"All right, we can talk all this out later. In the meantime, give me the keys to your Tahoe, and I'll get the gun for Harry."

"Thanks, and I'll finish going through the kitchen drawers."

After Hollis left the room, I realized I'd gone through all of the drawers already without finding anything of interest. But I had neglected to ask him if he had explored Rhinehart's bedroom or den, or wherever he kept his computer, television, or both.

The man had no doubt moved on to more sophisticated viewing

systems, and the thought of finding even more evidence of his vile pastime nauseated me to the core. Except now was not the time to fixate on my disgust; now was the time to home in on a possible killer.

I decided to check on Detective Bach, still sitting with our suspect in the front room, but as I opened the door, I noted they were no longer there. I stepped out of the kitchen and began searching for the two men.

"Over here, Maggie," Al called from a short hallway.

I moved closer.

"Mr. Rhinehart needed a restroom break."

"You're not worried he's got a gun stashed in there?" I whispered.

"I asked Hollis to check it out before he went outside. But I decided not to ask him why he was going back outside."

"Harry's here," I said, whispering again.

"That's a smart move."

"Harry's a smart guy."

Rhinehart knocked from inside the bathroom. The detective stepped closer to the door and told him to come on out, hands over his head. He did so, which surprised me some, and I wondered if he might be thinking what I was thinking. That he was on his way to living out the rest of his days in the Oregon State Penitentiary.

"Are you done yet?" Rhinehart asked me. "I've got better things to do this afternoon."

I held my tongue, only because I wasn't quite ready to drill him about his penchant for child pornography and possibly murder.

"Soon, Mr. Rhinehart. And then we'll have some questions for you."

I wouldn't know how to describe the look he'd just given me. Unfriendly, for sure, and with a mix of ice in his veins.

28

AFTERNOON, NOVEMBER 20

Once Hollis returned, I signaled for us to step outside for a brief conversation on the porch.

"What's up?" he said when we were alone.

"Where's Harry?" My voice quivered in the unexpected chill.

"He went to find someplace safe and out of earshot to test the gun."

"Makes sense. I wanted to ask you if you went through all the rest of the rooms on the first floor."

"Yeah, but given what we found in the kitchen, we should re-check the bedroom. That's where he keeps his computer."

"Makes for the best bedtime viewing, I've heard."

"Could be."

"All right, let's double-check the bedroom and move on to questioning the dude."

"He'll want an attorney present," Holly speculated.

"Probably. But we can already arrest him on child pornography charges. So, we'll start there."

We re-entered Rhinehart's abode and walked directly to his first-floor bedroom. Because the curtains were drawn and the afternoon light was already waning, I turned on the light. The space reeked of man cave and was set up with a large screen on the wall and a projector for whatever movie or television show his computer could access online, or had been previously downloaded and saved, or could be seen via DVD. The bed hadn't been made, proving the guy wasn't a complete neat freak, and that he was a fan of silk sheets.

Hollis sat down at the ladder-back chair tucked into the cramped table where Rhinehart kept his computer. "I didn't check it out earlier because I didn't think there was real reason to. We now have a real reason."

"No shit. Shall I get his password for you?"

"His initials and address number. I'm already in, and he's got a bunch of sites open."

"I sometimes think you're too good at this, but then I remind myself we're on the same side."

"All right, this guy makes me want to puke, and I've seen enough."

Hollis was normally far from being a judgmental sort, more than anyone I'd ever encountered, but it was refreshing to realize even he had his limits.

"Are you doing okay?" I asked him.

"No, but I will be once he's locked up. And I'd be even more okay if the people who produce this crap were locked up too."

"I'm afraid there are too many sickos out there."

"So I've noticed. Let's go talk to the scumbag."

———

Hollis stayed in the living room with our suspect, leaving me to debrief Detective Bach, but he deftly made a show of tightening his holster and looking blankly at Rhinehart before Al and I moved to a spot where we could speak privately.

We met in the kitchen, and after I explained what Hollis and I had discovered about Rhinehart, Bach was visibly shaken.

"Of all the evil in this world…"

"I know."

He sighed deeply. "What's your game plan, Maggie?"

"I guess I thought you would suggest what that should be. Wait, that's not exactly true. I think we should start with questioning him about the pornography. He'll be on the defensive and possibly more worried about the world knowing he's a devotee of watching children being molested and raped than he would be about anything else."

"So much so that he wouldn't mind turning out to be the hero who took revenge on the man who brutalized his daughter."

"You got it."

"You and Hollis, you're a really good team."

"Thanks, Al. But I wish we had been more attuned to Jenna's trauma."

I wasn't going to say it at this juncture because I hoped beyond all measure it was a wickedness she had been spared. But it would not surprise me if she had been a victim of her father's evil, or that other children might've been. And if so, why hadn't anyone brought that news to light?

"Let it go and do your job, Blackthorne," I said.

"Did I say something wrong?" Bach asked.

"Sorry, Al. I was just mulling over my own anger about all of this when I should just be doing my job. And it's rather past time to start our interview, I'd say."

"I'm ready whenever you and Hollis are."

"I've re-thought where we should start our questioning."

"Oh?"

"Yeah, we might as well start by asking him how his prints ended up inside the guard station. In part because earlier today, Harry learned the place was thoroughly cleaned on Monday the ninth. But I doubt Rhinehart knows that."

"Where did Harry hear about that?"

"Same lab tech who ID'd the prints called the Forest Service and asked about the cleaning schedule."

"He's thorough."

"Careful there. The lab tech is a woman named Christine."

"I'm old, but that's no excuse. Christine's thorough."

Detective Bach told Rhinehart we were all moving to the dining table to conduct his interview. He wasn't pleased about that, but then the three of us weren't looking to please him.

I retrieved my recorder from my pack, placed it in the middle of the table, turned it on, and read Rhinehart his Miranda rights. He signed a waiver and didn't ask for an attorney, but that didn't mean he wouldn't as we went along.

"Sheriff, how is it that your fingerprints ended up inside Desolation Guard Station?" I asked him.

"I was out there a couple times over the years looking for different suspects and people who were reported missing. That kind of thing."

"But that all ended after you resigned."

"What's that got to do with anything?"

"Have you been out to the guard station since your term as sheriff ended, what was it, six weeks ago?"

"No, I don't believe so."

"I have a question, Sheriff, if I may," Hollis said. "Did you keep a daily log while you were the elected sheriff?"

"Of course."

"So we would be able to look through public records, in particular the county's integrated electronic records management system, and be able to verify when and possibly why you traveled to Desolation Guard Station while you were at the Sheriff's Department?"

In a different setting, I'd be laughing my ass off at Holly's question.

Rhinehart blinked. "I guess."

Hollis continued. "Good to know there's a way to figure out a public official's coming and going. For instance, the Oregon State Police uses such a system. It tracks our emails too. Does the county's?"

"I suppose so."

"Thanks for bringing that up, Trooper Jones," I said. "The system also tracks our internet searches and activity. For instance, if I took a break and used my work computer to order something online, technically any member of the public or press, say, could learn from which company I'd ordered and also what I ordered."

I might have been exaggerating with that little digression, but it seemed

Hollis and I were making the point that when you work for the government, your online activities can be tracked and traced. And our suspect appeared to be thinking long and hard about that possibility.

"How easy is it for someone to get at that kind of information?" the detective asked.

"I could eventually dig it up," I said. "But for a savvy tech person—such as any teenager or Trooper Jones here—it might take four or five minutes."

Rhinehart cleared his throat. "Where is all of this going?"

"Well, for one thing, some people are really tenacious and eager to get to the bottom of things. For example, the State Police lab technician who identified your fingerprints also contacted the Forest Service. She learned that Desolation Guard Station received a thorough cleaning last Monday, the ninth."

"Proving what?" Rhinehart said.

Was he not listening?

"That you left your fingerprints at the guard station sometime after the ninth and before we found Charlie Archer shot dead on the thirteenth."

"So I visited after it was cleaned. So what? Doesn't prove I killed Archer."

"You told us you hadn't been there recently," Hollis pointed out.

"So I misremembered."

"You can't say you didn't have a motive for killing him. I know I was pretty shaken when I found your daughter wandering around out in the forest, beaten and bruised by the guy and in a state of shock," I nudged.

"Yes, that was a terrible, terrible thing. And I love my daughter, but I didn't kill her boyfriend."

"Do you love her?" I asked.

"What kind of a question is that?"

"Or do you desire her?"

He turned to Al. "Detective Bach, this questioning is out of line."

I wasn't about to let the detective interrupt the interview just yet. "We found your trove of child pornography."

I allowed that bit of news to drop before continuing.

"Did Charlie Archer know about that? I ask because we found those old cassette tapes in the box you tried to hide behind a false door inside your kitchen cupboard. That makes me think your ex-wife knew about your, shall we say, predilections. Maybe Jenna did too."

"But those tapes don't belong to me."

"Oh, who might they belong to?"

"I can't tell you that. I'd be betraying a friend."

"I happen to know you don't have any friends. Well, let me qualify. Somebody in the Sheriff's Office passed you the joint bulletin from the FBI and ATF with Charlie Archer and company's likenesses on it. Doesn't mean whoever did that is a friend, but they did you a favor. In addition, you left several kiddie porn sites open on your computer. So what friend do *those* belong to?"

"It doesn't mean anything."

"Other than you're under arrest for possession of child pornography."

I gave Hollis the nod.

"My pleasure, Sergeant Blackthorne," he said, rose from his seat, and handcuffed Rhinehart to the chair he sat in.

"You three are awfully smug. Lots of people watch this stuff." The fuck was smiling.

I couldn't help myself. "I love it when someone commits a heinous crime and tries to justify it with the *lots of people do it* defense."

"Who am I hurting?"

"Mr. Rhinehart, may I suggest you refrain from talking," Bach said.

"And if you don't know the answer to your own question, then you're sicker than I thought." Again—couldn't help myself.

"I need to use the restroom again," Rhinehart said.

Al surprised me. "It's not been very long. Let's finish the interview first."

"I might piss on the floor."

"The place doesn't belong to me, so if it comes to that, so be it."

Even more surprising.

There was a knock at the front door. I'd turned off my phone, but I was certain it was Harry come to give us a report regarding the forensics testing of Rhinehart's weapon.

"I'll get that," Hollis said. He moved to the front porch.

"What's that about?" Rhinehart asked.

"We'll soon find out," I said.

"I have a right to know who's knocking at my own front door."

I'd more than had it with the dude. "All right, I think it's UPS, maybe FedEx." Come to deliver justice, I hoped.

Hollis re-entered the house and again sat back down at the table with us. "Mr. Rhinehart, in the opinion of our forensic examiner, cartridge cases from your Glock 29 ten-millimeter semiautomatic match those used to kill Mr. Archer."

"I guess you'll have to prove all of this in a court of law."

"Not to worry," I said. "We fully intend to. And we'll start with reading off an inventory of your collection of recordings of men like you raping children. In fact, everything we found today related to child porn will be entered as exhibit number one. Followed by the fingerprints and the forensics report on your gun. And then we'll call your ex-wife and daughter to the stand and ask them exactly when it was you began abusing your own child."

"God, stop," he said. "All right, I killed the disgusting bastard, but only because I thought he was about to kill me."

Pretty rich, Rhinehart calling someone a disgusting bastard.

"He'd phoned me early that morning," Rhinehart continued. "Reminded me he had offed a cop and beaten the shit out of my daughter, and if I wanted to see her alive again, I'd meet him at that damn guard station."

"He admitted all of that to you?" I asked, fishing around for a direction to take this, other than down the self-defense road.

"Yeah."

"He was on the run after killing an Oregon State Police trooper. And you didn't consider getting in touch with our office?"

"It'd be a cold day in hell before I'd reach out to your office."

"What did Archer tell you when he called?"

"He said he'd had a fight with Jenna, and he'd gone off the deep end."

"Why would Mr. Archer admit that and call you out there?" Hollis interjected. "I mean, what was in it for him?"

"He wanted money. I think he was planning to leave the state."

"That's interesting. Because he moved to Dale in the first place to be in close proximity to a man he had pledged his loyalty to."

"Trooper Jones is correct," I said. "That's what the bulletin from the FBI and ATF was all about, remember?"

Rhinehart exhaled. "The feds and their bullshit was all that bulletin was about. I had even decided maybe Archer was okay when I first saw it."

He had a reputation for supporting right-wing causes while serving as the elected county sheriff, so it didn't surprise me he interpreted the feds' pursuit of POSSE as overstepping their authority.

"But that was before he hurt my Jenna, of course."

"I have a question," Bach said. "Mr. Rhinehart, did Mr. Archer bring up your child pornography hobby?"

"No."

"I don't believe you," I said. "He wasn't about to leave the area until he got the signal from Clifton Massey. But he was not above blackmailing you in the meantime."

"How would he even have known about that?" Rhinehart had lost a bit of the edge in his voice.

"Jenna."

"I protected her from all of that."

"Really?" I continued.

"When she visited as a kid, I made sure there was no sign of it around. She didn't know, I tell you."

"How about when she became a teenager?"

"No."

"Is it possible Anita told her?"

He smiled weakly. "Anita has her own dark secrets."

"Like what?" Hollis asked.

"Booze."

Holly kept on nudging. "No comparison to child pornography or murder."

"I told you that was self-defense."

"All right, addiction to alcohol is no comparison to owning, watching, maybe participating in child pornography."

The color left his face. "I never participated in that."

"So the children of the world are safe from you, at least." Hollis was on fire, or just royally pissed.

"It's time you learned, Trooper Jones. The children of the world are not safe, period."

"Why did you go into law enforcement, Dirk?" I asked.

"I liked the idea of it. Of being able to keep my community safe."

"Give me a break. You just said the children of the world are not safe."

"I meant it philosophically."

"I think there's plenty of evidence right here in your home that you have no standing when it comes to the safety of children. That's why Jenna told Charlie Archer about your movies, about the way you touched her as a girl, about what you did to her. She thought he would protect her from you, but she learned the hard way that neither of you were interested in protecting her."

"What did she say to you, Maggie?" he asked.

"You tell me."

"She told you I would make her sleep in my bed? That I would come to her room to say good night, and I would play with her pretty hair and fondle her? She said I would force her to touch me?"

"She didn't tell me any of that, but you just did."

He shot up from his chair, forgetting he'd been cuffed to it.

"Sit down, Mr. Rhinehart," Al said.

He did as he was told and looked directly at the detective. "Do you have children?"

"I do. A couple of them are around Jenna's age."

"She told me she never wanted to see me again. I'd even asked for her forgiveness, but her mother had turned her against me. Jenna was my precious little girl. Such pretty hair, the softest skin. I'd never felt such soft skin. I felt such love for her. But I got careless. I couldn't stop, couldn't help myself, couldn't leave her alone." He began to sob. "Anita came between my baby and me. Told me Jenna couldn't stay at my place anymore. After that, it was never the same between us."

We waited for Rhinehart to collect himself, but I, for one, was drained, and a tension had settled over the room, like the darkest cloud on a dark winter day. And I really didn't know what to do with what he had just told us. It hadn't been an out-and-out confession to sexual abuse of his child, but I knew I had to find some way to broach the topic with Jenna.

In the meantime, I was sure all three of us doubted Rhinehart had killed Archer in self-defense, but we needed a definitive admission from the man.

"Mr. Rhinehart," Bach said after a time. "We need you to explain exactly what happened at Desolation Guard Station."

"Like I told you. Archer said he wanted money, five thousand dollars so he could move. Said his unemployment benefits had been denied because Lyndon fired him. Said he knew I was addicted to…to child pornography. That Jenna had told him."

"So you lied when you said Jenna didn't know?" I asked.

He indicated he hadn't told us the truth and drew a deep breath. "He called me a disgusting creep and a bunch of other names. Told me to give him all the money I had in my wallet, and he'd come to my place to collect the rest the next day. I asked him where Jenna was, and he laughed and said, 'Not to worry, I roughed her up some, but she's still alive.' I came unglued at that."

"How so?" Hollis asked.

"I was shaking and screaming at him, telling him to shut up. But he just laughed."

"I know that would've put me over the edge," I said. "He beat Jenna, and you had no idea where she was or what her injuries might've been."

"I felt sick, literally sick. And I brought out my Glock."

Somewhere a ticking clock could be heard.

Rhinehart continued, "He tried to swipe the gun from my hand, but I moved faster than he thought I would. I pulled the trigger, and he fell back into an open closet. He was dead before he hit the floor."

I was curious about one other detail. "What did you do after that?"

For a moment he seemed not to understand the question. "I got in my pickup and drove home."

"You didn't try to find Jenna?"

"I was… All the years in law enforcement, I'd never shot anyone before, let alone killed anyone. Guess I was in shock."

Al sent me a look, giving me permission to make it all formal.

"Dirk Rhinehart," I said. "You're under arrest for the murder of Charles Archer."

He wiped away the last of his tears and turned to Detective Bach. "I'd like to use the bathroom now."

"Certainly."

"I'll escort him, Detective," Hollis offered.

"Thank you, Trooper Jones."

Hollis unlocked Rhinehart's handcuffs, and the two of us followed the man down the hall—a preventive measure in case he decided to take a detour out the back door or a window.

We stood outside the bathroom, heard him flush the toilet and then wash his hands. Moments later, he released a piercing howl, followed by a scream.

Hollis knocked on the door to ask if he was okay. There was no answer. Soon Rhinehart opened the door, a .22 pistol in his hand. I pulled my weapon from its holster.

"It's okay, Maggie," Hollis said calmly. He reached inside his pocket, brought his hand back out carefully, and opened it slowly. "Is this what you're looking for?"

Holly held several bullets in the palm of his hand. "Earlier, I found another of your false doors at the back of the bathroom cupboard. And the .22, of course."

"Place the weapon carefully on the floor," I said.

"What's going on?" Bach had joined us.

"I believe Mr. Rhinehart was planning to avoid going to prison. Hollis made sure that didn't happen."

"All right, let's escort our prisoner to the county jail," Al said.

After booking Rhinehart, I drove to McKay's Feed and Tack. Today was the last day of the Autumn Jubilee, the store's annual sale before winter arrived. It was also shortly before closing time, and the place was hopping.

I took a trip down a few aisles, waiting for the crowd to clear out. Finally the last customer of the day paid up, and Duncan locked the door and pulled down the shades. He noticed me standing at the checkout counter and beamed his beautiful smile.

"Hey, babe," he said. "What brings you here?"

"Kitty food for Raleigh Cat. Plus I have some news."

"What's that?"

"Our investigation wrapped up today."

He put his muscular arms around me. "God, I'm so happy to hear that. Let's go home and celebrate the end of the case and of this damn sale."

"I've got one more stop to make before I go home."

"All right, babe. But don't stay too long, okay?"

"You got it."

"Oh, and by the way. I hired Jenna Rhinehart today. She starts in a few weeks."

"That's great, Dun." I kissed him. "I'll see you at home."

From the feed and tack, I drove to Anita Rhinehart's house. The lights were on inside, so I parked, stepped to the front door, and knocked. I wasn't certain where I was going to begin my conversation with Jenna, but I knew it had to end with her knowing I recognized the terrible burden she had carried since her childhood.

Jenna opened the door. "Hi, Sergeant Blackthorne. Come on in."

I shut the door behind me. "First, I want to congratulate you on getting that job."

"Thanks. How did you find out so soon?"

"Well, it's not really a secret, but Duncan McKay and I are engaged."

"He's such a nice guy. Too bad there aren't more nice guys in the world, right?"

"In a way, that's what I've come to talk to you about. In private, if we could."

"Mom's gone out." Jenna peered at me warily. "This is about my father, isn't it?"

Motoring home afterward, I reflected on my conversation with Jenna. She had experienced tremendous trauma, and yet had not spoken of herself as a victim but rather as a survivor who was learning how to get on with her life. She had kept the worst of it—the years of Dirk's molestation—from Anita. She claimed her mother had protected her from her father as much as she possibly could. I hoped like hell that was true.

Unexpectedly, I thought about the new life developing in my womb, and a wave of emotion rushed over me. I decelerated, moved to the road shoulder, and wept.

Once I pulled myself together, I started to head back onto the highway, when my phone buzzed.

"Hi, Dun. I'm on my way right now."

"I had a thought today."

"Just one?"

"Well, my other thought was to close up shop a lot earlier than I did, but you saw how that turned out. Anyway, I was thinking about a name for our kid."

"Oh, really?"

"Yeah, I think we're having a girl, and I'd like to name her Belle."

"My middle name?"

"Yeah, I like it a lot."

"I'm about two miles from home. Let's talk about names when I get there, okay?"

"See you in a few."

As I hung up, I experienced the babe moving, more of the early quickening I'd recently learned about. It had been a few days since I'd last felt it, so I placed a hand on my growing belly until the fluttering subsided.

"Oh, Belle, or whatever your name comes to be, there's a lot of good love waiting for you when you arrive."

I glanced at the crescent moon overhead and drove the rest of the way home.

POISON SPRING
A Maggie Blackthorne Novel

When the murder of a beloved ranch owner shocks the entire county, Maggie Blackthorne must unmask a killer hiding in plain sight...

Ranch owner Mike Drake is a fixture in Grant County, beloved and respected by friends and neighbors alike. So everyone is shocked when his prize bull is found mutilated on his property near Poison Spring, just outside the village of Kimberly.

Police Sergeant Maggie Blackthorne and her partner Hollis Jones are called out to Poison Spring Ranch to investigate the slaughter—but they discover an even greater crime when they find Mike Drake himself, shot to death near his bull's carcass.

Residents throughout the county demand answers as Maggie and Hollis get to work on the case, but there are hardly any leads and too many contradictions. Almost everyone around had loved Mike Drake—but he seems to have been killed by a local with a grudge.

Maggie and Hollis must watch their step as they dig up dark secrets about one of the county's most upstanding residents. Particularly when their search takes them into the craggy, luminous fossil beds surrounding Poison Spring Ranch—it's dangerous terrain to wander around in...and the perfect place for a killer to hide.

Get your copy today at
severnriverbooks.com

ACKNOWLEDGMENTS

Thanks to all of my instructors and writer friends who have offered countless gems of wisdom and wit mostly for free: Dan Bern, Emily Chenoweth, Pat Dannen, Dan DeWeese, Charlotte Rains Dixon, Allison Frost, Jenni Gainsborough, Martha Gies, Debbie Guyol, Karen Karbo, Nam Le, Doug Levin, Dave Lewis, Ann Littlewood, Angela M. Sanders, Deb Stone, Colleen Strohm, Laura Wood, and Leni Zumas. I also want to give a shout-out to John Beer and Michele Glazer.

Thanks also to Julie Keefe, photographer extraordinaire! And to family, friends, and supporters Mary-Beth Baptista, Arlene Blair, Cara Busacker, Vicki Cartwright, Rachel Martin Crocker, Ann & Bill Griffin, Kari Guy, Annice Kessler Attoe, Charlie Landis, Sarah Landis, Duane Turner, Mark U. and Mark W.

An extra special thank-you to Lance Linder for his discerning eye.

I also want to thank the team at Severn River Publishing—Andrew Watts, Amber Hudock, Cate Streissguth, Mo Metlen, Keris Sirek, and my fabulous editor, Kate Schomaker.

Tom Griffin-Valade is beta reader, critic, cheerleader, and fan number one. Thanks, babe.

To our children and their partners—Shawn, Amy & Tony, Alexis & Ahmed, and Kai & Hannah—thank you all for believing in me and supporting me. To our grandchildren—Lauren, Logan, Piper, and Zio—thank you for reminding me of what's really important.

ABOUT THE AUTHOR

LaVonne Griffin-Valade was born and raised in the high desert country along the John Day River of eastern Oregon—a place that stoked her imagination and inspired her to become a lifetime writer of short stories, essays, poetry, and novels. She has worn many professional hats: elementary school teacher, mentor, education equity advocate, and Auditor of the City of Portland. Griffin-Valade has published essays and pieces of fiction in multiple publications including the *Oregon Humanities Magazine* and the *Clackamas Literary Review*. After receiving her MFA from Portland State University in 2017 she moved to fiction writing. LaVonne lives in Portland, Oregon and works as a full time writer. *Dead Point*, the first book in the Maggie Blackthorne series, is her debut novel.

Sign up for LaVonne Griffin-Valade's newsletter at
severnriverbooks.com